MW00872629

MARRYING A COWGIRL

CALLAHANS OF COPPER CREEK BOOK 2

NATALIE DEAN

KENZO PUBLISHING

© Copyright 2022 by Natalie Dean - All rights reserved.

In no way is it legal to reproduce, duplicate, or transmit any part of this document by either electronic means, audio format or in printed format. Recording of this publication is strictly prohibited, and any storage of this document is not allowed unless with written permission from the publisher. All rights reserved.

Respective authors own all copyrights not held by the publisher.

Cover Design by Deborah Bradseth (who has been amazing to work with! Thank you Deborah!)

Photography by Rebekkah Dubois (Love you Rebekkah! God bless your amazing old soul)

DEDICATION

I'd like to dedicate this book to YOU! All of my wonderful readers that have been following my stories over the years.

We're embarking on another new journey through Copper Creek. I hope you enjoy these stories as much as you've loved the Baker brothers!

Thank you to my biggest fans.... There's a lot of you! Jess, Bernie, Wren, Judy, Sherry, Vicci, Phyllis, Debbie, Indra, Jennifer, Carol, Jeanette, Margaret, Paul, and I know there's more I didn't list. But thank you all!

And I can't leave out my wonderful mother, son, sister, and Auntie. I love you all, and thank you for helping me make this happen.

Most of all, I thank God for blessing me on this endeavor.

~

AND... I've got a special team of advance readers who are always so helpful in pointing out any last minute corrections that need to be made. I'm so thankful to those of you who are so helpful!

EXCLUSIVE BOOKS BY NATALIE DEAN

GET THREE FREE BOOKS when you join my Sweet Romance Newsletter :)

Get One Free Contemporary Western Romance:
The New Cowboy at Miller Ranch, Miller Brothers of Texas Prologue - He's a rich Texas rancher. She's just a tomboy ranch employee. Can she make him see life can still be happy without all that money?

AND Two Free Historical Western Romances:
Spring Rose - A feel good historical western mail-order groom novelette about a broken widow finding love and faith.

Fools Rush In- A historical western mail-order bride novelette based off a true story!

Go to nataliedeanauthor.com to find out how to join!

OTHER BOOKS BY NATALIE DEAN

CONTEMPORARY ROMANCE

Copper Creek Romances

CALLAHANS OF COPPER CREEK

Making a Cowgirl

Marrying a Cowgirl

Christmas with a Cowgirl

Trusting a Cowgirl

Book 5 Coming Soon!

Book 6 Coming Soon!

Book 7 Coming Soon!

BAKER BROTHERS OF COPPER CREEK

Cowboys & Protective Ways

Cowboys & Crushes

Cowboys & Christmas Kisses

Cowboys & Broken Hearts

Cowboys & Second Chances

Cowboys & Wedding Woes

Cowboys' Mom Finds Love

Miller Family Sagas

BROTHERS OF MILLER RANCH

Miller Family Saga Series 1

Her Second Chance Cowboy

Saving Her Cowboy

Her Rival Cowboy

Her Fake-Fiance Cowboy Protector

Taming Her Cowboy Billionaire

BROTHERS OF MILLER RANCH BOX SET

MILLER BROTHERS OF TEXAS

Miller Family Saga Series 2

Humbling Her Cowboy

In Debt to the Cowboy

The Cowboy Falls for the Veterinarian

Almost Fired by the Cowboy

Faking a Date with Her Cowboy Boss

BRIDES OF MILLER RANCH, N.M.

Miller Family Saga Series 3

Cowgirl Fallin' for the Single Dad

Cowgirl Fallin' for the Ranch Hand

Cowgirl Fallin' for the Neighbor

Cowgirl Fallin' for the Miller Brother

Cowgirl Fallin' for Her Brother's Best Friend

Cowboy Fallin' in Love Again

~

Historical Romances

MARRYING A MARSHAL SERIES (Historical)

An Unexpected Treasure

The Dangers of Love

The Outlaw's Daughter

Falling for the Marshal

No Time For Love

MARRYING A MARSHAL BOX SET (includes the above five books, plus the previously unreleased 6th book of my Marrying a Marshal series)

LAWMEN'S BRIDES SERIES (Historical)

The Ranger's Wife

Benjamin's Bride

Carson's Christmas Bride

Justin's Captive Bride

BRIDES AND TWINS SERIES (Historical)

A Soldier's Love

Taming the Rancher

The Wrong Bride

A Surprise Love

The Last Sister's Love

BRIDES & TWINS Box Set / Mail-Order Bride Compilation (My best-seller! It includes TWO MORE unreleased heartwarming mail-order bride series)

LOVE ON THE TRAILS SERIES (Historical)

A Love Beyond Suspicion

Picture Perfect Love

Love of a Wild Rose

A Dangerous Time to Love

A Cold Winter's Love

Brides, Trails, and Mountain Men

Historical Western Romance Compilation

Includes my *Love on the Trails Series* plus an exclusive series titled *Marrying a Mountain Man*

BOULDER BRIDES SERIES (Historical)

The Teacher's Bride

The Independent Bride

The Perfect Bride

The Indian's Bride

The Civil War Bride

BOULDER BRIDES BOX SET

BRIDES OF BANNACK SERIES (Historical)

Lottie

Cecilia

Sarah

Though I try to keep this list updated in each book, you may also visit my website nataliedeanauthor.com for the most up to date information on my book list.

CONTENTS

1

James

James had been to the Callahan ranch several times under the cover of darkness. Beneath the moon and stars, he'd steal away with the one Callahan daughter who had been worth the trouble. No man with any amount of sense would date a Callahan girl for one reason.

Zeke.

The man was a terror to the young men in the county. One false move with his daughters and they could expect a shotgun pointed right at their chest.

But Brielle had been worth it.

He could feel her gaze drilling into his back as he headed for the barn with Constance. She prattled on about one thing or another, but every one of his senses was trained on the girl he'd walked away from.

Their relationship hadn't gone anywhere and the sneaking around hadn't been worth the trouble. Brielle wasn't willing to fight for him so he had cut the cord, gone to college, and returned as a veterinarian.

Seeing her around town was one thing. But seeing her this close and remembering every place they'd hidden to steal a forbidden kiss had him distracted. As much as he would prefer never to set foot on Zeke's property, he had a job to do.

"...the last time you were here?"

He started and gazed down at Constance. She wasn't little Connie anymore. When he'd dated Brielle, they were in high school and Constance was a year or two behind. He'd always viewed her as the little tagalong.

She'd grown up. Her large brown doe-eyes could suck a fellow in and hold him tight. Her hair was swept up off her neck in a small chignon.

Wait. She'd asked him a question.

What was she saying? Seeing Brielle had really messed with his attention span. It really was too bad that he couldn't take a pregnant horse off the ranch and care for it at the clinic. But then where would she give birth?

He gave Constance a chagrined expression. "What were you asking?"

Her wide smile made it clear she wasn't worried in the slightest. "Calliope's baby. I wasn't here last time so I didn't get a chance to ask you. Do you think she's going to have an easy birth?"

James peered down into her innocent, deep gaze. There was a small crease between her brows and her lips puckered ever so slightly into a frown. He stopped and placed a hand on her shoulder. "I think Calliope will do just fine. All you will have to worry about is what the foal's name will be."

"Oh, I already know that."

His lips quirked at the ends. "Oh?"

She nodded. "I'm going with Clio."

"Clio, huh?"

She nodded again. "She's a—"

"Muse."

Her lashes fluttered and the smile faded from her face. "Yes. How did you know?"

He chuckled. "I learned about Greek mythology in college. That, and the mother's name sorta gives it away."

Her smile deepened and a little dimple appeared on her right cheek just below the corner of her mouth. "I didn't realize that veterinarians took Greek mythology."

James turned, once again on his way toward the stall where they housed Constance's horse. "They don't. It was one of the classes I took for fun."

Constance hurried forward and placed a soft hand on his forearm. "Why did you want to learn about Greek mythology?"

He pulled open the stall door, then grabbed the lead rope that hung on a hook just inside. Calliope shifted, pawing at the ground. James held up one hand, then glanced back at Constance with a grin. "Why would *you* take it?"

"Because it's fascinating."

"My thoughts exactly. There's a lot we can learn from other cultures and the stories they pass down from generation to generation. I believe there might even be a tiny bit of proof in a lot of it. Who's to say that the gods the Greeks worshiped weren't just guardian angels that our God sent to protect his people?" James bit back a laugh at the stunned expression on Constance's face.

His theories weren't something he often shared with people in town. Most everyone who lived within a hundred-mile radius was Christian, himself included. Not many ventured far enough to learn about other people's religions. People like his mother frowned on such things. That was why he kept this sort of stuff to himself. But it was fun thinking up theories on how it *could* all tie in together. With their one true God of course.

James clasped the lead rope to the bridle Calliope wore and

Constance jumped back, holding the stall door open. He led the mare down the long aisle, her horseshoes clicking against the ground in an even rhythm.

Constance's hurried footsteps followed close behind and she finally caught up, walking by his side. "I love that theory. The Greek gods and goddesses are really just angels? I've never heard it before."

He chuckled. "As much as I'd like to continue our discussion, we should probably see about getting Calliope ready. I'd wager there isn't much time now."

"How soon do you think her baby's coming?"

James tilted his head, studying the horse's gait and how she carried herself. "It could be as soon as this evening."

She gasped. "Really?" That small crease appeared once more on the bridge of her nose. The rate of her breathing had increased as well.

He reached out and touched her forearm. "It's going to be okay. I promise. We'll get her set up in a nice, small pasture with some wildflowers, and she can find a way to get comfortable. Then when it looks like she's getting ready to deliver, you can give me a call. I won't be far."

Constance hurried around him, forcing him to stop. She shook her head. "I don't think you should go. If she's going to deliver, you should stay here. We have plenty of room."

"It will be *fine*. Calliope is a strong mare. She will know what to do. It's nature, Connie."

Her brows lowered. "Please don't call me that."

"Oh. Of course."

Constance pressed her lips tight in a firm line. "I know you don't believe me, but I have this feeling deep in my gut. Something is going to go wrong, and I think it would be best if you stay."

If she wasn't so scared, this whole situation would have been almost comical. He placed a firm hand on her shoulder and locked his eyes on hers. "I've got other animals to visit. I have office hours. I can only be here if there's an emergency."

"I know that. I *do*. But—"

"Look, I'll try to stop by after I visit some of my other 'patients.'" He gave her a warm smile, one that he hoped would settle her heart somewhat. But by the looks of it, he failed. She didn't brighten up. Her shoulders actually slumped even more. She let out a sigh and nodded, stepping out of his way.

He tugged on the rope and Calliope dug her hooves into the dirt beneath her. She shook her head and let out a shrill whinny. James tugged again, more firmly but got the same reaction. Strange. She should be fine to walk the next several yards to get to the corral they had set up for her.

James shot a quick look in Constance's direction. He didn't think it was possible, but she managed to look even more worried than before. She moved closer toward Calliope, but he held up a hand. "Don't."

She paled and stumbled back a step instead.

"She's distressed over something," he said.

"It's the baby."

He shook his head. "Not necessarily. She might just be tired, or she could be nervous. All we need to do is soothe her, calm her down so she'll be willing to get to that pasture. It's got grasses and a tree with some shade. I'd really like to get her over there rather than out here in the open."

Constance glanced over her shoulder in the direction they were supposed to go, then her gaze swung back to meet his. "I think you're wrong. She's upset, and I'm guessing it has to do with the baby. You need to do something right now."

"Do what?"

"I don't know! Aren't you supposed to be able to check her or something? Stick your hand in there and make sure the baby is facing the right way?"

"Constance, it's going to be fi—"

She gasped and her hands flew to her mouth as her eyes locked onto Calliope's backside. A bubble had emerged beneath her tail, with a hoof clearly visible.

James chuckled. "You know very well that this is how the process begins." He glanced toward the corral they had filled with extra straw. "Let's get her over there and I'll check her out." He gave her a crooked grin. "I never thought a Callahan would be so nervous."

She fidgeted beside him as they made slow progress toward the corral. "The last time Calliope went through foaling, it didn't survive."

His chest tightened. "I'm sorry, that's terrible."

Constance didn't look him in the eye. She twisted her hands together, wringing them so tightly that they turned white.

James nudged her with his shoulder. "Don't worry. I'm sure she'll do fine this time." He glanced back at where the foal was protruding and fought the instinct to go check while Constance was with him. Something looked wrong. As much as he wanted to assure Constance that everything was going the way it should, he got the distinct feeling he needed to do a thorough check on Calliope. His heart beat a little faster and he bit back a frown. It almost looked as though a hind hoof had come out rather than the front one.

They made it to the corral and Constance closed the gate behind them. He forced an encouraging smile. "Why don't you go get me a big bowl of warm water and some rags." He didn't need any of that, but he needed her gone so he could investigate.

Constance nodded, hopping through the bars of the fence and running toward the house.

"Okay, Calliope, what do we have going on?" He ran his hands softly yet firmly along her back as he moved closer to her rump. His stomach dropped to his knees and a dark cloud hovered overhead. He didn't want to be right about this one. He'd hoped he'd seen it wrong.

But there it was, plain as day. The foal's hind hoof had come out first. He pulled out his phone and dialed one of his assistants at the clinic.

Chloe Roberts picked up on the second ring. "Hello, Dr. Pratt. What a pleasure."

He turned and faced the house, making sure Constance didn't make a sudden appearance. The last thing she needed to overhear was that her foal might not survive this birth. James raked a hand down his face and sighed. "How soon can you bring some supplies to the Callahan ranch?"

There was a pause on the other end. "What do you need?"

"I'm going to need a horse epidural and some lubricant. The horse is displaying signs of dystocia with a posterior presentation. I'm going to try to turn the foal around, but only if you can get here in time. Otherwise, we'll have to make do and pull the foal out as fast as possible to prevent suffocation."

"I can be there in ten minutes. Maybe less if I speed."

"Just get here in one piece, will ya?" He hung up his phone and shoved it in his pocket just as he saw Constance emerge from the house with a large bowl in both hands. She had towels draped over her shoulders. Though she walked carefully, her pace was still a little too fast and the water sloshed over the side of the bowl with each step she took.

He opened the gate and gestured to where he needed her to place it. "I need you to find a few more things."

She nodded, her gaze wide. Shoot, she could tell. He could see it in the way her beautiful brown eyes darted toward Calliope, then back to him. It was almost like she was dancing from one foot to the other. "What do you need?"

"We need something to tie up her tail to keep it out of the way. And rope."

"Rope?"

He took a deep breath and let it out slowly as he placed both hands on her shoulders. "There's a complication."

Terror crossed over her face like a flash of lightning. She tore her focus from him and toward her horse. Constance attempted to pull out of his grasp, but he held firmly to her shoulders as she muttered, "I knew it. I knew something was going to go wrong. I don't want to lose another one. Last time the vet said this might keep on happening—"

"*Constance.*"

She was in a tailspin, and she wasn't going to do him or Calliope any good going down that path.

"I wasn't here last time. And we caught it early enough that I think I can turn it around. But if I can't, I need you to remain strong. You have to push aside all your fears and help me with this."

He hated the way she seemed to be crumbling in front of him. If he could, he would pull her into a hug and assure her that the foal would survive. But at the moment all he could say was what he felt, and that wasn't a guarantee. He tilted his head and studied her. "Do you think you can do that?

She nodded though she didn't look like she was convinced.

"Okay. Go get what you can find. I have my assistant coming to help. With a little bit of luck and some prayers, you should have a brand-new foal within the hour."

Constance sprinted toward the house once more. On the other side of the property, Dax was with his girlfriend Sarah working with a horse. If things went south, he might need Dax's help to pull the foal out. Hopefully, Dax didn't still hold the whole night at the country club against him. It appeared he'd patched things up with Sarah.

Once he made sure Calliope was stable, he made his way over to the couple. Dax stood on the outside, a proud smile on his face as he watched Sarah do the rounds with her horse. He glanced in James's direction but didn't let his focus linger.

"What do you want, Pratt?"

James folded his arms on the top metal rail. His eyes followed Sarah, but his mind was still back with Calliope and Constance. "Have you ever birthed a foal before?"

Dax lifted a brow and turned to face James. "I've helped once or twice. What's going on?"

"The foal is backward. If I can't turn it around, I'll need help pulling it out *fast*."

Dax nodded sharply. "I can help."

"Thanks." James pushed against the corral and headed back. He sent a prayer heavenward that this would all turn out the way they hoped. He hadn't failed a foal yet. He didn't want this one to be his first.

2

Constance

The heart in Constance's chest galloped, pounding hard against her ribs as she raced through the house to find the items James had requested. She wanted to believe him with her whole soul, even the parts of her that were usually pessimistic. From the curly brown hair on her head right down to her boots, she wanted to believe James was capable of delivering the foal without incident.

She'd even expressed how great James was.

There was only one problem. She'd never seen him in action. And the logical part of her brain was now insisting that she had too much faith in the guy. But what other option did she have? There weren't any other vets in the immediate area. As far as lifesaving skills, James was as good as it would get.

Every muscle in her body tensed as she stumbled into the kitchen and yanked open the drawer that had odds and ends. She could wrap a towel around Calliope's tail and secure it with packaging tape. That should hold all the hair out of the way. There had been some rope in this drawer, but now it was gone.

She slammed the drawer shut and whirled around to find Brielle staring at her with a strange look on her face. "Is everything okay?"

"No, it is most definitely not okay. Calliope might lose another foal."

Brielle's eyes widened. "What?"

Constance ignored her sister's question. "Do you know what happened to the rope in here?"

"Did you check the barn?"

"The only rope out there is lassoing rope. It will be too hard to use." She shoved past her sister and headed for the door. If Brielle was right and there was some out in the barn, she'd be lucky. For now, all she could do was check.

"What do you need the rope for?" Brielle called after her.

Again, she ignored her sister. Brielle never really seemed to like James. They'd gone to high school together and it had appeared they were friendly enough. But that was where their relationship ended. If Constance mentioned what James had planned, Brielle would most certainly make some kind of comment regarding his abilities, and Constance didn't need that negativity.

She ran for the barn, her hands holding tight to the hand towel and tape she'd found. Her feet hit the concrete in the barn with sharp thudding sounds. Her lungs burned and her heart ached. Rope. Where was the rope?

Constance got to the far side of the barn and dug through the tools and other odd items that usually found their way there. No rope, at least not any that would work. She could bring a lasso, but she wasn't sure if that would be what James needed.

It was all she could find.

She scooped up the rough, stiff rope and tossed it onto her

shoulder, then ran once more. By the time she made it to the corral, a new vehicle was pulling up onto the property. She'd only been gone a total of seven minutes tops. James was moving toward the car that drove up and came to a stop as close as they could get to the corral. A woman with her hair pulled back into a high ponytail exited the vehicle, and together they returned to Calliope's side.

Constance picked up the pace as much as she could and by the time she reached them, she could barely catch her breath. She wheezed and held her side.

"Oh, good. You've got it." James hurried over to her, wearing gloves with his sleeves rolled up to his elbows. He took the items she'd collected and told his assistant to start prep work. Their words grew quiet as James got to work. His brow was creased and drops of sweat dotted his temple. He didn't look confident at all which only made her stomach swirl even more. She moved closer, fully expecting him to tell her to take a step back.

Instead, his head snapped up and he beckoned her to his side. "I can't get the foal to turn around. We're going to have to pull on both of its legs when Calliope pushes. Can you fetch Dax for me?"

His words hit her like a train going through a tunnel, echoing through her mind. Numbly, she braced her still aching lungs to work hard once more as she charged toward the corral where Dax and Sarah were working with Sarah's new horse.

Dax saw her coming before she even got close enough to tell him he was needed. He called something to Sarah, then hurried forward and past her.

A severe feeling of lightheadedness threw her off balance and she had to pause before she passed out. The stress, along with the physical exertion, was wreaking havoc on her body. She steadied herself and headed back toward the group.

The others crowded around her horse, blocking Constance

from seeing anything despite standing on her toes or inching around. So rather than watch what they were doing, she moved around to stand in front of Calliope. She pressed her face against her horse's nose and wrapped her arms around the beast's neck.

"You're doing great. You're going to have a baby and its name is going to be Clio." Her words of comfort did little to ease the tightness in Constance's own chest. No matter what she did, she couldn't get her racing heart to slow. And she was almost certain Calliope could sense it.

She took a deep breath and released it slowly, letting only a little out at a time. Closing her eyes tight, she imagined a good outcome, hugging the baby foal, watching it scamper through the corral with its mother.

Suddenly an overwhelming peace overcame her. The heaviness that rested on her shoulders lightened and floated away. Calliope stopped her restless pawing and leaned into her.

"Pull!" James called out.

Constance kept her eyes shut tight.

"One more time."

The men grunted and then Calliope shifted, pushing even more against Constance. Eyes flying open, Constance tipped her head to peer around Calliope's large body to see James and Dax carefully lowering the foal into the straw that surrounded them.

The baby looked limp. Shouldn't it be more alert? Something had to be wrong, but Constance couldn't bear to go over and ask. She wasn't ready to be told that Calliope had lost another foal.

"Connie, come here."

Her jaw tightened, hearing James use her nickname from when she was a child. She wasn't one anymore. She was an adult who had to deal with the hard slaps that life flung at her. "I don't think I'm ready," she murmured against Calliope's neck.

Her horse attempted to tug away from her, like she wanted to investigate for herself.

"Clio is going to be okay. Come see. He's absolutely beautiful."

Constance's eyes flew open and she released her horse, as both of them came to inspect the newest member of the Callahan Ranch family.

Clio lifted his head and then fell backward into the hay. Calliope nudged him with her nose, nibbling at him and puffing air through her flared nostrils. The foal attempted once more to sit up and this time succeeded.

Constance gasped and her hands flew to her mouth. Emotion burned behind her eyes and in the back of her throat. He was going to be okay. She lifted her gaze to meet James's, finding him smiling at her. Without giving him any warning, she threw herself at him and wrapped her arms around his neck.

"I can't believe you did it." Her heart beat so wildly that she was sure he could feel it with the way their bodies were positioned. Relief draped over her like a warm fuzzy blanket.

James extricated himself from her arms and chuckled. "Didn't I tell you it would work out?" He glanced around the group, and she got the distinct feeling that he was concerned about how their interaction looked.

The flame of elation she'd felt during the last few minutes was doused with a bucket of ice-cold water. He was remaining professional. She was crazy if she thought he'd see her as anything other than the girl with the horse.

A twinge of disappointment sliced through her chest, but she smothered it, pushing it down as far as she could into the darkness of her mind. It was a crush. She'd get over it. She always did.

Constance scooted back a few more steps and tucked a

strand of hair that had come loose from the bun behind her ear. She offered him a smile. "Thanks for your help."

James nodded. "Of course. It's my job."

Only to Constance, it didn't seem like just a job. James had just saved her horse's foal. In her eyes, he was a hero. A ruggedly handsome hero with a jawline that could probably cut through steel.

Dax shook James's hand and headed back toward where Sarah was still exercising her horse. That left James's pretty assistant. She was young and attractive. Loose strands of her blonde ponytail framed her face and she wiped at her forehead with the back of her arm. She was smart, capable, and beautiful. Constance wouldn't be surprised if James had feelings for a girl like that, though she didn't really know his type.

She knelt down beside the foal and Calliope nudged her arm with her nose. Constance smiled and patted the horse's nose. "You did a good job, Calliope. He's absolutely perfect."

Calliope nickered and tossed her head.

Constance chanced a glance toward James and his assistant. She hated the way her stomach swirled each time the assistant laughed and touched James's arm. There was no telling what they were discussing, but Constance could tell they had a good rapport. They worked together. Why wouldn't they?

The knots in her stomach twisted and lumped together with each passing second. Never had she felt so insignificant around a guy she liked. Good grief. What was wrong with her?

She let out a sigh, returning her focus to Calliope. Constance got to her feet and rubbed her hands down the animal's back, leaning her body against the friend she had always been able to count on.

Her focus drifted toward the scrawny little rascal that was currently trying to get to his feet. After a few more tries, Clio finally succeeded, his legs stretched out at his sides like a tent.

A thread of pride strung through her insides, loosening the

knots that had refused to untangle themselves. She glanced up at James, hoping to share the moment with him. But where she'd expected him to be smiling along with her, he was frowning. His eyes were locked on Clio's hooves.

His assistant stopped talking, finally realizing he wasn't paying attention. He moved in closer to Clio and knelt down beside him. James's fingers gently prodded Clio's hind legs then he glanced up at his assistant. "Do you see this?"

She nodded. "Is that what I think it is?"

"What's wrong?" Constance blurted.

He massaged Clio's leg just above his hoof. "You see how his leg is dropping a little here rather than arching upward like his mother's?"

Clio attempted to take a step forward, but instead the foal appeared to be limping.

"What does that mean?" She peered at James, wordlessly pleading with him to assure her that everything was still okay.

He got to his feet. "It's what we call tendon laxity. It just means there's not much strength in the muscles back there. With a few controlled exercises, we should be able to remedy this. He will need to be monitored in case his hoof becomes overgrown or if he gets any sores. I'll check my schedule and see where I have time to drop in for a few hours every day. We shouldn't have to do it for more than a few weeks." James flashed her a smile. "It's more common in premature foals than you think. If it appears to be worse tomorrow, we can even put a lightweight bandage on it to promote relaxation."

She nodded, but all the words he was throwing at her went in one ear and out the other. She had no idea what half those words meant, but she didn't want to appear dumb in front of him.

"Keep them both in this corral until we're sure his back leg will be okay."

"I can do that."

"Great." He moved toward her and patted her shoulder.

Ugh. There was nothing about that gesture that suggested he'd ever think of her as more than just a client.

Constance shrugged out from his touch, then held out her hand. "Thank you again for helping. I'll see you tomorrow."

He shook her hand, then stepped back and gathered his things. Both he and his assistant moved toward the gate and left without another word to Constance.

Alone.

Despite having six sisters, Constance had always felt like she'd been overlooked. Her oldest sister was the smart one. The one who pleased their father. For all intents and purposes, Adeline was the golden child. Then there was Brielle, who was the problem child. Well, not as far as their father knew. He might have suspicions, but he didn't *know* of her late-night escapades. Then there were her four younger sisters. They might feel the same way as she did for all Constance knew. But to her, they were special in their own ways.

Dianna was great with children. Any kid she met, she could charm until they were best buds. Eloise was the peacekeeper. Anytime their father had a bad day—or anyone for that matter —she could calm them and help make everything a little brighter. Faye was a combination of Adeline and Brielle. She was loved by everyone, had brains and beauty—and as much as Constance wanted to hate her for it, she couldn't. Because Faye was practically perfect. Grace was the youngest. That made her the baby. She was calm and collected and had a heart of gold.

But Constance? She was the one with no particular skill. No excess beauty. Just a plain old Jane who would never catch the eye of anyone. It was probably a good thing Brielle wouldn't get married any time soon because if it was left up to Constance to marry, her younger sisters would never find love.

Constance turned toward Calliope, burying her disappointment in her horse's mane. James wasn't her destined love match, but she could still spend some time with him as friends. Maybe she'd learn a thing or two about foaling from the *expert*.

Then again, that could be a really bad idea. She knew from experience that spending more time with the person she liked usually caused her to like them even more. Could she deal with his dismissal if she willingly put herself in a position to be rejected?

Of course she could. She was a Callahan. If she couldn't get her crush to fall for her, then she'd stay preoccupied with other things.

The way James had known exactly what to do had been impressive. While she had been struggling to remain calm, he'd been a superhero. Maybe he would be open to training her in a few things.

Goodness.

Constance's rollercoaster of emotions hit her like a ton of bricks. The stress of the birth and the realization regarding her unrequited feelings for the doctor had officially given her a headache. She needed to take an aspirin and maybe a nap. Then she could revisit all of this tomorrow.

3

James

"Sean mentioned you had to help with a complicated foaling."

James glanced up from where he crouched holding the back hoof of a therapy horse. Shane's head was tilted and his arms were folded. It was a strange statement. He returned his focus to the hoof he had been examining. "That would be correct."

"Seems you're the resident hero over there."

James chuckled. "I wouldn't go that far."

"Come on, James. Don't sell yourself short. You're making quite a name for yourself. Word around the town is that you're exceeding me as the most eligible bachelor."

This time James let out a laugh. "Is that what you're worried about? You think I'm going to find someone before you? I didn't know you wanted to find someone to marry. Since you moved here, you haven't shown any interest in the local girls."

Shane shrugged. "I've been busy."

"So you aren't as invested in finding a wife."

"Maybe I am, maybe I'm not."

James rolled his eyes. "Well, you can rest assured that I'm not trying to steal your thunder. There was one girl when I was younger, but that didn't pan out."

"You never told me there was a girl."

James peeked at his new friend. There was a reason he enjoyed their friendship. Shane owned a new country club in town and was building a horse therapy center for people who'd experienced trauma. So they had a love of animals in common. Also, Shane didn't push too much, and he didn't know anything about the past mistakes James had made—namely the girl he'd fallen in love with, only to realize he had to break it off with her if he was ever going to be happy.

Things had changed drastically since the last time he'd seen her. Brielle hadn't been available before. She'd hidden any relationship from her father and from everyone who was important to her—even him. At the time she'd claimed it was because Adeline wasn't married and there were *rules*. But Adeline was married now. Brielle was free to date as she pleased.

He'd thought she would have sought him out. They could have picked up where they left off but be public about it. Only Brielle never did that. She didn't ask him out. She didn't check in at all.

Days turned into weeks and weeks into months until, finally, he'd gotten the courage to talk to her at the country club. He'd expected her to be excited to catch up, but instead she'd pushed him off onto her friend. Only Sarah wasn't available either.

So here he was in limbo, and there was nothing he could say to Shane that would clear any of it up quickly. Shane would probably laugh at him, and he wasn't in the mood to be made fun of.

He cleared his throat. "I never told you there was a girl because it's not an important part of my life. We've both moved on. Would I like to find a girl? Sure. Is that going to happen anytime soon? Not likely."

"Why not?"

Because his heart was still a little bruised from his last encounter with Brielle, even though it had been months ago. Catching even a glimpse of her when he'd gone to check on Constance's horse had been tough, and he wasn't looking forward to visiting the Callahan's ranch daily for the next few weeks.

As long as he didn't have to see Brielle, it would be fine. He just had to keep a one-track mind. But that wasn't as easy as it sounded.

Feeling Shane's eyes on him, James's gaze bounced up to meet them. "What?"

"You're jaded. You know that?"

James smiled. "Speak for yourself. I haven't met anyone who is as grumpy as you have seemed to become."

Shane scoffed. "Ouch."

"It's true. You run this amazing place. Women throw themselves at you. Literally everyone around you has a better excuse as to why they are single. But not you. I can't think of one reason you can't settle down."

Shane frowned. "You know very well the reason."

James got to his feet and brushed the dust off his jeans. "All I know is that apparently no one is good enough for you because you think they're all after your money."

"Exactly."

"Maybe you need to have a little more faith in people. I'm sure if you just opened your eyes, you'd be able to find at least one woman who doesn't care how much money you have. They'll just want to be with you because of..." He trailed off and let out a soft laugh. "Nope. Sorry. I can't think of even one person who could put up with that personality of yours."

Shane shot him a dark look. "Gee. Thanks."

"I'm just being honest with you."

He shook his head. "Okay, so what's the damage? How is she going to be?" He nodded to the horse that James had been inspecting.

James let out a breath through pursed lips. "It looks like she's got an abscess. I'll need to drain it, and then you need to keep it clean. I know you maintain good conditions for the horses here and this could just be a fluke where she got infected randomly. Or it could be due to something with her genetic makeup. I'll keep an eye on it as it heals."

They exited the stall and headed across the property toward the country club.

James raked a hand through his hair, his thoughts drifting once again to Brielle. There was a chance he'd bump into her after he left Shane's country club. As much as he didn't want to tell Shane about his past love life, a part of him was curious about what his advice would be. "I'll be able to stop by when I make my rounds at the Callahan's place. That foal needs some strategic intervention to strengthen his hoof."

"I'll make sure we're available for your visit." Shane's focus cut to James, seemingly able to delve into James's mind and read something that had remained hidden for so long. "I get the feeling that there's something else."

They stopped and James faced his friend. "That girl I mentioned."

A smile played at Shane's lips. "Yeah?"

"I had to break it off for a good reason, but there was—is—a small part of me that would have liked to see us reconcile if the timing was right."

"And is it?"

James lifted a shoulder.

"James…"

"No. It doesn't look like it will ever be right."

Shane tilted his head, his eyes searching James's and his lips pressed into a thin line. "I'm sorry."

"Yeah, me too."

"So find another girl."

James tossed back his head and let out a groan. "It's not that easy."

"Sure it is. Whenever you think about *her*, find someone else to think about. Associate those feelings for someone new."

James brought his head back around to gape at Shane. "Are you seriously suggesting I find a rebound?"

"If that's what you want to call it, then sure. Only make sure you find one who is worth it. Don't settle for something less when you deserve more."

James huffed. Shane's words were making things awkward —the exact reason why he didn't want to bring any of this up in the first place.

Shane laughed and clapped James on the back. "Just give it a try. Spend some time with someone new. Ignore the old flame like your life depends on it."

"Isn't that just the same thing as bottling everything up?"

"Perhaps. But it's probably the only thing that will work. Even *you* have to admit there's a reason why people go on the rebound."

For the first time since James had brought up this conversation, Shane had made a comment that actually made sense. They wandered through the club until they got to the front entrance. Shane held out his hand, and James shook it.

"And when you find someone worth rebounding for, maybe we can double," Shane said.

James rolled his eyes, knowing full well that Shane wouldn't have anyone to double with. He gave his friend a wave and skipped down the steps toward his truck. If he was lucky, Brielle wouldn't be there.

"He's looking pretty good," James assured Constance. She hovered nearby, watching every single move he made. It was somewhat unnerving the way she wanted to be so close to everything. But then, he supposed if his horse had been through the trauma that Clio had, he'd be clingy, too.

Constance held her hands behind her back as she watched with sharp eyes the way he massaged and examined Clio's hind leg.

"He's getting some strength back here just by following his mother around. Has he been eating regularly?"

"I think so. I don't see them apart very often. And Calliope is very patient. She doesn't wander too far or go too fast."

"That's great." James rose to his feet and moved to where Calliope grazed. "How has she seemed after giving birth?"

Constance shook her head. "She's bounced back really fast."

He nodded. "That's what I want to hear." James ran his hand down the mare's glistening coat. It was clear that Constance adored her horse and took great care of her. There wasn't a speck of dirt on her body that James could find, and her mane and tail were in great shape as well. "You're very good with her."

Constance beamed. "Thank you."

His gaze lingered on her smile and the way it had lit up her whole face. It was stuff like that he didn't really notice on anyone after he'd dated Brielle. Maybe it was because of his hope that he'd end up with her again one day.

No. He wasn't going to think about that.

He needed to find something to distract himself.

James turned back to Constance. "Have you ever—er—considered working with animals in more ways than you do here?"

Her brows lifted in surprise. "Like what you do?"

James nodded. "Sure. You might find you enjoy taking care of the animals."

"Actually, I was going to ask you—"

Motion in the corner of his eyes captured his attention and he shifted his focus to the far side of the property where the barn was located. A familiar figure emerged from the structure, leading a horse toward a corral.

Brielle.

His chest tightened and his stomach lurched. He had to tear his eyes back to where Constance was—finding that she now stared at him expectantly. James blinked and searched his brain for any clue as to what she was going to ask him. He used to have the ability to recall things that were said when he wasn't one hundred percent attentive. But those were his college days. Now he had a harder time retrieving such information.

He cleared his throat. What kind of thing could she possibly ask that he would refuse? He couldn't think of a single thing. James nodded. "Of course. I don't see why not."

Constance's concerned expression went from grey to bright. Like dusk to a full-blown sunrise in a matter of seconds. Her brown eyes almost looked caramel colored, the way they shined with excitement. "Really? That would be wonderful. When do you think we could start?"

Uh-oh. Why had he let himself get distracted? Brielle wasn't worth it. She was in his past, and he needed to look toward the future. He just didn't know what that future would entail yet.

He shifted, putting all his weight on one foot. "Well, what do you think?" It wasn't the best response. But it was probably the safest one he could go with.

"I'd love to start as soon as possible. I know that there are going to be educational courses and tests to take if I want to be a real vet. But I figured if you'd let me shadow you, then I could help out around here in case you couldn't make it on time."

Oh.

He had to admit, her words made perfect sense, especially considering where their conversation had started. She wanted some form of training when it came to caring for the animals at her ranch.

Brielle's distinct voice floated over to where they were, and his attention flitted in her direction unbidden. Her graceful stance in the saddle, the way she could move with the horse she rode, all of it had his heart reaching for memories that needed to remain hidden.

His focus landed on Constance once more. Shane had said to find someone he could distract himself with. Suddenly, spending time with Brielle's younger sister didn't seem like such a terrible idea. He was going to be here to help her with the foal, so why not spend some extra time helping her with the basics of being a vet? It sure would be nice to have the extra help on hand for next time something came up.

James nodded. "Well, I've got a full schedule for the next couple of weeks, so I don't know if I'll be able to have you shadow me at other places. That being said, when I visit here, you can ask as many questions as you'd like. I'd be happy to share what I know with you."

The grin on her face didn't fade one iota as he gestured toward the foal. "First, let's give this little guy a bit of a workout. Can you go get us a lead rope? We'll have Calliope make the rounds and stay close to Clio to make sure he doesn't get overworked."

Constance nodded and hurried away. Without meaning to, he gazed once more at the corral where Brielle ran her own exercises. She'd always been a good rider. There was no doubt about that. But it was the way she carried herself that had captured his attention when they were in high school. He knew from the moment he'd met her she was something special. There was no one quite like her.

While they dated, he'd thought he was the luckiest guy on the planet. To have Brielle Callahan's arms around his neck was like heaven.

Did he regret breaking it off with her?

That was the million-dollar question.

Sometimes he did. Had he been more patient, they could be married right now. Then again, he'd like to say he knew Brielle pretty well. If she wasn't married by now, she might just not want that sort of thing in her life.

Regret or no regret. He'd made the right decision.

Maybe if he kept telling himself that, he'd finally believe it.

4

Constance

She had a skip in her step and she felt lightheaded. James had said yes. He'd agreed to mentor her as much as he could. That meant she'd be able to learn a few things about caring for the health of the animals on their ranch, but it also meant she'd be able to spend some quality time with him.

Stop it.

You're being ridiculous.

James wasn't interested in her. He probably had his eye on someone else in town. Maybe it was his assistant.

Her steps slowed, her hand tightening on the rope in her hand. The threads of the rope dug into her skin, pinching her sensitive palm as she observed him.

James was staring at Brielle like a fool.

Of course.

How could she be so naive? Everyone loved Brielle. She was the beauty, but she was also the brave one. Everyone who ever dated her was willing to do it behind her father's back because of who she was.

Constance bit back the emotion in her throat, swallowing the bile of disappointment as it threatened to erupt. James would be disappointed when he found out that Brielle didn't like him at all. She thought he was too full of himself. What would he say if he heard that?

She snorted.

Guys who liked Brielle didn't care if she refused to give them a chance. They were willing to get their hearts broken if it meant they could steal one kiss from her. Constance had lost count of all the times her older sister had snuck out in the middle of the night to go dancing or spend time with the newest flavor of the week.

Dr. Pratt deserved better than Brielle. He deserved to find someone who thought the sun and the moon rose and set for him.

Someone like Constance.

Her face flushed hot and probably a deep red color, forcing her to turn around and face the barn. She refused to be caught staring at him. And he would definitely never see her blush over him. James Pratt was just a guy.

A guy she could never call her own no matter how much she wanted to.

She let the cool air brush over her, settling the blood cells that had insisted on making a home just beneath the surface of her skin.

When she climbed through the fence of the corral, he was still staring like an idiot. She sighed as she brushed past him. "She doesn't like you."

He jumped, his head snapping around to stare at her so fast that his neck had to be hurting. "What?"

Constance shrugged, placing the rope around Calliope's face and securing it. "Brielle thinks you're just full of hot air.

She doesn't like you." Her back faced James, so he couldn't see the way Constance grimaced as she probably crushed his spirit. Why did she feel the need to tell him that? He could have just as easily learned it himself if he'd bothered to talk to her in person.

"Why do you say that?" His voice made her jump, the low timber rumbling through her body and vibrating her bones.

Still refusing to meet his gaze, she fingered the rope. "She said so herself the other day."

"You guys were talking about me?" Now, instead of simple curiosity, his voice held notes of amusement.

Goosebumps rose on her arms and legs, her skin prickling with the sensation. Finally, she turned to face him. "We weren't talking about you specifically." Alright, that was a bold-faced lie. But how could she explain why she had brought up how she felt about him? He didn't need to hear how she practically worshiped him.

And that feeling had only gotten more pronounced after he'd saved Clio. Goodness. She was in so much trouble. She should have seen this coming. The lump in her throat had done exactly what the Grinch's heart had done—it had grown too many sizes and now was cutting off the air to her lungs.

James was right in front of her—literal inches from her. She could smell the soap he used and that, combined with his closeness, had her stomach knotting up like it had the day before. If humans were so evolved, why couldn't they control the way their insides went haywire whenever they were near someone they were attracted to?

He tilted his head and her mouth went dry. He seemed to be studying her, delving into her mind to find every last dark secret she held there.

Well, she wasn't going to let him be successful. James Pratt had no right to her innermost thoughts. Not now, not ever.

Unless she started dating him.

Nope. Not even then, her mind argued.

If he found out how much she liked him, then she would never hear the end of it.

Constance edged away from him but then held out the rope. "What do you want me to do while you exercise them?"

He stared at the rope in her hand, then lifted his focus to her face. "I figured you'd be the one walking her around the corral. I'll stay close to Clio."

Her fingers tightened around the rope as she closed it into her fist. "Okay then." Without further prompting, she started walking. Calliope followed without much pressure. The bond they shared was deeper than most relationships the horses here had with people. That was probably due to the fact that she'd raised Calliope since she was a foal.

Constance had high hopes she'd be able to do the same with Clio.

Slowly, they made the rounds once, twice, three times. Clio did well keeping up with his mother, and Constance was able to avoid meeting James's curious glances in her direction. That would have to change, though.

If she truly wanted to learn how to help the animals around Copper Creek, she'd have to be okay with their close proximity. She peeked at him over her shoulder. "Do you enjoy being a veterinarian?"

A soft smile filled his face, though his focus remained on Clio. "Of course I do. That's a strange question."

"But what if you lose a patient? Or your patient's owners don't like the treatment you can offer to their animals?"

"There's risk in almost every job. Mine is no different." His voice was soft, thoughtful even, and it made her want to ask him to expound on it, but she didn't know if it was inappropriate to get so close to him.

She fiddled with the rope in her hands once more, unable to hold back the question after all. "What kinds of risks?"

"It's like you said. Losing a patient has got to be one of the biggest ones. No one ever wants to experience that kind of loss. It's painful, to say the least. But it can also be psychological." James's voice grew quiet as if he was reflecting on something really important. "Have you ever heard of imposter syndrome?"

"No."

"It's simple. Almost exactly what it sounds like. When you choose a career, you want to make sure you're cut out for it. You attend classes, you study, and you inevitably compare yourself to others in your field. I don't care what career you pick, if you're like the majority of the population, you will have experienced this sensation at least once in your life."

Constance slowed and turned to face him. "What sensation?"

"Comparison. When you compare yourself, all you see are your flaws and the things you need to improve. Then you look at others and all you see are their strengths and what they excel at. You can't possibly fathom them failing at anything and you feel like you're an imposter. You start to doubt your abilities, and that's when it gets really hard."

It was strange to hear him talk about this sort of thing. He'd always appeared so confident in what he was doing. She thought back to how he'd acted when he was delivering the foal. Not once did she feel like he didn't have control.

"Were you scared yesterday?"

He didn't break eye contact for even a moment. "Yes."

Her eyes widened and that familiar sense of anxiety returned with full vengeance. He'd been scared. What if he'd been wrong? She could have lost so much.

James's quiet voice dragged her from her reverie. "But you want to know the dirty little secret no one tells you about imposter syndrome?"

She remained silent. Whatever it was that he was going to say must be important. Otherwise he wouldn't have started closing the gap between them. Her skin felt like it was on fire with each step he took to be closer to her.

"You need fear."

"Huh?"

He nodded. "It's healthy. I don't think I would ever trust someone who is so confident that they don't experience fear. It's what drives us to improve or be better. It's what makes us slow down and really think about what we're doing so we don't make the *big* mistakes. Fear is the missing ingredient for a lot of people."

"I've never thought of it that way."

"I don't think many have," he mused. "So when you decide if you want to move forward with an official education to become a veterinarian, remember that if you want to become great, you will always have that fear in the back of your mind. It's necessary to push you forward."

He was standing directly in front of her, mere inches away once more, and she hated the way it unnerved her.

Flashes of the day before when she'd thrown herself into his arms plagued her all night and refused to leave her alone today. That had been an inappropriate response, and he'd suggested as much when he'd stepped back.

But now that she knew why he'd acted that way—namely his interest in Brielle—somehow it made it all worse.

She took a careful step backward, not wanting him to notice the effect he was having on her. Crushes were for teenagers. She was not a child anymore. Perhaps if they were able to get to know each other a little better, he'd be the one to take the first step and ask her out.

But that wouldn't happen if he had feelings for Brielle, secret or otherwise. He probably didn't even realize what he was doing. Man, guys were so oblivious sometimes. She shoved the lead rope into his hands and took two more steps backward. "I just remembered that I have to check on the goats."

James arched a brow. "Goats?"

She nodded. "We use them for goat's milk." She could smack herself in the forehead right now. He probably already knew what goats on a ranch were for.

"Mind if I tag along?"

"Mind if you... why would you want to do that?"

"I haven't seen a goat since—" He cut himself off and rubbed the back of his neck. "You know what? Never mind. I'm just going to head out, if that's okay. I'll be back tomorrow same time if that works for you."

She nodded, her voice stuck in her throat.

"Great. Then we can discuss some other little things you can look for when you're taking care of your animals. You'd be surprised at how often it's those small things that go unnoticed that turn into bigger things." He chuckled. "I was at the country club and Shane has a horse with an abscess. I'll be getting my supplies and draining it. He didn't notice until the horse started limping, but he might have caught it sooner if he'd checked her hooves more regularly." He waved his hand dismissively. "You don't need to know any of that."

She moved closer to him. "But I do. That's exactly what I'm talking about. I need to know what to look for on a daily basis so I can give early intervention if necessary."

He gave her a funny sort of look, his eyes appraising her. It was that discerning stare that made it difficult to sit still for very long. But it was also that look that made her feel seen and listened to.

Life was so utterly confusing sometimes. Her hormones needed to get their act together and start listening to the boss. And the boss said that James Pratt was definitely off-limits.

Friends.

That's all that they would be.

With maybe a professional respect for one another.

She inched closer to the gate and gave him a small smile.

"I'll see you tomorrow then." Without waiting for a response, Constance spun on her heel and strode out of the corral and toward the house. She'd made it to the porch before she realized that she'd told James she was going to check on the goats. If she turned around now, it would appear as though she'd been distracted. And he'd probably think it was he who had been the culprit. But if she went inside, then he might think she was lying only to get away from him.

Slowly, she turned around and stared at him from across the property, only to find that he'd gotten swept up in watching Brielle once more.

Constance's hands tightened into fists at her sides. Why couldn't she ever make someone look at her like that? Honestly, it didn't even have to be James. She just wanted to be seen—to have someone know her from the inside out.

But there was no one. She hadn't dated a single person in high school. Nor did she date anyone after she graduated. She'd followed her father's rules, yes, but it wasn't that hard when there wasn't anyone to tempt her.

But now? The temptation stood only fifty yards away in a corral with the horse he helped bring into this world. And the only one he had eyes for could care less about him.

She let out a groan and whisked her way into the house, letting the storm door slam shut behind her.

5

James

Shane was an idiot. It didn't matter how much James tried to distract himself from her; all he wanted to do was watch Brielle. Something in his brain must be broken. Hadn't the breakup been _his_ idea? He'd realized what was best for the both of them and he'd made it happen.

So why was he standing in the middle of a corral watching the one woman he let get away and wishing he could turn back time? The temptation to charge across the dirt and grass and confront her once again was stronger than he'd like to admit.

His foot took one step, and he just about took another when a truck he didn't recognize pulled up to the house. James stood stock still as a tall man in a cowboy hat, black shirt, and jeans emerged from the cab. Brielle pulled her reins to the side and urged her horse into a canter toward the side of the corral where the stranger stood.

James's whole body burst with jealous energy forcing him to turn away as Brielle slid from her saddle and closed the distance between the two of them. She perched on the railing and grabbed his hat from his head to put on her own head.

He could hear her laughter all the way across the property.

There was one thing he knew without a doubt at this point. Brielle wasn't as broken up about their history as he was. She didn't seem to be interested in him in the slightest. Whoever this cowboy was, he wasn't a local. James hadn't seen him around town. He could be from another county or from out of state.

What was he doing?

Torturing himself, that's what.

James clenched his hands into fists. The energy it took to ignore what was taking place over there was completely overwhelming.

James called out to a young man headed toward the barn. "Hey, where are the goats?"

The kid jumped as if he wasn't used to being noticed by anyone. His brows creased and he glanced around like he wasn't sure who James was speaking to.

With deft fingers, James untied the rope he had around Calliope's nose, then he practically swam through the thick layers of straw that lined the ground before he climbed through the rails. "I need to know where the goats are. Can you show me?"

"I'm actually supposed to be giving this horse a—"

"Then if you don't mind, you could just tell me. I'm sure it can't be all that hard to find."

The young man nodded and lifted his arm, pointing in the opposite direction Constance had taken just a little while ago.

"Are you certain?"

He gave James a funny look.

Of course he was certain. He worked here. But now James had a new puzzle to solve. Why had Constance lied about visiting the goats? It was probably nothing. Wherever she went, she had a good reason. But that meant if he headed over to where the goats were located, he'd be there by himself looking like the idiot that he was.

Whatever. He needed to get away from the blatant flirting that was occurring several yards away.

It had been years.

Years.

When he'd dated Brielle, they had been young and inexperienced. He'd had an optimistic view of how relationships were supposed to go. He'd even been naive enough to believe that Brielle's father would approve of him and give them a pass.

He might have, too, if he had pushed Brielle to finally tell someone about them.

But none of that mattered anymore. She was the same old Brielle, but he was different. He'd grown. He'd matured. And he knew better than to pine after a woman who wasn't going to do him any good.

What James needed to do was bury himself in work. Relationships would only distract him. And now that he had two horses on therapy, he would need all the focus he could get.

The bleating of the goats reached him before he turned the corner of the barn and came across a pen full of white, brown, and spotted goats. Their strange eyes blinked at him and for a few minutes they went quiet. He wandered toward the fence and rested his folded arms on the top bar.

It must be really easy being an animal, driven by innate desires. They only ever needed to worry about where their next meal would be coming from. That was it. Eat, sleep, and die. At the moment, that sure sounded preferable to dealing with the anguish in his chest that shouldn't even be there in the first place.

Shane had a point. Trying to forget Brielle by putting someone or something in her place might be the only option he had. There was only one problem. Work wasn't doing it for him. So a relationship—or maybe a new friendship—could do the trick. He just needed to stay busy.

"What are you doing out here?"

He jumped and turned his head, finding a young woman he hadn't met before. Her blonde hair was a little darker and could be mistaken for golden brown. She had the same brown eyes that Constance had. They were soulful and warm.

While he'd spent a lot of time with Brielle when they'd dated, she had never let him meet any of her family. The only times he'd interacted with anyone in her family had been after he'd graduated college and started practicing as the town vet.

There was only one thing he knew about this family. They were named alphabetically. But seeing as all the Callahan daughters were old enough to be out of high school, it was getting harder and harder to tell them apart.

He cleared his throat. "I should know your name."

She arched a brow. "Why are you out here?"

James let out a sigh and sent his gaze toward the goats. "Constance said she'd be out here—something about checking on the goats."

The girl's lips quirked into an amused grin. "Constance doesn't take care of the goats. I do. Lately, she's been trying her hand at breeding and training. Dad let her start with Calliope but based on the way the last foal was born, she might have to find a new interest."

"I'm sorry. I don't think you told me your name?"

She moved forward, coiling a rope she held in a large circle. "I'm Dianna."

"So, Dianna. What do your other sisters take care of?"

Dianna peeked at him. "Faye and I help with the barnyard animals. Adeline and Brielle have been dealing with the administrative stuff. Though, Adeline carries most of the work." She shook her head with a wry smile. "Constance and Eloise are more interested in the horses. And Grace is still figuring things out, I guess."

"Did you all choose what you wanted to learn about?" He had to admit it was intriguing to find out that everyone on the ranch had a purpose. Had Zeke planned it that way?

Dianna opened the gate to the pen and wandered inside. She readied her lasso and gave him one more look. "I guess we did. Dad just expects us to help out... whatever that may be. Of course we all have jobs or college classes right now, so we do most of our work in the mornings or evenings. The ranch hands fill in the rest."

"Your dad is a really lucky man to have such hard-working daughters." Was it his imagination or did her smile fall just a little bit? Brielle had never said much about her father other than his strict rules on dating. It was reasonable to assume he had other strict requirements while he raised his daughters.

They all seemed very well adjusted and happy for the most part. The only thing he could see being a problem was how restrictive their love lives might be.

Dianna deftly wrangled a goat, then pulled it toward the gate. She offered him a smile as she passed but didn't say another word.

If anything, his last words to Dianna only made him feel guilty about how he'd ended things with Brielle.

Enough moping.

James pushed against the fence and spun around to head back toward the corral where his real patient was and collided with someone new. His hands shot out and he grasped Constance's upper arms to keep her from stumbling to the dirt beneath them.

She gasped and her wide eyes lifted to meet his. "Dr. Pratt. I'm so sorry. I had to run inside for a minute..." Her cheeks filled with color. "Did you need something?"

Perhaps it was seeing those brown eyes on Dianna, but

being up close to Constance, he realized he was mistaken. They were not the same pair of eyes. While Dianna's were warm and inviting, Constance's seemed to glow. Golden flecks speckled her irises when the sun hit them just right.

He shook his head and released her. "Sorry, what was that?"

"Did you need something?" she repeated.

There was nothing he needed. Not really. There was a whole lot he would've liked to have happen, but he had already decided that he wasn't going to dwell on the past anymore. Movement out of the corner of his eye caught his attention and he shifted his focus. Brielle was headed right for them with that cowboy beside her.

James glanced down at Constance once more. "Would you like to go get a coffee?"

Her brows lifted and her wide eyes rounded even more. "We have coffee here—"

"No. I'd like to take you to coffee and..." Shoot, he needed an excuse. Anything. "...pick your brain about a few things. You said you wanted to learn more about being a vet."

"True. I did say that." She blinked, but her focus never wavered from his eyes.

"I ran into Dianna and she said you're more interested in horses than anything else around here."

She nodded. "I suppose she's right about that too."

"So how about we discuss your interests over a cup of coffee? There's a big need for on-call veterinarians who can assist in foaling. With the right education and training, I think you'd make a good candidate."

This time her face scrunched into a look of disbelief. "Why would you say that? Did you even notice me during Clio's delivery? I could barely keep my eyes on Calliope. I was terrified."

Brielle and her *friend* continued to get closer.

"That's one of the signs of a good doctor. You care so deeply about your animals that you will do whatever it takes to help them. Now you just need to get a little bit of training and some confidence, and one day you might be better than me."

She let out a shy laugh. "I don't think that could be possible."

"Sure it could." He glanced once more at the oncoming couple. "Are you busy right now? I have some time between this appointment and the next one."

"Really? Yeah, sure. Let me just get my things." She hurried off just as Brielle arrived from the opposite direction.

She watched her younger sister scurry off before she met James's gaze. "Still here? Is everything okay?"

From the second he'd seen her coming, his whole body had grown tight. From his toes to his thighs, to his chest, and now his jaw—James was about ready to crack from the pressure of it all. He forced a smile and nodded. "Everything is perfect. We're just going to get some coffee."

There was a brief moment of vindication when he noticed something uncomfortable flash across her eyes. Brielle glanced up at the cowboy and gave him a wide, flirtatious smile. "How about you go check out the goats for a minute while I have a word with the doctor."

The cowboy's eyes cut from Brielle to James and back. He nodded, touching the brim of his hat before slipping into the pen.

"The goats are pretty popular today," James said.

"I'm not here for small talk." Her voice wasn't harsh or overly mean, but the direct statement seemed to sting just a little.

"Then what are you here for?"

"Did you tell her we dated?"

James's brows furrowed. "Tell who?"

Brielle rolled her eyes. "I'm not in the mood for games."

"Who's playing games?"

"James. I asked you a question. Did you or didn't you tell Constance that we dated?"

"That's a weird question."

She let out a groan. "Just make sure you don't tell her, okay?"

There was a twinge of concern threaded through her tone.

"Please?" she added.

James nodded. "Sure. I won't tell her."

"I mean it. I don't want her knowing."

He frowned. "Why? Does this have something to do with your father's rules?"

Brielle pushed past him and entered the goat pen. "Sure, let's go with that. Just don't tell her and we'll be golden."

As much as he would have liked to extend their conversation, he knew deep down that was impossible. She was no longer available to him.

Constance materialized as if from nowhere. She had her purse and it looked like she'd put on some makeup.

But to be honest, she didn't need makeup. He thought she was prettier without it.

And just like that, the thought occurred to him. Constance *is* pretty. Not to mention she loves caring for the horses, just like he does. Maybe this coffee date wouldn't be so bad.

6

Constance

He asked her out. This was really happening! Her high school crush asked her out!

Constance's hands trembled slightly in her lap. She stared out the truck's front window, unable to quell the nerves that refused to leave. Acting like this was ridiculous.

She was probably overthinking this. He hadn't shown any real interest in her. It's like he said. He wanted to discuss her interest in being a vet.

Okay, she was *definitely* overthinking. This wasn't a date. James didn't like her. But she'd take whatever she could get. It wasn't like she could date anyone officially anyway—not with Brielle in her way.

Constance chewed on the inside of her cheek and glanced at James out of the corner of her eye. He kept his hands firmly on the wheel and his focus on the road. He was clean-shaven, unlike a lot of the cowboys out in this part of the state. And with his chiseled bone structure, he could totally pull it off without having too much of a baby face.

Just looking at him gave her stomach a fresh wave of tangled knots.

Brielle was right. Constance had a crush on the doctor and there was nothing that would fix it. Why did her crush have to be so interested in Brielle?

Constance turned her attention to her window. The last thing she needed to do right now was dwell on the things she couldn't change.

They parked along the street in front of the coffee shop in town. James darted from the vehicle before Constance had a chance to unbuckle her seatbelt. He hurried around the front of the truck and opened her door.

She snickered when he held out his hand toward her.

"What?" he asked.

Constance shook her head, unable to keep the smile from her lips. "Nothing." She was too much of a hopeless romantic, and he was quickly becoming the guy she wanted for her prince charming.

His hand was free from callouses, but still strong. She grasped it tightly, letting him pull her to her feet. Constance had to be careful not to bump into him. His touch lingered longer than it needed to and, for a split second, she thought he was studying her. The thundering in her chest resumed, but it was the only part of her that was active. She froze beneath his gaze, and she could almost feel like they were more than just two people getting a coffee.

But then James pulled his hand from her grasp and gestured toward the entrance of the coffee shop. She expelled a heavy breath and nodded, pulling her lips into a smile. "Thanks."

Together they took the handful of steps toward the door. James's warm hand rested on the small of her back, sending chills throughout her whole body. The universe was a cruel place. She wanted so much for this to be real.

James held open the door as they entered the shop. The scent of mocha and vanilla beans wrapped around her like a comforting hug. Constance took another deep breath, telling herself that she was doing so because she loved the smell of this place.

But if she were honest with herself, she had to admit that she was taking deep breaths because she needed to remind her heart to stop doing flips inside her chest cavity.

She turned to face James when he put his hand on her shoulder.

"What do you want?" he asked.

Constance's gaze cut to the counter where the barista was taking orders, then ricocheted back to James. "I'll have an iced vanilla latte."

He nodded. "Go ahead and find us a seat. I'll put in our order."

Her focus swept through the coffee shop. It was moderately busy with about six couples and a handful of people sitting alone with a tablet or a computer. There was a table near the entrance right by a window offering a clear view of the street.

Constance slipped into the booth and picked up a little laminated menu card with a list of pastries. The croissant drizzled with warm chocolate hazelnut looked absolutely divine and her stomach growled in response.

She put the card away and placed her hands in her lap. What she should be doing right now was figuring out what she wanted to learn from James in the first place. He had offered his expertise, and to squander it wouldn't be wise.

What was more important? Her crush? Or the possibility of having a career that would serve her well into her future.

It shouldn't even be a question, which was why she was going to lock away all her hopeless romantic notions. She scowled at the tabletop. It wasn't going to be easy, but she'd be able to do it if she put her mind to it.

A cup and a paper bag were placed in front of her. Constance snapped her head up just as James took his seat. He pried off his cup's lid and poured a little packet of sugar in, then stirred it.

Constance eyed the paper bag with curiosity until James chuckled. "They have the most amazing croissants here. Have you tried them?"

Slowly, she shook her head.

He nudged the bag closer to her. "I hope you like it. I grabbed two of my favorites."

She didn't move.

James laughed. "Well, it's not going to bite you." He grabbed the bag and opened it up, then pulled out a croissant with a napkin. He placed one in front of her and the other in front of himself.

Constance stared at the dessert, dumbfounded. It couldn't be. "Is that chocolate drizzle?"

"Chocolate *hazelnut*."

There wasn't even anything in her throat, but she must have inhaled wrong. Constance coughed and held her hand to her chest as she gasped for some air.

His brows furrowed. "You okay?"

The laugh that attempted to slip from her lips sounded more like a wheeze as she still fought the itch in the back of her throat. Constance nodded and reached for her drink. But it didn't satisfy her needs.

Her face flushed and she covered her mouth to prevent herself from spewing the sip she'd just taken. When she finally got herself under control, Constance nodded once more. "Sorry, you just surprised me."

He gave her a strange sort of look. "That doesn't sound good. At least your reaction wasn't."

"No, no. It's fine. I—it's really silly, actually. I was just thinking how good those croissants looked." She gestured toward the pastry in front of her. "That one specifically."

A hint of a smile touched his lips.

She touched the corners of the napkin with her fingertips and rotated the croissant a few times. "Thank you," she murmured. "This was really sweet of you."

"Don't mention it." He took a bite of his, then wiped his mouth with a napkin from the box at the end of the table. "So, let's talk."

She arched a brow. Right to business. To expect anything else would be equally silly. Constance cleared her throat and took another sip of her drink. Time to dive in. "You said you were willing to let me shadow you, at least at our property anyways."

James tore off another piece of his treat. "What are you interested in exactly? Is it just to help with birthing the horses, or do you want to do more?"

Goodness. That wasn't the question she was expecting. She hadn't considered what opportunities would be opened up to her if she asked. Her brows pulled together. "What does that even mean?"

James leaned back in his seat and offered her a smile. "It means whatever you think it means."

She huffed. "My dad wouldn't let me go off and become a vet. Not a *real* one. He's really protective and that might mean going away for college."

"Not necessarily. You would have some courses that you would need to take in person, but a great deal of the classes can be completed online. Then there are a certain number of training hours you would need to complete. But I could help you with all of that."

"You're kidding."

He shook his head. "If that's what you want, then I'm sure

we could make it happen. But if all you want is to learn a few tips and tricks when it comes to your horses, then we can do that instead."

Constance worried her lower lip. Until he'd brought it up, she hadn't even considered getting the education to be a veterinarian. Doing so would open a lot of doors for her. If she wanted to move away from Copper Creek, she could make a new life for herself. She wouldn't be tied down, and better still, she'd be able to help animals.

She leaned forward, gripping the table with her hands. "But what if my dad doesn't want me to? I have savings, but I don't think I'd be able to manage everything it would take. I'd need his help."

James tilted his head to the side. His eyes traced over her face making her feel almost naked. "You know, I've been looking to hire a new vet tech. That's a two-year degree unless you can really add on your credit hours. What would you say if I gave you a scholarship and when you finished your associate's degree, you worked for me while you completed your bachelor's requirements?"

Her eyes widened. "Work for you?" she stammered. "Why would you do that?"

That charming grin filled his face once more and he shrugged. "I like you, Constance. And I—I used to be good friends with your sister. It would be my pleasure to help you out, and I would get to have some great company along the way."

The blush that had come and gone like the tides of the ocean returned with a vengeance. She glanced away. He didn't mean he *liked* her. She needed to stop with all this wishful thinking. James was a good guy. He was talented and smart, and anyone in town with an interest in animal medicine would jump at his offer.

She lifted her gaze to meet his. "I would love to take you up on your offer."

"Great! We'll have to look into the specifics of it all, but I'm sure we can figure out all of that stuff later."

"There's just one thing."

He stilled, holding his drink mid-air.

"You're going to have to convince my father."

James chuckled. "That's going to be easier than you think. All I have to do is give him the facts. How nice it will be to have a trained person on Slate Rock Ranch. If anything were to happen to even one of your animals, you would have the training and the know-how to fix it. Of course not everything will turn out the way you want it to, but just by being present, you increase the likelihood of a better outcome than if you weren't there. I can't be everywhere at once. This town really should have more than one veterinarian." He finally took another drink, then replaced his cup. "And maybe you can be that person."

His words warmed her as if she were a marshmallow cooking over an open flame—all gooey and toasty inside. She couldn't hold back her grin if she wanted to. When he'd first arrived on the Callahan property, she would have been thrilled if he had given her even a small smile.

Turns out... she'd gotten much more than that.

CONSTANCE BURST into the house and hurried up to her room. The plan wasn't going to start until James had a meeting with her father, but according to him, it was a done deal. He'd insisted he was good with men who had a sense of business.

And her father was nothing if not a strong member of the community due to his business sense.

She flung herself onto her bed, then grabbed her pillow

and rolled onto her back to stare at the ceiling. James still left her feeling weak in the knees and wishing there was a chance for something more between the two of them. But this opportunity was a close second on the scale of dreams coming true, and he would be the one to help her make it happen.

A quiet rap on her door drew Constance's attention. She sat up, still hugging the pillow to her chest to find Brielle standing in the doorway with a concerned look on her face. "Where did you go with James?"

"He took me to coffee."

"Coffee." Her tone made it clear she wasn't convinced.

"Yes. Coffee. And it's none of your business, but he was sweet and helpful and he's going to help me become a vet."

Brielle's features softened a little. "That's very sweet of him to say those things, but you can't get your hopes up." She settled onto a rocking chair just a few feet from Constance. The wood creaked as she rocked back and forth.

"Why are you saying that like you think it's not going to happen? I am going to take some classes, and he's going to help me become a vet just like him."

Brielle's patronizing smile was like scratching Constance's fingernails on a chalk board. It set her teeth on edge and all she wanted to do was wipe it from her sister's face. Brielle ran a hand through her perfect locks. "I know you like him and all, but just because he says he'll do something doesn't mean he'll follow through."

"What do you even know? You used to be friends with him when you guys were in high school. People change, Bri. And you might not know him as well as you used to."

"I know him better than you think," she shot back. Then she closed her eyes briefly before standing up. "Besides, you're forgetting one thing." She waited for a few minutes before finishing her statement. "Dad."

"James said—"

"James isn't part of this family. He doesn't know the rules as well as we do. What do you expect him to do? Talk to our father about letting you participate in whatever this thing you're trying to do is called?"

That was the one thing Brielle could have said that burst Constance's happy bubble. Somehow hearing it out loud was just enough to make Constance realize just how ridiculous she'd been. James wasn't part of their family. He might be a charmer, but Constance had yet to see any sign that her father would succumb to anything when it had to do with his daughters.

She frowned and fell back on her bed. Maybe she wasn't going to have her dream after all.

Brielle's movement shuffled through the room. She sat on the edge of the bed and patted Constance's knee. "It will be fine. You can still learn some stuff from him. But it's probably best to tuck that dream away for the time being."

She was right.

Of course she was right.

Maybe Constance didn't really deserve to have anything that she wanted.

Not her dream job.

And definitely not James.

7

James

After coffee, James had promised Constance that he'd speak with her father when he got a chance sometime over the next several days. Vet tech courses weren't due to start for a few weeks and there was still time to register.

As much as he'd like to say he fully believed Zeke would be on board, he wasn't quite sure. He didn't want to let Constance down after their conversation, which only added to the feeling of being on edge as he strode toward the house.

In the evening, most cowboys still finished up their work for the day. Zeke should be on the property and available to visit. Now, all James needed to worry about was how to approach the subject.

Constance knew her father better than James ever would. If she didn't think this was possible, then James had his work cut out for himself. He just needed to do what he said he would and bring up the important points.

James rapped his knuckles on the door and waited as the

sound of heavy boots hitting a wood floor echoed through the entryway. The door swung open and he started, stepping backward for a moment as he stared into Brielle's eyes.

Those eyes were the ones that had kept him up at night. They were the ones he saw when he regretted his decision to let her go. They didn't belong to him anymore.

Brielle glanced behind her as she pulled the door shut so quietly that it only clicked. The surprise left her gaze and her eyes narrowed as she folded her arms. "What are you doing?" Her even voice was strong and sharper than he expected.

"I'm not here to see you." It was the only thing he could think of to say to her.

She snorted. "I *know* that. What are you doing with Constance?"

His head reared back. "What do you mean?"

Brielle took one step toward him, and he compensated by backing up. Her lips were pressed into a thin line. "What is it, James? You and I couldn't make it work so now you're trying to date my sister?"

Her words were like a splash of ice-cold water. A small bark of laughter escaped his lips. "I'm not trying to *date* her. Is that what you think? Why? Are you jealous?"

It was her turn to look taken aback. "What? *No.* She's my sister, and I'm not going to let you mess with her just because you can't date me."

A huge wall came up around him, protecting his heart from the implications of her words. He shoved his hands in his pockets and frowned at her. "Just because we couldn't make it work doesn't mean I'm still pining over you." That was a huge lie. And if she could read his mind, she would've put him in his place.

James swallowed hard and stepped toward her, rolling back his shoulders to stand a little taller. "Constance is a bright woman. She has a real interest in taking care of injured animals. She'd make an excellent veterinarian, and I want to help her get there."

Brielle's suspicions faltered. Her gaze swept over him and she relaxed somewhat, her arms dropping to her sides. "You realize my dad isn't going to go for that, right?"

"Why not? I'm sure even he could see the perks of having a vet in the family."

"Sure. But I can tell you right now he's not ready to relinquish the control he has on our lives."

James rolled his eyes. "That again? Honestly, I'm beginning to think that you are just making all that up. Admit it, you didn't want us to get serious so you refused to tell anyone about us. I would wager that if I had done what I thought was right and told your father we were serious, he would have given us his blessing."

"You don't know anything," she sneered. "My father's rules were the only thing keeping him from falling apart after my mother passed away."

"If that's true, then he's using it as an excuse. Your mother passed over ten years ago."

She gasped.

Shoot. He hadn't meant to say that. He really should have just kept his mouth shut.

Brielle's eyes flashed with fury and her voice lowered to a menacing hiss. "Stay away from my sister."

"I told you. I'm not trying to date her."

"Looks can be deceiving."

"What is *that* supposed to mean?"

She snorted. "Why don't you tell me?"

James had a hard time not gaping at her. Their conversation had taken such an unexpected turn he didn't know what to say. Was she implying that he was interested in Constance? She appeared to have a similar mindset as Shane. What was it with people trying to get him to move on by dating someone new?

Constance was pretty. Her soft smile and bright countenance had definitely captured his attention. But he hadn't considered her a possibility as a rebound in that sense. His offering to help her had been purely to keep himself busy. In no way had he thought about her romantically.

Wait a minute.

James blinked. "Are you suggesting that Constance might have feelings for me?"

Brielle threw her hands into the air. "I'm not having this conversation with you. Just do what I say and stay away from her." She turned to head inside, then stopped. "And keep our past relationship a secret."

It was instinct. James reached out and touched her shoulder, causing her to spring away from him. He nearly forgot what he was going to ask her, but then he forced everything from his mind and set a steady gaze on her. "Why is it so important that no one knows?"

She snorted. "I don't care if anyone knows. I just don't want *Constance* to know."

"Why?"

Brielle rolled her eyes. "You're smart. You can connect the dots. Goodbye, James."

"I still need to speak to your father."

"He's in the barn."

A whoosh of air blew across his face as she slammed the door shut. James rubbed the back of his neck. Brielle had changed so much since they'd dated. She used to be so full of light, so happy. Over the years she'd grown more jaded. Maybe it was just him she acted that way towards. He'd seen the way she smiled at that that cowboy a few days ago.

He hurried down the steps and glanced once more at the house. Whatever the reason, Brielle hated him now. There was not a single doubt in his mind. Their conversation had left a bitter taste in his mouth and knots in his stomach.

James picked up his pace, jogging toward the barn as if putting more distance between himself and the house would help ease the ache he felt. He made it to the entrance just as Zeke emerged.

Mr. Callahan smiled warmly at James. "Dr. Pratt. What can I do for you? Constance should be inside if you need to see her about her horse."

"Actually, I had something I wanted to discuss with you."

Immediately the warmth left the man's face, replaced by suspicion. James had never been on this side of things with Zeke. In that moment he could see a hint of what the girls meant when they said he wasn't to be trifled with when it came to the wellbeing of his daughters.

A lump formed in James's throat and he tugged at the collar of his T-shirt. "It's not what you think." If what he was thinking regarded James's interest in dating his daughter. "Constance has shown an interest in the veterinary field."

Zeke raised one brow and he folded his arms, but he didn't say anything so James continued.

"There are several programs that would allow her to remain here while studying and she could put in some hands-on hours with me. I'd be happy to train her and pay for her education."

The way Zeke studied him made him feel vulnerable, like he could see every misdeed James had ever done—including dating Brielle without his blessing. He took a deep breath with his lips pursed and let it out slowly. "Constance hasn't mentioned her interest in becoming a veterinarian."

"I think it's a newly formed interest."

"Hmm."

That wasn't a "no." James might have been right after all. "I think her education would make a great addition to your ranch. She'd be on site if any of your animals needed care. And I personally believe that she's—"

"I suppose that's fine."

"—a natural... Really? It might take her away from some of her work here at the ranch. But the investment in time isn't much—"

"James, you've struck oil. Stop drilling."

James forced out a chuckle that probably sounded more like a dying animal. "Right. Well, I'll help her register for her classes, and she can start shadowing me immediately."

Zeke grunted his acceptance of the plan, though his features had seemed to soften. All it had taken was for James to make it clear he wasn't interested in Constance in a romantic way. It had almost felt like he was being hunted by some kind of predator and the moment he'd jumped into the river, they'd lost his scent. Ridiculous, but that's exactly what it felt like.

Zeke stared at him expectantly as James stood there awkwardly for a few minutes, then he brushed past James and headed out of the barn.

James exhaled as he watched Zeke put more distance between them. Man, Zeke was just as scary as everyone had claimed him to be. Perhaps he'd misjudged Brielle's opinion on how things worked around here.

He shook his head and dug his fingers into his hair. No, he refused to believe that if one of Zeke's daughters stood up to him that the man couldn't be moved enough to change his mind on his dating rules.

JAMES REACHED into the bed of his truck and pulled out a box labeled "textbooks." Constance's gaze locked on the box he hefted into his arms and her pink lips parted, drawing his attention. They were full and soft... and he had no right to be thinking of them.

Shoot. Brielle had gotten into his head. Now there was a

part of him that wondered if it would be so bad to date the third daughter in the Callahan family.

He cleared his throat and tilted the box so she could see its contents. "These are the ones I used when I was studying. I can't guarantee that they will be the ones your professors will have you buy. But you're welcome to use anything I have." She reached for the box and he chuckled, tucking the box closer to himself. "I'm not going to let you carry this thing all the way to the house."

Constance frowned. "What? You don't think I'm capable of carrying a box?"

"*No.* I think that you're a lady and I'm a gentleman. I'll take it in for you, and after that you can do whatever you want with it." He bit back a smile at the surprise that flickered across her face. She hadn't expected him to do it, which made him wonder what kinds of guys she'd spent time around. They weren't even involved and he wouldn't have made her take the box into the house.

The thought of other suitors affected him unexpectedly. He shivered and attempted to brush off the strange irritation that had settled around him. He nodded toward the house before heading in that direction.

Constance fell into step beside him. She tucked a strand of hair behind her ear and glanced at him. "What comes next?"

"What do you mean?"

"Do I start shadowing you now? Or do I need to take some classes first?"

He peeked at her. Constance had this glow about her that he had started noticing more and more frequently. It was like a manifestation of her inner beauty. She was meek and kind, but he'd seen small fractures of moments where she could be bold.

Once again, James found himself shaking off these strange thoughts. "What did you ask?"

Her lips quirked into a small smile. "What do we do next?"

"Right. Well, I think it would be wise to have you shadowing me now. I don't know about you, but I learn best when I can observe things firsthand."

Constance nodded. "I'm the same."

"Great."

She hurried ahead of him and pulled open the door for him to enter. His arm brushed against hers and an unexpected shock traveled between them. Their eyes met and she smiled as she rubbed her arm. "Sorry."

James hovered in the entryway. "Where—"

"Oh! Can you take them up to my room?"

He hesitated. If her father saw him wandering through the house, he might not like it very much. And that wasn't even being in her room. James swallowed and nodded. "Of course. Lead the way."

She scurried past him, careful not to touch him—or at least that was how it seemed. This was the first time he'd been in the Callahan's house. Nothing was unexpected. It was a typical house where a cowboy raised his daughters. The décor was more rustic. A lot of brown tones and wooden furniture in every room. They made it to the end of the hall where there was a wall full of pictures. Images of the girls and their mother when they were younger. There were pictures of Zeke on his wedding day. Most of the frames contained memories from a long time ago. He couldn't find even one picture where the girls resembled how they looked right now.

Constance slowed, having noticed that he wasn't with her. She took a few steps back to stand beside him and study the familiar pictures. Her hands were behind her back as she stared at the one where her mother was surrounded by most, if not all, of her daughters.

"You must miss her."

"Every day," she murmured. "But we each have mentioned how at one time or another, we've felt her with us."

Chills crawled up his spine and his blood seemed to chill. He glanced at her once more. It must have been really hard to have grown up without her mother. James couldn't even imagine. His own parents were still very much alive, though he tried to keep them out of his personal life. Daphne Pratt was one of the more notorious gossips in town. Keeping his relationship with Brielle from her back in the day had been a feat all its own. She had a tendency to come to conclusions on her own that weren't right and then spread that information to whoever would care to listen.

He hadn't even told her his plan to train Constance. He could imagine what she would do with that information.

James's chest tightened. He'd kept his relationship with Brielle a secret much like she had. But he'd done it to make her happy. She'd done it because she feared what her father would do. There was a difference.

Facing Constance, James offered her an empathetic smile. "I'm a firm believer that the love of people who have passed stays with us. Perhaps it's her way of keeping you safe from everything you have to deal with while she's gone."

Constance worked her jaw, keeping her eyes trained on the pictures. If he had to guess, he would have assumed she was having a hard time keeping her emotions contained. "My mom's favorite part of the ranch was taking care of the animals."

"Oh?"

She nodded, still not meeting his gaze. "I think if it were up to her, she would have gotten a degree to be a vet, too." Finally, she lifted her focus to his face. "I think she would have been really proud of me. I think she would have wanted me to follow this dream."

As much as James wanted to say something intelligent, he couldn't come up with anything. He didn't have any experience with this sort of thing. She was following a path that was going to make her happy, but she was also doing it in remembrance of her mother. There was nothing more admirable than that.

Constance let out a heavy sigh. "Come on. My room is upstairs."

He followed her up a curved stairway and down a hall with a few doors. She pushed open the last one on the left and disappeared inside.

James came to the doorway and froze. His eyes landed on her sister who sat on a bed on one side of the room. Constance pointed to a desk by a window. "You can put it here."

Dianna glanced at him, her eyes full of curiosity.

He didn't move immediately, locked in place by her gaze. Clearing his throat, James adjusted the box. "How are the—erm —goats?"

She laughed and turned back to the sketchbook she had in her lap. "They're fine."

Constance gave him a funny look but didn't say anything. He crossed the threshold into her room and placed the box on her desk. "You still have time to register for classes until the end of the week. I put a list of the ones I'd recommend taking first in that top book." He motioned toward the box and her gaze followed.

He continued, "Other than that, I suppose if you'd like to start shadowing me, you can start tomorrow."

Constance nodded, leaning against the desk. "I'd like that."

He returned her smile. "Me, too." The tightness in his chest returned. She was so different from Brielle—so much more open and softer somehow.

And completely off-limits. He couldn't forget that part.

8
———

Constance

"*W*hat was *that*?" Dianna cackled.

"*What*?" Constance leaned against her closed bedroom door after she'd said goodbye to James. Her skin was flushed and her heart beat rapidly. She'd long ago given up on controlling the way James affected her. It was more than the way he looked—so much more.

While he was handsome, what really drew her to him was his intelligence and his love for animals. He was so special, and she couldn't believe he hadn't already settled down with someone.

Brielle.

She couldn't believe that Brielle didn't see what Constance did. Her eyes swept through the room to Dianna, finding her shrewd gaze locked on Constance.

"You know what I'm talking about," Dianna said.

"*No*." Constance's face burst into flames. "I have no idea what you're talking about."

Dianna rolled her eyes. "Oh, come on." Her voice rose a few octaves and she clasped her hands together over her heart. "*I'd like that.*" Then she lowered her voice dramatically. "Me, too." Her gaze drilled into Constance. "What are you doing? You know as well as I do that there is no way you or I or any of us is going to get married. Ever. Not with Brielle standing in our way."

"It's not Brielle's fault."

"Isn't it? She's the one who gets to be married next, and she's not doing a single thing about it. Adeline knew what was at risk. At least *she* did something." Dianna picked up her pencil and dropped her eyes to the sketchbook in her hands. "Face it, Connie. We won't get a happily ever after. We will be too old and brittle when Brielle finally finds herself and the *one* she wants to marry."

"That's not fair and you know it." Constance collapsed across the bottom edge of Dianna's bed and stared at the ceiling. Her eyes traced along the designs overhead, making patterns in the textures. "Dad is the one who decided all this. What would he do if we all decided that his rules aren't going to be followed? He can't afford to have all of us leave the ranch."

Dianna stilled, and when Constance turned her head to gaze at her, she found her younger sister staring at her with an unreadable expression.

"What?"

"Would you really do that? Go against Dad's rules? What if he did kick you out? You wouldn't have anywhere to go, nothing to fall back on. There are only so many jobs in town. We can't all get a job at Sal's Diner. And there's too much work to do to keep Slate Rock Ranch running."

Constance sighed. This was what she was afraid of. Her sisters had been raised to believe there weren't any other options. Why couldn't they just see what she saw? They weren't locked into this life they led. There were ways out.

If her dad followed through with his threat to kick her out of their family, then she'd have the job at the vet clinic to fall back on. They couldn't keep living in the stone age.

Dianna still stared at her, obviously waiting for a response to her question.

"Take it easy, Dianna. I'm not thinking about doing it."

Her sister gave her a disbelieving look.

"*Okay*. I've *thought* about it, but I'm not going to *do* anything about it. Happy?"

None of Constance's words appeared to have the soothing effect she'd hoped them to have. Dianna shook her head. "Whatever you decide to do, I hope you consider all the outcomes and how it will affect our family. You saw how hard it was for dad to lose Mom. I think it would be even harder to lose one of us."

"*That's* why he shouldn't have any of these crazy rules."

Dianna ducked her head and scribbled something onto her paper. "*That's* why he made these rules in the first place. He can't keep track of the whole ranch and all seven of us. It's too much."

"But we're adults, Dianna. We should be able to make our own decisions." Even as Constance said it, she knew she wasn't going to win this fight. Dianna was too set in her ways, too brainwashed to see what Constance could.

She'd never mentioned any of these ideas out loud before. Dianna had been the first one she'd dared share these thoughts with. And there was a reason for that, too. If Dianna wasn't on board, there was no way the rest of them would be. If no one was willing to go up against their father, the status quo would remain.

Constance rolled off the bed and moved toward the box of books on her desk. She picked up the one on top and flipped open the book to find the sheet of paper that James had left for her. She traced her fingers over the chicken scratch and smiled.

She could almost imagine him writing all this information down for her.

He'd done it with her in mind.

No one had ever paid her enough attention to warrant a thoughtful note like this even though it was just a list of classes in the order that he recommended. But it had taken him time, and that was enough.

"YOU SEE THIS?" James pointed along Clio's hind leg.

Constance was finding it hard to concentrate with her proximity to James. She had to be close in order to see what he was showing her. His cologne or deodorant or shampoo was messing with her, making her realize just how much she relied on her sense of smell. She blinked and gave a sharp shake of her head.

His brows furrowed. "This. Right here." He reached for Constance's hand and placed her fingertips along the spot where he'd pointed before. His hand was warm and softer than she remembered. A lump formed in her throat and she forced herself to pay better attention.

"Okay."

"Do you remember when he was born how this curved toward the ground and he couldn't put much pressure on it?"

Constance nodded.

"Feel how his muscles have strengthened. They're not where I want them to be yet, but if you examine him, you can feel the difference." He moved her hand to Clio's other hind leg. "See this? This is where he should be." James's face was so close to hers. It would take hardly any effort to lean into him and have her cheek brush his. It was like they were playing a game of Twister.

She fought the blush she knew was lying in wait. James's

hand still held onto hers firmly as he moved it up and down Clio's leg. If she attempted to pull away from him, that would be strange. He would think that she didn't like to be touched or that she wasn't interested in what he had to teach her. Neither of which was true.

The real problem was that she couldn't focus with his skin against hers. And their contact was mild compared to how a normal couple would treat one another.

Constance let out a slow breath through pursed lips and forced a smile when James glanced at her. His eyes lowered briefly down her face. When they landed on her mouth, he released her so suddenly that she nearly fell backward.

He shot to his feet, startling Clio and causing him to take off in an almost amusing run. James dusted off his jeans, his gaze following Clio. He pointed toward the young horse. "Have you noticed how much faster and surer he's become?"

She rubbed her nose as she glanced over to where her horse was now prancing toward his mother. His strength had gotten much better. Her chest swelled with pride and she got to her feet. "It's amazing how much things can change in only a few weeks."

"It is."

Feeling his gaze on her, Constance turned toward James once more. But the second she sought his eyes, he looked away. "So what's next for today?"

He cleared his throat, shoving his hands into his pockets and rocking back on the heels of his boots. "I've got some therapeutic work with one of Shane's horses out at the equine therapy center."

"Really? That's exciting."

James arched a brow as he brought his focus back to her, causing her to blush right then and there.

"I mean, it's not exciting that the horse needs therapy. But I didn't realize you worked with Shane. I guess that makes sense.

You *are* the best vet in the area." She choked out the words as her blush grew hotter with each sentence that forced its way into the fray. "When will the therapy center open? Do you know?"

His lips twitched, pulling up at the ends. "It looks like Shane is doing a slow roll-out. He's got a few clients who utilize his services, but the grand opening will be in a few months. I think he's shooting for early December. So we need to make sure all of his horses are in good shape for that. Shane is really busy training the horses, and I hear Dax and Sarah are providing the foals for him to work with. There are a lot of cogs in motion here."

"Wow."

James nodded, glancing at his watch. "We have about an hour before we need to be out there. What do you say we get some lunch?"

Like a date?

Of course not. This was a work lunch. They'd probably *only* be discussing work.

And that was exactly what ended up happening. Constance sat across from James in Sal's diner, taking a bite of apple pie à la mode as James drilled her on her coursework.

"What about animal anatomy? That class was usually pretty fun."

She wrinkled her nose. "Yeah, if you like learning about the tissue and organs of animals."

He chuckled. "Being a vet isn't all gold and silver. You have to deal with the nitty-gritty stuff too."

"Please tell me I won't have to dissect anything."

"Sorry."

Her gaze shot up to meet his. Ugh. She hadn't gotten that far in her syllabus. It made sense she'd be dealing with that sort of thing. But she'd hoped that most of her coursework would include diagnosing problems that animals struggled with —externally.

"Don't worry. It's not as bad as you might think. It's just the smell you never really get used to."

Constance grimaced and pushed her plate across the table. "Ugh. And now I've lost my appetite."

James eyed the half-eaten pie and motioned toward it. "Does that mean it's up for grabs?"

She nudged it farther. "Go for it."

He grinned and grabbed her plate, quickly making the dessert disappear.

"What made you want to be a veterinarian? I mean, was there a moment when you knew for certain it's what you wanted to be?" Constance twisted her glass of water around, then traced the edge at the top.

He swallowed the bite in his mouth and reached for a napkin to wipe his mouth. "I suppose I knew I wanted to be a vet when my dog was hit by a car."

Constance gasped. "Your dog died? That's terrible."

"I was three when it happened."

She frowned. "I'm so sorry."

He shrugged. "It was hard, especially at that age, but to be fair we do live out in the country. Life. Death. We see it all. It's part of our lifestyle."

"True." Her thoughts turned to the first foal Calliope lost. Constance hadn't handled it as well as she would have liked. "It's kinda funny."

"What is?"

"That you wanted to be a vet after the death of your pet, and I wanted to be one after the birth of mine."

His handsome face brightened, a smile spreading across his face from ear to ear. "That's an interesting point."

It was rare moments like this when she could take advantage of the fact he wasn't engrossed in their work, so she could get to know him better. "Why did you decide to come back home? You know, instead of starting a clinic somewhere in the city."

James took a sip of his drink, his eyes growing distant. He wasn't focused on her, which gave her a chance to study him without being caught. She loved how he was so clean-cut. Every hair was in the right place. Even his clothes were pressed. "I suppose I came back because I knew that Doctor Cliff wasn't going to be around much longer and the next closest option for animal health care was in the city."

Once again, he was showing proof that he thought of others before himself. He was *always* thinking of others.

"If you had a chance to move somewhere else—anywhere —where would you go?"

He cocked his head and his eyes seemed to shine a little brighter. "I don't know. I haven't really thought about it. I suppose there really isn't anywhere I would prefer to go. I love it here. I wouldn't want to leave my family—however *interesting* they might be."

And he was a family man.

She knew getting to know him over the course of her training might cause her some regret. But she didn't think it would affect her this much. The more she got to know the person inside, the more she realized her first impression of him had been spot on.

"Why aren't you dating anyone?" The second that question escaped her lips, Constance stiffened and her face flushed. She hadn't meant to ask him that. The question burst from her before she could contain it. There was no brushing it off because the way he stared at her made it clear he had figured out why that question interested her. She pressed her lips together and looked away. "I mean, anyone with eyes can tell you're a catch. It doesn't make sense why you aren't *with* someone." It was a stupid excuse, and she couldn't bear to meet his gaze while she waited for the answer.

"I guess I haven't found the right girl yet."

That statement both thrilled and disappointed her. He hadn't found anyone, which meant she might have a shot. But he'd also spent quite a bit of time with her and he still hadn't found what he was looking for. Once again, she found herself in the in-between.

They finished their meal and James paid their bill, then they were back in his car and on their way to the country club. Constance's face was still warm, refusing to return back to a normal temperature. Her question had been highly inappropriate and there was no telling how it would backfire on her.

9

James

After two weeks of spending time with Constance on a daily basis, James had started to realize something.

It wasn't good either.

For how much he'd argued with Brielle over her assumption that he was interested in Constance, he had finally succumbed to the fact that she was far more interesting than he'd given her credit for.

She was smart.

Boy, was she ever smart. What he wouldn't have given to have been able to catch on to some of the concepts she'd managed to with an incredible speed. She had focus and drive, and at times it made him feel far inferior to her. Within the next couple of years, he wouldn't be surprised if she managed to surpass him in his training.

One day, she could move across the country and help animals in parts where they desperately needed someone with her skill.

His hand gripped the steering wheel just a little tighter. Why did that thought make him uneasy? He had been telling himself that the reason was simple. He was paying for her education. Most companies didn't do that unless they got a return on investment. If Constance left to work elsewhere, then his investment went with her.

There was a clause in the document they signed that stated she needed to stay put for at least two years after graduation. Maybe he should have made it longer.

She sat beside him, a book in her lap and a highlighter in her hand. Her hair fell forward, blocking some of her face from his view like a waterfall blocked what was hidden behind the glittering wall. Constance brought the highlighter to her lips, nibbling on the end of the lid. He itched to move the hair back behind her ear but touching her in that way would be highly inappropriate. They were working together. He was her superior. And he was technically her sponsor.

There had to be an ethics problem in there somewhere.

James faced forward, focusing on the road. He still needed to get Brielle out of his head. She had been the one he wanted. She had been the one who had made his heart yearn for something more.

But instead of seeing Brielle's face in his dreams, he saw another.... Constance.

He let out a groan, causing Constance to tuck her hair behind her ear and glance at him. "Is everything okay? Did you forget something?"

James stiffened. "What? No. I'm fine."

She stared at him for a few more moments, then turned back to her textbook. "Did you know that a horse's eye is the largest of any land mammal?"

He choked back a laugh. "Yeah. I think I knew that." James grinned as he watched her skin fill with color.

"Right. These were your books."

"To be fair, it's been a few years since I read some of those books. You might be able to surprise me yet."

Her blush slowly faded and she closed her book to stare out the window. "How well do you know Shane?"

James tilted his head. "I suppose I know him pretty well. He's one of my good friends."

"But he only moved in a few years ago."

"Yes," James drawled, "but that was about the time when I moved back as well. I think our friendship developed over that fact a little easier than some." He peeked at her. "Why do you ask?"

Immediately he knew she didn't want to tell him why she was curious. Her face flushed and she fidgeted again. Without meeting his gaze, she traced her finger on the armrest between them. "He's like you, isn't he?"

James had no idea where Constance was going with this one.

"What I mean to say is that he's been around for a few years. He's one of the town's most eligible bachelors, and he's not seeing anyone. Right?"

"I don't believe he's dating anyone."

This time she did meet his gaze. "Can I ask you a personal question?"

Uh-oh. The way her voice softened, carrying with it an almost timid tone, didn't sound like her question would be something he'd want to answer. Then again, this was Constance. How bad could it be? "Sure."

She traced her finger around her ear, but there was nothing for her to tuck. "What are you looking for in a girl?"

Back to the dating thing. He should have known. "I don't really have a *list*."

"I don't believe that for a second."

He bit back a smile. Constance probably shouldn't know how much she was amusing him. He didn't believe that he had the power to influence anyone, but if Brielle believed that Constance was already interested in him, he should play it safe.

Keep it professional.

"A list. Okay. If I had to pick some characteristics about the woman I'd be interested in, I'd have to say she needs to make me laugh. But she can't be a clown. She needs to be intelligent and willing to fight for what she wants. But also know when to step back so I can feel like I'm needed." He peeked at Constance. "None of that made sense, did it?"

"Oh, I think it did," she murmured quietly before she turned to look out the window.

"Kind."

"What?" She glanced at him, then pulled her focus away.

"She has to be kind. I want to find a girl who, just by looking at her, I know she has a good heart. Those sorts of women are hard to find these days."

"Yeah," she murmured. "I suppose the same could be said about men, too."

"I think you're right."

James's thoughts took on a life of their own as he turned into the country club's parking lot. They drove along the paths leading out back where the barn, corrals and object courses were located. Sean was in a corral, doing some training. There were other ranch hands working with various other therapeutic animals.

When he shot a look in Constance's direction, he was momentarily distracted. Her eyes lit up like a Christmas tree. They darted back and forth, soaking in every single detail that she could.

"I knew Shane had started developing this part of the club, but I didn't realize just how far he'd come. There has to be enough room for one hundred horses at least," she said.

"I think he plans on filling every single stall."

She turned wide eyes on him. "You're kidding."

He shook his head, secretly loving the excitement in her voice.

She continued, "I guess he'll be keeping you really busy."

"You, too."

Her brows creased and her focus darted out to the fields, corrals, and track that were all set up. "What do you mean?" she asked.

"Remember when I said he wants to have a grand opening in December? Well, I figure you'll be coming along for every visit by that point. We'll both be busy."

Constance grinned. "Really?"

"Of course." He motioned for her to follow him toward one of the barns. "I have other people helping out at the clinic. But when I have to make site visits, I like to bring someone with me. Seeing as you're still training, I assumed that would be you."

She'd fallen behind and had to run to catch up to him. "That sounds amazing," she said breathlessly. "I'm looking forward to learning as much as I can. I was talking to my sister the other day and I realized that I need to have something to fall back on."

He slowed his steps. "Something to fall back on?"

"Yeah," she hesitated. "If something were to happen and I had to move away or..." She shrugged. "I just want to make sure that I can take care of myself."

James faced her. "Is this something I should be concerned about?" He asked it, but already he knew the answer. She was worried about her stability, and that worry seeped into his mind with a force he hadn't been prepared for.

Constance shook her head quickly and smiled, though it wasn't as bright as her other grins. "Everyone should have a fallback plan, right? I'm sure you have one or had one at some point."

He frowned. What she said made sense, but he knew too much about her family to just take her reasons at face value.

On the other hand, she was a Callahan and if he pushed too hard, he knew he'd be met with resistance. Even Constance could be capable of that.

James jerked his chin toward the barn. "Come on. We have a horse to work with."

The happy spark returned to her face and her step appeared lighter. "Do you think there's enough work for me to stay in town?"

He peeked at her. "That's a strange question."

"Not really. There are only so many people who live in this area. Everyone knows you. They might only want you to care for their animals."

He stopped suddenly and held up both hands. "Hold up. Are you saying that when you're done with school and training you would want to start your own veterinary clinic?"

Constance's face paled momentarily. "Is that not okay? I thought when everything was said and done that you'd want me to venture out on my own."

James's chest tightened and his heart ached. It was sudden and sharp, and he almost thought that he was having some kind of episode. But that sensation left before he could examine it further. He folded his arms and considered her for a moment. "In answer to your question, I had assumed if you were to stay in town, that we would continue working together. But I suppose if you wanted to start your own business, then I would support you in that if that's what you wished." He rubbed the back of his neck. "Sounds like you've already come up with a few thoughts on the matter."

Her boots kicked up some dust as she shifted from one foot to the other. "I haven't decided anything yet. I—" She gave him a wry smile. "I guess I just thought that you wouldn't want me tagging along everywhere."

He placed a firm hand on her shoulder. "You couldn't be more wrong. I would be happy to have you as part of my team."

That sounded so dumb. He could have come up with a more articulate way of assuring her that he had expected her to stick around. He opened his mouth to make a better attempt but was cut off.

"James! Good, you're here. I think she's gotten worse." Shane waved them over toward the barn.

James snapped his mouth shut and jerked his chin in Shane's direction. "Shall we?"

They made it to Shane, and he didn't give them any time for introductions.

"I noticed that she's limping worse than she had the other day." Shane strode toward the stall where the horse was being held. Every so often he'd turn around, walking backward as he spoke. "Is that an indication that she's not healing right?"

"I don't like it, but I'd have to see just to be sure."

Shane opened the stall door and let James in. Constance stayed on the outside of the stall, resting her folded arms on the door the second Shane closed it. They stood side by side as James knelt down and lifted the animal's back hoof. It didn't appear to be any worse than it had been the last time he'd visited. The likely cause could easily be that she was favoring her good side.

He glanced up to say as much and his words died in his throat. Shane was leaning his side against the door and facing Constance. He smiled broadly, and they were speaking quietly. Shane was pulling out all the stops. He ran a hand through his hair and made a comment that elicited a laugh from her lips.

Constance glanced away and laughed again when he commented once more.

James's stomach churned with an uncomfortable sensation. The back of his neck was hot and every muscle in his body had tightened, coiled and ready to spring. He cleared his throat and the two of them glanced in his direction. "It looks like she's just favoring her good side. Could be nothing. But it would be a good idea for me to observe her while Constance exercises her."

Constance straightened, the excitement in her gaze returning. Witnessing that small shift caused a small amount of relief, but not enough to put him at ease. He stepped forward. "Shane, will you hand me that lead rope behind you?"

Shane turned, putting a few feet of distance between himself and Constance to pluck a rope from the wall. He returned with it, but rather than handing it to James, he gave it to Constance. "I guess you're the one who's going to need this."

She reached for the rope, their hands brushing.

James watched their interaction and once again, he cringed. Seeing Shane with Constance gave him the strangest urge to shove his friend aside and demand he leave Constance alone.

She slipped into the stall, brushing past James to put the lead rope on the horse. Shane's eyes followed Constance until James stepped between the two of them. Folding his arms, James lifted his chin. "Are you still on track with the opening in December?"

Shane nodded. "I believe so. We won't have all the horses I want for the opening. It's turning out harder than I thought to get them trained in time. But we should have enough that we can start bringing folks here for treatment."

"That's good."

"It is. Right now, I'm working with a few charities to get the first six or so clients to have a free session. I want to show the world how good it is for kids and adults alike to spend time with animals." His gaze darted to Constance and he lowered his voice as he leaned forward and nodded toward her. "Is she the girl?"

James's brows pulled together. "What?"

"The one you were talking about?"

James's eyes widened and he charged out of the stall, forcing Shane to come with him as they wandered down the aisle. "No, and I'd appreciate it if you didn't bring that sort of thing up in front of her."

Shane laughed. "If she's not the girl, then why does it matter?"

He ignored the question. "The things we discuss as friends aren't meant to be repeated in front of my employees."

"*Oh*." Shane winked. "I get it. She's a potential rebound."

James glowered. "Of course not. I'm teaching her how to be a vet. That would be highly inappropriate."

They stared each other down for a moment before Shane glanced back toward Constance. "Then you wouldn't mind if I ask her out?"

It was on the tip of his tongue. He wanted so bad to tell Shane to stay far away from Constance.

He could state several reasons. There were rules in her household, for heaven's sake. She wouldn't be able to date anyway. Shane hadn't been interested in looking for a serious relationship.

But something inside James knew those weren't the real reasons he wasn't thrilled about Shane's interest.

At some point he'd started to develop an interest himself. As much as he hated to admit it, he wanted to explore the possibility of starting something with her. But where would that put him?

In the exact same place he had been when he'd dated Brielle.

It would be unwise to put himself through that again. And yet he was willing to do just that. Or at least a part of him was willing to do so.

James shook his head. "Don't bother. She's a Callahan. Her father wouldn't let you get near her."

Shane tilted his head and chuckled. "I see."

"No, you don't."

He laughed again and started for the barn entrance. "Say what you will, James, but it doesn't mean I believe it."

James hurried after him. "If you're insinuating that I'm trying to get closer to her—"

Shane slowed, giving James a sideways glance. "You're not?"

James groaned. "It's like I said. Her father—"

The sound of approaching horse hooves from behind stopped him midsentence. Constance smiled at them as she passed. "I'll take her to the closest corral."

Shane nodded. "We'll be right there." He waited until Constance was out of earshot before he turned to face James. "Either you want her for yourself, or you don't care and I can take a crack at her. Speak up now or I'm going to ask her out."

Before James could argue, he strode from the barn, leaving James to scramble after him. But by the time he caught up, he was too late.

10

Constance

Constance clicked her tongue and urged the pretty dapple grey horse to shift into a canter. Movement out of the corner of her eye drew her attention and she glanced up to find Shane hurrying toward her with James a few yards behind.

Shane's handsome smile filled his face and he moved with purpose. The only way she could describe James's expression was one of terror. It was enough to make her chuckle. She hadn't realized they were so comfortable with each other. Based on the way they were talking in hushed tones in the barn, she would wager they were actually pretty good friends.

Opposites must attract in this situation. Shane was far more confident in the way he carried himself. He was a born salesman, so that made sense. He had the ability to command attention, too. He was tall, put together, with dark hair and the most piercing blue eyes she had ever seen.

Shane was the kind of guy she would expect to find on the

cover of one of those romance novels that made her blush. But he wasn't really her type.

Constance's focus shifted to the one who was. James was still the only man she had eyes for. She couldn't explain it. That was just the way things were.

"Constance, I have a question for you," Shane said.

Her gaze bounced to Shane once more and she let the horse slow down. James arrived a moment later.

Shane continued, "Would you be interested in going to dinner with me?"

She froze. James leaned over, his hands on his knees, puffing. He didn't even bother looking up at her. Boy, she wished he would. If she could get even one glimpse of how he felt about this situation, it would help her decide.

But Shane was expecting an answer. It would be easy to tell him no. There were rules. She wasn't supposed to date anyone. Technically, she wasn't supposed to get serious with anyone. She'd gone on a few dates in high school—mostly dances. But boyfriends weren't allowed. And even the sporadic dates were better left secret, though she couldn't imagine her father not knowing.

One date couldn't hurt. Besides, James obviously didn't have an interest in her; otherwise he would have said as much. He would have asked her out, right? She cleared her throat, then smiled warmly at Shane. "I'd love to go to dinner." But to be on the safe side, she'd keep her father in the dark on this one.

James's head snapped up. Unfortunately, she couldn't tell how he felt about her answer. He kept his opinion hidden behind a wall.

Shane glanced at James, then swung his head around to Constance. "Wonderful. I'll pick you up—"

Her blood ran cold and she shook her head. The last thing she needed was to have her father see Shane Owens picking her up for a date. "I can meet you here."

"Don't be ridiculous. I'm a gentleman. I would be happy to—"

"It's not that. I'd just prefer meeting you here rather than having you come all the way out to the ranch."

"If you're certain." Shane shoved his hands into his pockets. "Well, I'll see you Friday night? Let's say six?"

She nodded.

Shane gave James a slug in the shoulder. "When you're done, you can find me in my office." He left without another word, leaving her alone with James. The air felt like it had grown colder and heavier. James moved through the fence and took the lead rope from Constance's hand. He didn't say anything, which was strange.

Constance couldn't help it. A small thrill ricocheted through her body. Based on his reaction, she would guess he wasn't happy with the course of events that had just taken place. Granted it could all be in her head, but a little voice inside her insisted it was because he didn't like the idea of her dating someone else.

She stood by his side, watching the horse make her rounds. It was hard to contain her emotions when they were so close and he was showing signs that he might actually like her. Constance bit the inside of her cheek. Up until a few weeks ago, she would have remained silent and meek. That's how it had always been.

But this new job, the opportunity to become her own person, working with James—it was spurring on a part of her she had never known existed. "You okay?" she murmured.

James gave her a look out of the corner of his eye. "Yeah," he grunted.

"Are you sure? Because it feels like something is wrong."

His jaw tightened. That was the only reaction she got.

"It's just that when we got here, you were more—"

James faced her. "Doesn't your father have a rule that you can't date anyone until it's your turn?"

Immediately her face seared with heat. "Technically—"

"Enough with the technicalities. The whole town knows about your father's rules. I knew about it even in high school. You realize that's the reason all of your sisters are single even though you are all well-within a reasonable age to get married and start families."

Her mouth dropped open. This was not where she'd envisioned this conversation going. Nausea churned in her stomach and she looked away.

Shame. Or guilt. Something now plagued her, but she couldn't tell if it was because she was more embarrassed over her family's dirty laundry or if it was because she shouldn't be going on a date with Shane.

"Tell me something, Constance." He turned away from her, focusing once more on the chore at hand. "Even if you could go on dates but the marriage thing was off the table, it's clear that Shane doesn't care about the rule—"

"What if he doesn't know?" she blurted before she could catch herself.

"He knows. I can guarantee it. And since he knows and he's so willing to go against your father's wishes, why would you even want to spend time with a guy like that?"

Her defenses exploded around her in angry colors of red and orange. "Have you considered that maybe I don't agree with the rules my father placed? Maybe you could accept the fact that I'm a mature woman who should be able to make her own choices."

James snorted. "If that were true, why hide the date?"

"What are you talking about?"

He shot her a dark look. "You don't want him to pick you up. You're hiding this date from your father and the rest of your family. Sure doesn't sound like you're trying to take charge of your life. Seems to me that you're sitting on a fence where you don't have to make a decision one way or another."

She huffed, throwing her hands down at her sides and curling them into fists. "You ought to know better than anyone."

He stiffened. No, she'd imagined it. There was no reason for him to be uncomfortable beyond the fact that he'd started this argument in the first place.

"I told you that I was interested in this job—this career, so maybe one day I could leave the ranch and head out on my own. I'm essentially a middle child and yes, my father has that stupid rule that he's holding over my head. But I'm not there yet, so I'm doing what I can to keep the peace." Her chest started to hurt, then she realized she wasn't taking deep enough breaths. "I'm going to live my life the way I want to, and you don't have any say in the matter."

"I never said I did," he muttered.

"Then why are you lecturing me on how I spend it? If I want to go out on a date with Shane, then I'm going to do it."

He whirled around to face her. "Have you even considered that maybe I'm having this argument with you because I wanted it to be me?"

Frozen. Stuck in the mud with nowhere to go. That's how it felt at that moment. Her little voice had been right. James was indeed interested in her. He just hadn't acted on it.

James moved toward her, the three inches in height he had on her making him appear even taller in this moment where she was frozen in time.

She swallowed thickly. Her tongue felt swollen, unwilling to move or do much of anything as James stared down at her with an expression that appeared to be a mix of disappointment and longing. His slender fingers tucked her wayward strands of hair behind her ear and she shivered. She expected him to say something—anything to break this tension that was thicker than the ice on a pond in the wintertime.

Instead, he let out a sigh and stepped backward. "Just forget I said anything, will you?"

She blinked three times, then shook her head and closed the distance between them. "Why?" she demanded.

"Why what?" There was a sadness in his voice now. He had resigned himself to whatever decision he'd kept from her. The thrill, excitement, and longing she harbored was quickly being overthrown by desperation and anxiety in a battle of wills. If she had told Shane no, would that have given James the opportunity to speak up?

She gave his arm a little shove, but he didn't move. "You can't just say something like that and tell me to forget you said it."

"That doesn't answer my question."

She shook her head. "Seriously? What do you think? If you wanted to be that guy so bad, why didn't you just ask me out?"

"Didn't you hear a single word I said? Your father—"

"Is not responsible for my happiness as much as he believes he is. He can't decide my fate any more than you or anyone else could."

James's scowl deepened. "I'm not the kind of guy who's willing to sneak around. I deserve more respect than that. So do you *and* your father."

Once again, he'd managed to make her feel small. Although hiding this sort of thing was what each of them did at one point or another, Brielle was the only one who consistently partook in that kind of game. Why couldn't Constance have a little fun once in a while? Why couldn't she enjoy the company of a man who was interested in her? She clenched her teeth and her fingernails dug into her palms. "Once again, you find yourself telling me how I should lead my life. The fact that some random guy asked me out isn't going to hurt my dad."

James wasn't looking at her anymore. It was almost as if he couldn't stand to. "I'd hardly say Shane is some random guy.

He's the most eligible bachelor in the area. If you married him, you'd be set for life."

"*What*?" She practically screeched the question. "Who said anything about *marriage*? You realize that this is the twenty-first century, right? Just because a woman goes on a date with a guy doesn't mean she's looking to make it official. He asked. I said yes. That's all there is to it. And honestly, I had been hoping that *you* would be the one to ask me out. But I guess we can't all get what we want in this life, can we?"

Constance spun on her heel, prepared to go storming off toward his car when his hand shot out and his fingers wrapped around her wrist to prevent her from moving even a foot away from him. His intense, dark eyes studied hers, shifting his focus on her face back and forth.

She looked down at where he held her wrist, then returned her gaze to meet his. "You can let go now."

He shook his head. "Do you mean that?"

"Do I mean *what*?" Her brain was all muddled, making it hard to piece together their conversation.

"Did you—do you—would you like to go on a date with me?"

The bark of laughter that bubbled up her throat and flew into his face had convulsed from her without her permission. "You can't be serious."

His confused frown said otherwise, causing her to sober.

"You just gave me this long speech about how it was inappropriate to hide this sort of thing from my father, and now you're asking me if I want to go out with you, too? You realize that if I were to say yes, I wouldn't be able to take it any further than a date with you either. I don't intend to disobey my dad even though I disagree with him." She pulled her hand from his grasp and took a step away from him. "Based on what you said, I think it's safe to say you would be uncomfortable with even going on a date with me. I'm going to head back to the car now, unless you'd like to continue bossing me around and trying to make me feel bad about going on a simple date."

She slipped through the corral and hurried toward the car, not looking back. Technically he *could* boss her around. He was her *boss,* after all. But when it came to her personal life, there was no reason for him to butt in at all.

The door was locked and she wasn't in the mood to go back to where James worked with the horses just to get his keys, so she leaned against his car for a few minutes, then found a tree to sit beneath.

She plucked at the grass growing beneath the tall branches and rubbed them between her finger and thumb. A pair of familiar boots filled her view and she glanced up to find her oldest sister standing over her with her hands on her hips.

Adeline cocked her head to the side, then glanced around the area before bringing her focus back to Constance. "Aren't you supposed to be working or training or somethin'?"

Constance groaned. "I'm taking a break, not that it should matter to you. What are you doing here anyway?"

Her sister arched a brow. "You're in a mood."

"Yeah, well, you would be too if some guy was practically telling you that you were living your life wrong."

That got Adeline's attention. She settled onto the grass and peered at her sister with those deep, soulful brown eyes of hers. "Oh boy. What's going on?"

Constance shook her head. If she told Adeline, she could almost guarantee her father would get wind of it.

"Connie, you know I'll figure it out eventually anyway. You might as well tell me so we can cut to the chase and I can go get some lunch with Sean."

She wasn't going to give up. That was Adeline's MO. When she wanted something, she figured out how to get it. It was what made her the perfect choice to run the ranch when all her sisters finally found the guy they wanted to marry.

Constance sighed. "Shane asked me out." She half-expected Adeline to gasp or tell her she needed to say no. Adeline had been the one to follow the rules from the get-go. Except when she'd told everyone that she was pregnant when she wasn't. Now she was going to have a baby in a few months, so it appeared everything had worked out the way she wanted it to.

Instead, Adeline just gazed at Constance with curiosity. "Shane Owens? Sean's boss? The guy who owns this place?"

Constance nodded. "One and the same. Apparently, he's friends with James."

"I thought you liked James."

"I did—do." She sighed again, but this time it was more vocal and her groan carried. "*I do.*"

Adeline shook her head. "I'm sorry. Now, I'm confused. Why are you going on a date with Shane when James is the one you want to spend time with?"

"Shane asked me first."

"Oh." They sat there in silence for a few moments, each one of them picking at the grass before tossing it aside. "Maybe *you* should ask *him* out."

Constance laughed. "*He's* the one who's telling me that I can't live my life the way I want. He's upset that I'm willing to hide my date from Dad."

Adeline groaned. "You too? I thought that Brielle was the only one doing that sort of thing." She set her somber gaze on Constance. "Seriously, you should just tell him. Believe me when I say you shouldn't hide anything from our father. He'll figure it out eventually."

"Yeah, like the way he figured out you weren't pregnant?"

Adeline grimaced. "*Not* my finest moment. But to be fair, most of that was Sean's fault."

"You could have easily gone into his office and told him up front."

Her sister leaned back on both of her palms. "Yeah. Maybe.

Think of it this way. My mistakes have been the ice breaker between you guys and Dad. Now that I'm married with a kid on the way, the rest of you should stick up for yourselves. We put too much faith in why he gives us these rules in the first place."

"Speak for yourself," Constance muttered.

"I mean it, Connie. If you want to date someone, then do it. But take it from me. Dad should know and you should give him the benefit of the doubt. He was willing to see past all of Sean's imperfections. I'm sure he'd be thrilled you're not marrying a Baker brother."

They both laughed.

"You're probably right."

"I *know* I'm right." She grunted as she got to her feet, then held her lower belly. "I know you probably won't take my advice. At least not right away. But think about it, okay? Dad needs to realize that we're not little girls anymore. He has to let us grow up and become our own people."

Constance got to her feet as well. "Then maybe you should say something."

"Do you honestly think I haven't? I've tried. Dad thinks you're all too happy to continue with the status quo. If you want change, you're going to have to risk an unpleasant conversation with dad. I'll see you back at home for dinner, okay?"

Constance nodded, watching Adeline waddle toward the last place she'd seen Sean. Her sister was right, and Constance knew it. But that didn't mean she was willing to be the first one to break her father's heart. She let out a heavy sigh.

But there were no other options as far as she could tell.

Perhaps if things got serious with someone, then she would make the sacrifice. But it was hard to even envision that when it was so far off in the future. For all she knew, she'd end up an old maid anyway and there wouldn't be a need to have that awkward conversation with her father.

11

James

James threw open Shane's office door and stormed inside, letting it slam shut behind him. "What are you doing?"

Nothing was more infuriating than Shane's grin as he continued reading a document in his hand. "I'm sorry, I don't know what you're talking about." He didn't even look up to meet James's angry gaze.

Fists clenched, head pounding, James strode through the office, only recalling one other time when he'd felt this riled up. He shoved those thoughts aside and drilled his gaze into Shane's forehead until his friend lifted his head. "You know *exactly* what I'm talking about."

Shane tossed his paperwork on his desk, leaned back in his seat and let out a chuckle. "You okay, James? Cuz you seem a little off."

"*Off*? I told you to leave her alone. But you went and asked her out."

"Ah. I get it now. I *did* give you a chance to ask her out first."

James snorted. "No, you didn't. You told me to do it, then you took off and asked her out yourself. You realize why she doesn't want you to pick her up at her house, right? It's that rule her father has. Do you honestly think that you are above it all? I don't care who you are, Zeke Callahan will not let anyone—"

Shane twisted his office chair back and forth. "Constance is an adult. She can make her own choices. It's not up to me if she wants to keep something from her father." His friend steepled his fingers together. "That being said, if you're so upset about this, then maybe you need to ask her out like I suggested. To be honest, I figured if I asked her out, it might light a fire under you to do the same. Looks like my plan worked."

James's head reared back. That wasn't the direction he thought this conversation would turn. He hated the way it gave him pause. But more than that, he hated the hope it gave him. It wasn't that simple. He couldn't just ask Constance out on a date. She had already said yes to Shane. Not only that, but he knew from experience that being the secret boyfriend wasn't a good fit for him.

But Constance was unique. His relationship with her could turn out differently. He shook his head. No. He refused to fall prey to that lifestyle again. James threw up his hands and spun around. "You know what? Go ahead. Learn the hard way. I've been there and it isn't great." He shouldered himself through the office door. The whole way toward the entrance of the country club, his vision blurred and the anger mixed with something he could only describe as desperation.

As much as he'd like to give up and let Shane do whatever he wanted, he knew he had to entertain the idea of building something deeper with Constance.

His heart and mind were being pulled in a dozen directions. Every bad memory he had while dating Brielle came to the surface. The heartache he experienced was only a small part.

There were so many good memories, which made losing her that much harder. But those feelings had dissipated with each passing day that he spent with Constance.

James hadn't wanted to find a rebound girl. The term was insulting. Constance was not a rebound. He had simply found someone who was able to help his heart find purpose again.

Once again, he had to bury those kinds of thoughts. They threatened his sanity. He knew better. It didn't matter how much he wanted to be part of Constance's life in that way, it wouldn't work out.

His car sat in the parking lot and Constance leaned against it, looking at her phone. She lifted her head when he drew near, then shoved her phone in her pocket. Her smile didn't quite hold the glow that it had when they'd arrived. Something had shifted between them.

He didn't know what it was, but he knew he didn't like it.

Danged ole Shane. He was the one who'd done this.

James's jaw tightened so hard his teeth ached. He yanked his keys from his pocket and unlocked his doors. He headed around to open her door for her, but Constance had already climbed up into her seat. So he made his way back around and climbed behind the wheel. She didn't say anything which only made things even worse.

They drove back to Slate Rock Ranch in silence. He pulled in front of her house and waited for her to climb out, but she didn't. Instead, she fiddled with her hands in her lap, then turned toward him. "Are you upset with me?"

The word "yes" was on the tip of his tongue. But that wasn't fair. He wasn't upset with *her*. She wasn't the one who'd asked Shane out. It was the other way around.

No, he wasn't mad at her. He was furious with his friend. Shane didn't say as much, but deep down, James knew that he was aware that feelings were developing between them. And he'd asked Constance out anyway.

James kept his focus trained in front of him. One look at her would only bring him more trouble. "Does it matter?"

"Yes. I value your opinion. If you think I shouldn't—"

He huffed. "I'm your boss—your mentor. The only thing that should matter is how I feel about your work ethic." James sighed and faced her. "What you do on your personal time is your business, not mine. Now if you wouldn't mind, I have a few more stops to make before I can head home."

Her brows creased and she opened her mouth, but nothing came out. She almost looked hurt. Good. The last thing he needed was to be tempted to do something stupid. Even now, his focus dipped to the frown that marred her face and all he could think about was pulling her close and stealing a quick kiss.

Just that thought alone was enough to prove to himself that he wasn't in a good head space. For all he knew, this infatuation for her that he was feeling would be short-lived. They might not even be compatible. He was attracted to her personality and her beauty, but if there wasn't any chemistry, then they'd end up at a dead end.

He forced a smile and nodded toward her house, hoping that his expression was one that demonstrated a degree of goodwill. "How about you take tomorrow off and use that time to study. I'll still swing by to run Clio through some exercises."

"But I want—"

"You'll have a date to get ready for, right? I'd hate for you to not have enough time to get to the country club without your father noticing." He leaned over her seat and pushed the door open. "I'll see you on Monday."

Every part of him crawled with remorse. He probably shouldn't have said any of that. He was supposed to remain professional. And right now, he was letting his personal feelings get in the way of that.

He could feel Constance's gaze on him as she sat unmoving

in her seat, but he refused to meet it. If he had to spend even one minute longer with her, he might lose what little control he had left. James straightened in his seat and placed his hands on the steering wheel, waiting. He almost thought she wouldn't take the hint, but then she finally left the truck. Surprisingly enough, she didn't slam the door like he expected her to.

His gaze followed her toward the house until she disappeared inside, then he slammed his truck into gear and drove away.

The remorse mingled with a hint of regret but for a different reason. A part of him wanted to take Shane's advice and go against everything logical. But deep down he knew he had made the right decision.

Lies and secrets always ended in pain.

JAMES SHOVED a file into the cabinet and slammed the drawer shut, then yanked open another one. Out of the corner of his eye he noticed Chloe glancing up from her place at the reception desk for the third time.

"Is there something I can help you find?"

His fingers rustled through the edges of the pages and the thick file folders, and he shook his head. "No. I'm fine."

"Really? Because you've been looking for something for the last hour and we're technically closed. You could just go home—"

"I'm *fine*, Chloe."

"Is this about the Callahan girl?"

His fingers froze mid-air, muscles ridged. A coldness hit his core as he forced himself not to look in her direction. How could Chloe know about Constance? He'd been training her, but every time he was with her, they had been nothing but professional.

Slowly, he turned his head and stared at his assistant. "What are you talking about?"

Chloe sighed, putting her paperwork on the desk. "Seriously? You can't believe that the whole school didn't see you and Brielle whenever you two snuck off to be alone."

The tension in his muscles eased somewhat. He continued to stare at her, waiting for her to make the point she obviously wanted to make. His thoughts tumbled and snowballed in his mind. How many people knew about Brielle? And if there were a lot, then how had Constance been left in the dark? Chloe had been in his grade. But Constance was a grade or two behind.

It was difficult to dig up the memories of his relationship with Brielle. At the time he'd only had eyes for her. He wouldn't have known much about her younger sister.

Chloe let out an exaggerated sigh. "It is, isn't it? You're back on the Callahan's ranch and now you're reminiscing over your past relationship. What did she do? Tell you that she didn't want to reconnect?"

His brows pulled together as he met her gaze. "No. Well, yes. But that's not what I'm upset about."

"So, you are upset."

He glowered and spun back to the filing cabinet. "I'm fine."

"No, you're not. You're taking all your anger out on that cabinet and soon we'll have to get a new one. You might as well tell me what's going on because I'll figure it out anyway."

James huffed. If she thought he was upset about Brielle, there was no way Chloe would put two and two together. She hadn't figured out that he was interested in Constance now.

Boy, if she figured that out, she would be having a lot more to say than pointing out his abuse of a large piece of metal. He yanked a file out without looking at its contents and shut the drawer. "There," he lied, "found it."

Chloe's gaze dipped to the folder, then up to his face. "I can tell when you're lying. You might as well just tell me so I can give you some advice and we can get past this whole thing."

He moved through the reception area and toward his office. "The day is over. You can go home, Chloe."

But instead of hearing her get up from her seat and move toward the door, he heard the chair creak and her shoes following him across the commercial tile. The tightness in his body returned and he spun around to face her. "What do you want?"

She folded her arms, her features set in a hard line. "You're my boss, and yes, technically you can tell me when I should leave and when I should arrive. But you're also my friend, and if you're going to let whatever is bothering you mess with our workday, then I'm going to make sure that you get it figured out. I refuse to work in an environment where you're going to sulk over a girl."

"I said it wasn't—"

"Fine. It might not be Brielle. But it's *someone*. I've never seen you this riled up before."

He let out a harsh breath. "We haven't been working at this clinic for very long. You don't have much to compare it to."

Chloe rolled her eyes. "Stop making excuses and just tell me what's going on."

James tightened his jaw, then turned and marched into his office. He threw the file down on his desk and whirled around to face Chloe where she now stood in the doorway. "Fine. If I say it's Brielle, then what? Give me advice for something you know nothing about."

The corners of her lips twitched, and she leaned one shoulder against the door jamb. "I'd say that if she's making you feel this bad about something, then you obviously care more for her than you're willing to admit to yourself."

She made a good point. However, it wasn't Brielle he was worked up over. It was Constance, and he didn't really know her at all. How could this mean so much to him if he didn't know what he was missing?

Chloe continued. "So tell me what happened. Is she trying to hide your relationship again?"

"No," he muttered. "How do you even know about that? We were really good at keeping our relationship a secret. Not even her family knows."

This time Chloe ducked her head and her cheeks colored.

He took a step toward her. "You said that it was obvious that we were together, but that doesn't make sense if no one else noticed."

She peeked at him and the coloring in her cheeks deepened. "I might have had a crush on you in high school." She blew out a harsh breath. "Don't worry. I don't anymore. But I always thought that Brielle didn't know how precarious her relationship with you was. I could tell you weren't happy then. And you definitely aren't happy now. Why would you even want to go back to her?"

He ran a hand through his hair, trailing it back to his neck then he let out a resigned sigh. "I'm not trying to get back with Brielle."

Confusion flitted across her face. "But you *are* interested in someone who doesn't return your feelings."

"I don't know. And this conversation is highly inappropriate to be having with my employee."

She frowned. "I'm your friend, too, James. I'm just trying to help."

"Well, thank you for your help, but I'd rather figure this out on my own."

Chloe threw her hands up into the air and stormed away. His muscles relaxed as he settled back on the edge of his desk. There was only one thing that came from this conversation. If Chloe had figured out that he had feelings for someone just by the way he was acting, then maybe she was right.

But having feelings for someone didn't mean he was in love. He was frustrated that he couldn't act on what was probably just a glorified crush. Constance was literally in the same position that Brielle had been when he'd dated her. She was unavailable and unwilling to do anything about it.

Right now, she was probably sitting in a fancy restaurant across from Shane while a waiter asked them what kind of wine they wanted to go with their expensive meal. Shane would treat her like a princess, James was sure of it. And once she got a taste of being with him, she wouldn't ever give James a second look.

12

Constance

Constance stared at her phone. The text message she'd sent Shane had been brief and apologetic. She just couldn't bring herself to go on a date with a stranger when she saw the person she really wanted to spend her time with every single day.

The way James had practically pushed her out of the car the other day had made her feel so sick to her stomach she couldn't get much sleep. All morning, she tried to study for her classes and ended up wasting hours staring at blurred pages.

This wasn't how her life was supposed to be going. She'd resigned herself to not getting James's attention, but lately it didn't even appear as though he was interested in Brielle anymore. Anytime her sister wandered through the property, James practically ignored her.

It had gotten to the point that Constance thought he might actually want to ask her out. She'd caught him staring a few times. But then again, that could have been when he was making sure she was listening.

She sat in her truck, and her head flopped back on the seat as she stared up at the big sign over the veterinary clinic's building. There was a car and a truck in the parking lot. One was James's, but she couldn't be sure who the other one belonged to. Probably his assistant.

The fact that they were both here late didn't sit well with Constance at all. What if she walked in on them and they were having an intimate moment? She hadn't thought that they were interested in one another, but then again, she hadn't been paying much attention to Chloe the few times she interacted with their boss.

Constance groaned. She really shouldn't be here at all. What did she think she was going to do? Just walk in there and lay everything out on the table? That sounded utterly terrifying. Of course James didn't seem like the type to laugh in her face, but even if he let her down easy, she didn't want an audience for that.

She tossed her phone aside and gripped the steering wheel before pressing her forehead on top of her hands. What had happened to her resolve? She'd *finally* managed to convince herself that she didn't need to act on her crush. They could just be friends.

Well, that resolve was broken, shattered and splintered on the side of the road where he'd opened the car door and insisted that she leave. If there was even a chance that James was interested, she had to find out.

Constance straightened, pushed open the door and climbed out. Her steps were slow at first, but as her heart rate quickened, so did her movements. She tightened her hands into fists to help distract her from her rapid breathing and the way her body felt like it was going to explode.

Through the glass door, she could see Chloe hunched over

the reception desk, but James was nowhere in sight. Constance hovered outside the door. She gripped the handle, but it was as if her resolve had withered and died. If she went inside and told James that she'd rather be on a date with him, there were only two possible outcomes.

He might tell her he felt the same and she could rejoice that she'd made the right decision.

Or he would tell her he had no interest in her and firmly shut the door to any relationship they might have been able to have.

Did she really want to go inside and find out which path she would now follow? Could she continue working with him if it was the latter?

As if against her will, Constance pulled open the door and entered the clinic. A little bell tingled overhead. Without looking up, Chloe murmured, "We're closed, but you can make an appointment..." She finally lifted her gaze and her eyes locked on Constance. A fleeting smile was replaced with shock. Then she glanced over her shoulder in the direction of the office before turning her head back around to look at Constance. "Hey, Connie. What are you doing here?"

Constance cleared her throat, her hands now clasped behind her back as she shifted her weight from one foot to the other. "I was wondering if James was here."

Once more, Chloe shot a look over her shoulder then a wide smile filled her face as she thumbed in that direction. "He's in his office. You can go on back." She got to her feet and tapped the stack of paperwork on her desk. "You'll let him know I left for the evening, won't you? I'm meeting my brother for dinner."

"Of course."

Chloe grabbed a jacket and edged around the reception desk, brushing past her before exiting out the front door.

Constance stared back toward the office, now full of the

trepidation she'd experienced outside. This was it. If she turned back now emptyhanded, she'd have no one to blame but herself.

She moved toward the door that was only open a crack, blocking her view from anyone who might be inside. Each step she took made the walk feel so much longer than it actually was. She just had to bite the bullet and tell him how she felt.

Simple.

Slowly, she pushed the door open. The metal hinges creaked, but other than that, the only sound she heard was the rustling of papers. James's back was toward her as he sat in his chair facing the wall.

"Enough pushing, Chloe. I told you it isn't Br—" He'd spun around and his words died. His eyes widened as they swept over her form and he scrambled to his feet. He leaned to the left, his focus shifting behind her. "Is Chloe—"

"She said she had dinner plans with her brother."

James gave her a short nod. His cheek twitched and he brought up his hand to rub it. "Aren't you supposed to be on your date?"

She fought the need to flinch. Instead, she lifted her chin and moved into the room. "You weren't very nice yesterday."

He opened his mouth, but she held up a hand to stop him from speaking.

"I don't understand you sometimes. It's like one second, you're really pleasant and we're getting along, and then there are these brief moments when you act like I'm this person you can't stand to be around."

"Constance, I—"

"Let me finish, *please.*" She shut her eyes briefly and pushed aside all the fear and anxiety that attempted to consume her. She'd come this far and she wasn't going to just walk away. Constance opened her eyes and peered at him. "I need to tell you something and I don't want you to interrupt. Can you agree to that?"

His cheek twitched again and he moved to the side of his desk. "Okay."

Her stomach swirled unsteadily. Her legs were weak and her skin tingled on every surface. She squeezed her eyes shut once more and pressed her lips together, praying for the confidence she needed to finally confess her feelings.

"Constance," he whispered. Too close.

Her eyes flew open and she found him mere inches away from her. His head was tilted slightly and his lips were turned down into a concerned frown. "If this is about the other day, I'm sorry for how I acted—"

"I like you," she blurted. Her face burst into flame and her voice cracked. "I've had a crush on you for as long as I can remember. But working with you this month has only increased those feelings."

Shock. That was the only thing she could read on his face. He didn't move, didn't show any indication of how he felt regarding her confession. Why wasn't he saying anything?

Her throat closed up and her heart pounded against the walls of her chest. "I'm sorry, this was a mistake. I should have never come here." She turned, ready to escape out of his office. "It's wildly inappropriate—"

James's hand caught hold of hers, successfully stopping any prayer of getting out of there unscathed. He pulled her back so that she was forced to stand before him, vulnerable and in the process of breaking. This had to be the most embarrassing thing she'd ever done in her entire life. Why couldn't she have left well enough alone?

Constance stared into his intense eyes, waiting for what felt like an eternity for him to let her down easy. That's what a gentleman would do. He was probably involved with someone else and she'd been too blind to see it.

"You're right," he said softly.

She blinked. Right about what? That he couldn't stand her? That it was inappropriate to talk about this sort of thing when they should be maintaining a professional relationship? Constance swallowed hard and tugged on her arm to move away from him. She didn't need him telling her that she was doing something wrong. She already knew that.

His grasp on her remained firm and his eyes grew more serious. "I wasn't nice when I found out about your date, and there's no real excuse for it."

Constance froze. This wasn't where the conversation was supposed to go. She'd been prepared for him to patronize her, to tell her *thank you* for her interest, but he didn't share the sentiments. He should have told her that she was right about being inappropriate and that their relationship would be better if she'd make sure to keep those thoughts to herself.

This was not that.

"If I was in the habit of making excuses, I'd take this chance to tell you that the reason I wasn't kind was out of jealousy."

She sucked in a small breath but only managed to make herself cough on the little bit of spittle that came with the air. He didn't seem to notice, because he continued as if nothing had happened.

James blew out a breath through pursed lips. "I can't tell when it started, but one thing's for sure... I'm falling for you."

This wasn't real. It couldn't be real. He was lying to make her feel better. That's what he was doing. That was the only thing that made sense.

Still, her heart hammered harder than it had ever done in the past. Her palms had grown sweaty and her legs were about to give out. She shut her eyes and shook her head. "I'm sorry, what?" When she opened her eyes, she figured he'd be smiling at her, laughing at her expense.

No, that was a little harsh. James was too nice to do that.

Instead, his features remained serious. He continued staring at her as if expecting her to say something back.

She hadn't planned for this.

In fact, when she'd marched into his office, she hadn't thought past telling him what was weighing on her chest. All she knew was that he needed to know what was in her heart.

He let out an anxious-sounding chuckle. "Will you say something?"

"I—" She snapped her mouth shut and swallowed hard as she shook her head. "I'm the one who said it first." Goodness, that was lame. "I mean... I don't know. What do you want me to say?"

James released her and stepped back to lean against his desk. He folded his arms, and the way he studied her made her feel even more naked than she'd felt when she'd confessed her feelings for him. "I guess we have to figure out where we go from here."

"What do you mean?" There was probably a simple answer to that question. But it appeared that any brain cells she'd had before this conversation started had completely disappeared. Maybe it was because she'd had a crush on him since the very beginning, and somewhere inside her heart, she had settled with the understanding that he wouldn't return those feelings. She stepped toward him. "Are you suggesting you want to try... to see if things..." Her face flushed and she looked away. There was no delicate way to say it that didn't sound like she was some fifth grader asking a boy out for the very first time.

"Do you want to go out with me?"

Constance snapped her head up and gazed at him, a smile tugging at her lips. "Really?"

"I don't see any other path, do you?"

"You could tell me that you're not interested in destroying a perfectly good working relationship and—"

"Constance," he said firmly, "it's clear to me that we have

feelings we'd both like to explore. How about we do that? No strings. Just a date."

She couldn't hold back the smile any further as she clenched and shook out her hands. "Yeah, okay."

"Yeah? How about next weekend?"

Constance nodded. "I'd love to go on a date with you."

"Great." He walked around his desk and sat in his chair.

She hovered awkwardly. This was when she should say something cute and leave—leave him looking forward to seeing her again. Think. What could she say that would do just that?

James glanced up at her as he picked up the document he'd been reading when she'd interrupted. His eyes shifted to the door and back to her. "Was there something else?"

Constance shook her head. "No, nothing."

"Alright. Well, I'll see you on Monday, I guess."

"Yep. Bright and early."

"Goodnight, Constance."

"Goodnight, James. Love you." She spun around and took two steps before realizing what she'd just said. Slowing, she cringed, then glanced over her shoulder at him. "I didn't mean to say that. It was just—"

He shook his head, a small smile touching his lips. "See you Monday."

"Right." As swift as her feet could carry her, she was out of his office and into her truck. Her face was still flushed and her hands shook as she gripped the steering wheel. Constance's lungs didn't seem to want to cooperate with her as she sucked in breath after unsteady breath. That had to have been the most embarrassing and terrifying thing she'd ever done. The fact that she hadn't reacted to Shane like that was proof enough that she wasn't meant to be with him.

James was the one she'd wanted since before she could remember. He was always so nice to her when he'd come over to help Brielle with her homework when they were younger. He was smart, sweet, and he'd matured in a way that she couldn't resist. There was nothing that could change the way she felt about him.

13

James

ames's eyes locked with Constance's for what felt like the hundredth time as they worked with Clio in the corral on Monday morning. Tension between them still hung thick, wrapping around them, pulling them closer and tying them together.

She'd smile and pull her hair behind her ear. He'd return her smile with one of his own. They shared this small secret—unless she'd told her sister about it. That didn't seem likely considering he hadn't had a visit from Brielle since he'd arrived. They'd simply spent the morning in the middle of their usual routine.

He wiped his brow with the back of his hand. "I think that does it today."

Constance knelt down beside Clio and rubbed her hand up and down his leg, massaging it. "It looks like he's all better."

"He's improved a lot. I think we'll be able to cut back on the exercises, but we'll want to keep an eye on him to make sure he doesn't regress at all."

She rose to her feet and rubbed her hands down his back. "You hear that, buddy? You're getting nice and strong." She moved toward his head and hugged his neck. A breeze drifted between them, offering a cool reprieve from the hard work they'd accomplished.

James could say a thousand things right now—bring up their conversation from last weekend or talk about their upcoming date. He could even ask her to elaborate on the crush he'd had no idea about.

But he thought better of it. If Brielle were to happen upon them, he'd get another earful. It was better to pretend that everything was status quo. Then if their first date went well, they could figure out how to tell everyone that they were dating.

He frowned. Wait a minute. When she'd accepted a date with Shane, she'd been very upfront with wanting to keep her relationship a secret.

James glanced at her as he coiled the rope around his arm. Would she desire the same thing when she went out on a date with him? A familiar sense of uncertainty roiled in his stomach. He didn't want to go through that again.

Constance wasn't Brielle. Just because she wanted to keep her date with Shane under the radar, didn't mean she felt the same about him. She'd been the one who had told him that she was interested. This was different.

They took Clio back to his stall and then spent the remainder of the day checking up on other animals. Every hour he spent with her seemed to add just a little more weight settling over him. There was a heavy instinct that he should bring up his concerns before this went even further.

But how was he supposed to bring it up when there wasn't a guarantee they'd click? It could wait until their date on Friday.

While in the car between visits, Constance would pull out her textbooks and study. Every so often he'd glance in her direction and watch her. She had this quiet serenity about her that he'd only recently started to notice.

She couldn't be more different from Brielle.

Constance must have felt his eyes on her because she lifted her eyes from her book and stared at him. "What?"

He shrugged and stared out the window. "Nothing." When he glanced at her out of the corner of his eye, she was still focused on him. "Our last stop is the country club."

The book in her lap snapped shut. "Okay."

"You never told me what happened on your date."

"Nope I didn't."

He gave her a side-eyed stare. "You can tell me, you know."

She snickered. "Do you honestly want to hear me tell you how Shane held my hand over dinner and rubbed his thumb across my knuckles?"

James stiffened, his jaw clenched. Shoot. She was right. If he had to listen to her recount everything that happened, he didn't know if he'd be able to talk to Shane until he came to terms with it.

"...or how he walked me to my front door and kissed—"

"Nope. Nope, you're right. I don't want to know."

A smile spread across her face. "Good. Because it didn't happen."

His head snapped around and he stared at her for a moment before returning his attention to the road. "It didn't?"

She folded her arms and turned away from him, focusing on the landscape out the window. "I canceled our date and that's when I came to see you."

"Why?"

Constance let out a huff but didn't meet his curious gaze. "Everything I said at your clinic was true. What would you have done? Would you have gone on a date with someone when all you could think about was someone else?" She peeked at him. "You know, it's funny. I used to think that you had a thing for my sister."

And just like that, he felt like the air had been sucked right out of his lungs. He could tell her right now that she'd hit the nail on the head. He could confess that he'd spent a lot of his formative years with Brielle.

Only, Brielle had all but threatened him if he even so much as whispered a word about their past.

And what would it accomplish? To tell her that he'd dated her sister first—a woman who was so different from her— could be unsettling. With how much he hated the idea of her going on *one* date with Shane, deep down he knew she wouldn't be thrilled about knowing this little tidbit of information.

Suddenly Brielle's threat made more sense. If Constance found out about Brielle, their relationship could suffer as well.

He cleared his throat and forced a chuckle. "That's funny."

"Is it?"

"Sure is." His grip on the steering wheel tightened and relaxed. "We were friends in high school, but you knew that already."

"Yeah," she murmured quietly. "So you've never had feelings for her? I'd understand if you did."

James glanced at her, noting the worry lines on her forehead and the way her mouth had tightened into a thin line. There wasn't any harm in keeping this kind of information from her. Nothing would change based on her knowing or not knowing. But a bold-faced lie would be harder to hide. "I might have had a little crush on her, but you know the rules."

Her features scrunched and her frown deepened. "What rules?"

"When you were younger. Your sister couldn't date until Adeline was hitched." Once again his stomach tightened uncomfortably. Right here. This was the best time to bring it up. But if he did, he'd have to tell her why he was so against her keeping their possible relationship a secret. Everything would come out and he'd already fibbed.

Sacrifices would have to be made.

Once again, Constance stared out her window. "Yeah, I know."

There was something in her voice that just tore at him. It was clear she wasn't thrilled about the rules either. "Why do you put up with it?"

"Hmm?"

"Your father's rules. Why do all of you put up with it? You're adults. What could your father possibly be holding over your heads to make you comply?" He didn't know what he was expecting her response to be, but it wasn't the scowl that she had on her face.

"What?" she said, her eyes squinting a little.

James swallowed hard. She wasn't asking him to repeat himself this time. Her tone said it all. He'd offended her.

"Look, I know you don't understand it. No one does. But my father—all of my sisters—we're all each of us has. We're not going to go against my father's wishes because we love him. His heart is in the right place, even if we don't agree with it. It's a crazy rule he made after our mom passed away. I think it's his way of keeping us close. We're not going to do something that would break his heart."

"But isn't that what you'd be doing if you go on our date on Friday? Especially without Brielle being married?"

She let out a harsh breath. "If you're going to make this a big deal, then maybe I was wrong."

"It's just a question, Constance. I didn't mean any offense." His words tasted bitter and the growing silence did little to relieve the frustration that they were both feeling.

"I accepted your offer because I know I deserve to be happy too, despite my father's rules. That being said, I'm not going to intentionally hurt his feelings over something that might not even last."

"Ouch." The word escaped his lips before he had a chance to think better of it.

Constance sighed again. "I didn't mean it like that. What I meant to say was—"

"You're right."

"I am?"

He nodded but refused to meet her gaze. James could feel her eyes drilling into him, questioning him. "Neither one of us knows whether this date will even go well. We're flying into it blindly based on the infatuation that has developed over the last few weeks. We could spend the evening trying to come up with something to say that isn't work-related and realize that we don't have anything in common."

Her silence did nothing to bring him peace. In fact, it made him feel even more worried. If he was smart, he'd just break it off before they made it to Friday.

James all but slammed on the brakes and parked the car. He climbed out of the vehicle, not even sure why he was upset besides the disappointment that threatened to suck the life out of him. There were too many moving parts for a relationship to work with Constance. His secrets, her secrets. None of this felt right, but at the same time he couldn't tear himself away from it.

He stormed around the car, not bothering to wait for her. She'd follow when she was good and ready. The few short minutes he had before she arrived might give him some clarity. Sure, he could go talk to Shane about what had transpired, but he was still mad at his friend over the whole debacle last week.

Hurried footsteps followed him.

Shoot! She was faster than he'd given her credit for.

"James! What's going on with you today?"

His brows lowered and he shoved his hands into his pockets, not slowing down his pace. "Do you ever wonder why we are so interested in doing things we know aren't good for us?"

"Are you talking about our date this weekend?" she asked.

"It doesn't matter what I'm talking about. It's a simple question." They'd made it to the shelter of the barn and he spun around to face her. "I've been told to stay away from you."

Her head reared back and her mouth dropped open.

"Yeah. And somewhere deep down, you know you should stay away from me."

"Don't you dare try to put this on me. You have no idea what's going on inside my head," she sputtered, her face growing redder by the second.

James moved his face closer to hers, fighting the fury that threatened to overwhelm the disappointment. Maybe he should just give in. Maybe the anger would be more tolerable. He lowered his voice as a ranch hand wandered past them. "The truth is, we're both being pulled as if *we're* the stock and some higher power is dragging us to where it thinks we're supposed to be. But we're not cattle, Constance. Sometimes we have to make a choice because it's best for us."

"Are you crazy?"

He stilled.

"That's the stupidest thing I've ever heard," she threw the words back into his face. "We're not animals, but we have been gifted with an instinct about certain things. If you're drawn to me and I'm drawn to you, there's a reason for that. For all we know, God is telling us we should at least test the waters."

He snorted. "God couldn't care less about who you, or I, or anyone dates. There are bigger issues that are going on in the world."

Constance's eyes widened. "*Please* tell me you don't really believe that."

Her question gave him pause. He was a good Christian man. He believed that there was a higher power. But being a man of science had a tendency to cloud his judgment when it came to the little things.

"God cares about his children, James. Even the little things. I don't have any clue why it's been so hard to get over my crush on you. But I can't believe that there isn't a reason for it." Her eyes shone bright with a conviction that once again put him in his place.

Goosebumps erupted on his skin and as if against his will, he was forced to acknowledge that she had a point. He ran a hand through his hair and his shoulders relaxed. "I've been in a relationship before that didn't end well because there were too many secrets."

Her brows creased, but she didn't ask him to elaborate.

"I don't want to fall into bad habits. It puts me on edge just thinking about keeping this a secret from your father."

"I can't tell him, James. Not yet."

"Okay. Then how about this. If our relationship progresses, would you consider telling him? Even if Brielle isn't getting married yet?"

She chewed on the inside of her cheek and stared at her hands. Before she met his gaze, she nodded. "Yes. I will consider it."

He closed the distance between them and hooked his finger under her chin. She peered at him with so much innocence that the small tendril of hope that had been brought to life was smothered. How could he stand in front of her demanding candidness when he was holding back?

Because they were holding back for two different reasons.

He needed to protect her from finding out about Brielle even though his past with her didn't matter anymore. Not to mention, his not being up front had a lot to do with Brielle's insistence on Constance not knowing. Constance on the other hand, was hiding something because she loved her father.

James quickly shoved those thoughts as far into the recesses of his mind as he could. He didn't want them to get in the way of possibly having something good with her.

The light that shone from her eyes and her face was enough to ease the ache that lingered. His gaze dropped to her mouth, noticing the way her soft, full lips parted as if she were surprised at how close they'd become. It wouldn't take much at all to taste her lips right here and now.

If he could show her that they could make this work, perhaps she'd be more willing to start a much-needed conversation with her father about her own freedom.

But he wouldn't do that—he couldn't promise something only to have it not work out in the long run. Constance deserved better. She deserved to be treated with respect. Brielle hadn't cared—not about their relationship, nor about her father's feelings. She'd been interested in her own desires, which was clear by how many guys she'd taken through the wringer. Maybe James was being too judgmental of Constance's older sister. Constance was better, more loving in this respect. And that was why he couldn't say a word about his experience with Brielle. He couldn't have a frank conversation about why lying to her father was a bad idea.

He dropped his hand and stepped back, forcing a smile he had to dig out of the pit of darkness that threatened to swallow him. "I guess we're still on for Friday, huh?"

"I guess so."

14

Constance

onstance had nearly lost her chance with James. It had been a close call and something she was quickly losing control over. It was clear James didn't want to hide anything. But *he* didn't have to live under the same roof with her father like she did.

One day, she might be able to get the courage to tell her father about him, but not anytime soon. The risk wasn't worth it. And the relationship was too new.

All week long, she'd kept her weekend plans close to her heart like a hand of cards. No one was to know about her date nor who she was going to go out with. As far as her sisters were concerned, she was still "little miss perfect" Constance who couldn't do any wrong.

She'd done a pretty good job at keeping things under wraps. But one thing bothered her from the moment she'd had that conversation with James in the barn.

Who had told him to stay away? She couldn't imagine her

father saying something like that. He'd been far more supportive of her learning the vet trade than she'd expected, and that required daily interaction with James. It appeared they had a good rapport going.

So that meant one of her sisters had said something.

Constance could rule out Adeline. Ever since she'd gotten married, she'd been more vocal about her sisters getting more freedom. The problem was she'd been shot down time and time again. Their father was having none of it.

Her youngest sisters were also less likely to be paying attention to this sort of thing. They had their own problems to worry about. And with Brielle elbow deep in suitors, she probably couldn't care less about what James and Constance were up to.

That left Dianna.

Constance sat on the edge of her bed on Friday afternoon after taking a quick shower. She'd told James she'd meet him at the clinic before dinner. There was only one thing she had to do first. She needed to confront Dianna.

They were all free to make their own mistakes. Dianna should have never butted into Constance's affairs. If James hadn't been told to stay away, there was no telling how far their relationship would have been by now.

Constance wove her fingers through the soft curls in her freshly dried hair and rose from her bed. She had about twenty minutes before she had to leave to meet James. She probably should just leave well enough alone. But one thing bothered her. Why would Dianna keep Brielle's secret but judge Constance for the exact same thing?

She scowled as she grabbed her purse and strode from her room. Dianna was in Brielle's room, and Constance could see the light on beneath the door. Constance pushed the door open and her younger sister glanced up from a book she was reading on Brielle's bed. Her expression was blank—completely void of anything that would suggest she had a clue what was about to transpire that night.

Constance folded her arms, the scowl still on her face. "Why did you do it?"

"Why did I do what?"

"Why did you tell James he should stay away from me?"

At first, Dianna's brows lifted, then she laughed and put her book aside. "What are you talking about?"

"James said that you told him to stay away from me."

Dianna scooted to the edge of the bed and swung her legs over the side. "James said *I* said that?"

"Well, no. Not specifically, but—"

"Then maybe you should ask *him* before you come accusing me of—"

Constance shifted her weight from one foot to the other and scanned the room if only to avoid looking directly at her sister. "I don't have to ask him. I know it was you."

Her sister got up from Brielle's bed and moved across the room, her once smooth features beginning to take on a more irritated expression. "How would you know that?"

"You're the only one who makes sense. None of the others would care whether or not I had a crush on a guy or if I wanted to act on it."

Dianna threw up her hands. "Brielle dated guys all the time and I didn't butt in on her relationships."

"*Exactly.*"

The indignation that was written on Dianna's face was almost worse than the irritation from earlier.

"Why do you think I'm so upset? Why are you so insistent on putting your nose in my business when I'm not doing anything different than Brielle had done?"

"Because I *didn't* say anything to him." Dianna sighed and shook her head as she moved back toward her bed. "You know my opinion on breaking this rule. We talked about it recently, in fact. I don't need to go talking to the guy you like to get my point across. If you want to go do something stupid, that's on you."

"But—"

"Who's doing something stupid?" Brielle materialized in the doorway. How on earth she'd managed to open the door without being noticed, Constance didn't have a clue.

Constance whirled around and stared at her older sister, then pointed a finger at Dianna. "She told James to stay away from me."

Brielle shot a confused look in Dianna's direction who only shrugged. "She doesn't believe me. I did no such thing."

"I *know* you did it. But joke's on you. He asked me out anyway." Constance smirked.

"He *what?*" Brielle's sharp voice broke the momentary silence in the room, causing both Dianna and Constance to glance in her direction.

"He asked me out, and I said yes."

Brielle's face turned red and she glowered at Constance. "You can't do that."

"Why not? You did it all the time."

Her older sister paled briefly then her cheeks returned to that bright shade of red. "I—"

Dianna chuckled. "Looks like you found the person who would have told James to stay away. The question is why."

Constance's head swam. Brielle was the one intervening in her life? How could that be possible? She'd been the one notorious for sneaking out and dating guys before she was allowed to. She glared at Brielle and took one quick step in her direction. "*Hypocrite!*"

"What? No, I'm not," Brielle sputtered. "I didn't tell him to stay away because I didn't want you dating. I said it because—" She snapped her mouth shut, glancing from Dianna to Constance again. "He's not good enough for you!"

A sharp bark of laughter exploded from Constance's chest. "He's not good enough for me? That's ridiculous. He's probably the most eligible bachelor in town except for Shane Owens— who, by the way, asked me out last week."

Brielle's eyes almost bugged out of her head. "What's the matter with you?"

"What's the matter with me? What's the matter with you? I'm just doing what you were doing a few years ago." Fire and ice combined in Constance's chest. The pressure continued to build and a deep seeded ache overwhelmed all her senses. "I'm allowed to be happy. And when the guy I've liked my entire life finally notices me, I'm going to leap at the chance."

"You're not." Brielle's jaw tightened.

"I don't know why you of all people are taking this so seriously. I'm an adult and I deserve to be happy. And if you're so selfish that you can't get out of our way so we can have a chance at it, then you can suffer in your own pit of unhappiness for all I care."

Brielle reached for her, grasping her forearm. "I mean it, Connie. He's no good. There are so many other guys that would be worthy of you."

Constance jerked away from Brielle and snorted. "Somehow, I think if it had been any other guy, you still would have reacted the same way." Constance shoved past Brielle and hurried down the stairs. She wasn't about to give Brielle the chance to chase after her, or worse, stop her.

The whole drive to the veterinary clinic, Constance grew more and more agitated. Brielle was such a fraud. How could she go around dating as many guys as she wanted, come home and brag about them to anyone who was willing to listen, then turn around and tell Constance she couldn't do the same?

If there was one person Constance thought she could count on to be in her corner on this one, it was Brielle. Now there was no one she could talk to. No one she could get advice from.

Constance knew exactly where Dianna stood. And apparently Brielle had changed her tune the second she was given the green light to date whomever she wanted.

By the time Constance pulled into the parking lot, she didn't even know if she wanted to go on this date. She wasn't going to be very good company. It would probably be better to turn around and call James with the bad news.

She put her truck into reverse, prepared to do just that, when the front door to the clinic opened and James stepped out.

Well, now she had to go through with it.

He waved at her, then turned around and locked the door before striding toward her truck. She rolled down the window and peered at him in the darkness. "Hey," she murmured.

"You look—" James shook his head. "You're beautiful."

It started with a small tingling sensation, but it grew the longer he appraised her. He pulled open the door and held out his hand. "Are you ready?"

Constance stared at his hand like it was a snake ready to strike. She lifted her gaze up to his face and bit down on her lower lip. "I was thinking..."

He shook his head resolutely this time. "Nope. None of that. No backing out just because you're worried it's not going to work out. We're going—"

"It's not that at all." She grasped his hand and allowed him to pull her from the truck. He nudged the door shut behind her, then moved toward her, causing her to lean against the vehicle.

"Then what is it?" His voice had grown husky, its low timber enough to cause a chill to race down her spine.

"I'm not having the best evening."

"Maybe I can fix that." James said gently. "Tell me what happened."

She swallowed hard. This wasn't how she wanted their first date to start. It would be better to shove aside her frustrations with Brielle and just move forward. She'd been looking forward to this date for longer than she could remember. Constance shook her head. "How about we just start tonight off right?"

The corners of his mouth lifted. "I know just what to do." He took hold of her hand and tugged her toward his car.

"Where are we going?"

"You'll see."

Her sour mood didn't have a chance. The excitement overthrew everything that had been frazzling her nerves for the past hour. James reached to open the door, then stopped. Her gaze dropped down to where his hand was, then lifted to his face. Was there something wrong?

He glanced at her eyes, his blue eyes scanning her face as if he could read her innermost thoughts. James tucked a strand of hair behind her ear and his fingertips trailed along her jawline. Her skin tingled with electricity. She sucked in sharply, then exhaled with effort.

"Whatever happens tonight—whatever happens moving forward, I want you to know that nothing compares to how I feel about you right now."

Her brows creased. "That sounds ominous."

James chuckled, his head dipping momentarily before he lifted his eyes to meet hers again. "There's nothing like starting a new relationship. Excitement, anxiety, even wondering if you're doing the right thing."

She tilted her head to the side. "Do you think we're doing something wrong?"

His features tightened. Right. He didn't like the fact that she refused to tell her father who she was dating. If it were up to him, she'd march right up to her father and tell him that she was going to be in a relationship with James, regardless of the consequences.

But that wasn't going to happen. At least not until she was done with her classes. James would just have to be patient. She reached for the door handle, her skin grazing his. Their eyes met and James moved in front of the door, blocking her from being able to open it.

"There's something I've been wanting to do for over a week, and I feel like if I don't just do it, then it's going to be harder and harder to do." The tail end of his statement came out in a whisper. His eyes were serious as they dropped to her mouth, then slowly met her gaze once more. "Would it be okay if I kissed you?"

15

James

That had to be the dumbest thing he'd ever asked a girl. Usually, he would just judge the situation and steal a kiss. But something held him back. He couldn't tell if it was due to the state in which she'd arrived or if it was because of his past relationship with her sister.

He still hated the way that secret weighed on him, but he knew he was making the right choice. In this moment, he felt like he was a teenager again. What would he do if she said no? He couldn't imagine anything more humiliating than to ask her permission only to be turned down.

Over the next few seconds, time slowed to almost a standstill.

Constance worried her lower lip before it was pulled into a small smile. She nodded. James cupped her cheek with one of his hands, dipping his head lower. He could smell her shampoo —a sweet and almost floral scent. Her breaths shortened and her lips parted.

An aching pleasure flooded his body as his lips caressed hers. His free hand rested against the top of the car just over her left shoulder as he kissed her gently. Constance sucked in sharply, her arms wrapping around his neck and drawing him closer.

She tilted her head back and shivered. Desire wrapped around him like a rope, growing tighter and more restrictive.

Carefully, he disentangled himself from her embrace and rested his head against hers, his eyes shut tight. His breaths were shallow and his heart continued to beat even faster. He longed to pull her against him once more, to explore every curve of her body.

But he was a gentleman.

When he opened his eyes, her gaze was clouded with a yearning that mirrored his own. He chuckled if only to break the tension. "We should..."

She let out a slow breath and nodded. "Yeah."

James reached around her to open the door. He could still taste her sweet kisses which only made him crave more. If he wasn't careful, he'd put them in a situation they might regret.

Constance peered up at him from where she sat in the car. In her eyes, he could see so much. At least he thought he did. Hope, desire, excitement... dare he say love?

No, it was too soon to even consider that.

It was something that could happen in the future. He wouldn't completely disregard the possibility. There were just a few things they needed to figure out before they started on that path.

HE TOOK them on a drive up the mountains and parked in a lot when they couldn't go any farther. Constance climbed out of the car and stared up at the trail they were going to take. She smiled at him as she gestured toward it. "How many girls have you taken up there?" There was a teasing note in her voice, but beneath the surface he could hear her uncertainty.

James grinned at her. "I can honestly say I've never taken anyone up there that I've kissed like I kissed you."

A pretty blush filled her face and she ducked her head, letting some of her hair cover up the rosy hue of her skin.

James reached out and brushed it away. "Why do you do that?"

"Why do I do what?" she whispered.

"Hide your face like you're embarrassed?"

"Maybe I am."

He studied her. Based on what he knew, she hadn't dated anyone before him. He wouldn't be surprised if she'd never been kissed. "You don't have to be."

A smile tugged at her lips and she tore her gaze away from him. "You say that like you can change the way I feel with one statement."

"Maybe one day I'll be able to accomplish that."

Constance let out a self-deprecating laugh and fidgeted. "I don't even know why you wanted to go on a date with me. You might as well get used to me acting a certain way until I figure this out a little more."

He cupped her cheek with his hand, letting his thumb trace over her cheekbone. "Then I guess I'll just have to help you see what I see."

She bit her lip again as if the gesture would help her hold back how much it pleased her to hear his words. This was good, he was on the right track.

They walked side by side on the trail leading toward the peak. This particular lookout allowed spectators to see the whole valley and then some. They'd be able to see the city lights two hours away.

He'd been telling her the truth when he'd said he hadn't

brought a girl up here whom he'd shared such a kiss with, but Constance wasn't the first woman he'd brought out to this place. It was a great location for a picnic, and that's exactly what he had planned on doing.

The picnic basket in his left hand bounced against the back of his leg with each step he took. Every so often Constance would meet his gaze, but most of their hike was completed in silence. There was so much that hung in the air between them.

He would have liked to discuss that kiss for one. And then there was the obvious secrets she planned on keeping from her family. But instead, he chose a safer topic.

"How are your classes going?"

She fiddled with her hair, meeting his eyes again. "Really good. Some of my online classes allow me to go at my own pace and I'm about ready to take two of my finals."

"That's great."

Constance nodded. "It is. But I'm not sure if I'm going to be able to go through the other classes as quickly."

"It's fine to take your time. Don't feel like you have to rush any of this. Enjoy it." His right hand brushed against hers and his fingers twitched. He probably should have held her hand when they'd started the hike. Doing so now would seem strange.

James cleared his throat. Think. Something else he could talk about that wasn't related to work. The harder he attempted to come up with something to say, the more he drew a blank. What would she even want to discuss?

She beat him to it. "Have you told anyone about our date tonight?"

He could sense the hesitation in her voice. It was almost like she hoped he hadn't said a word. James stepped over a fallen branch and attempted to collect his thoughts. He hadn't said a word to his mother or father.

Shane was the only one who would be aware of James's

infatuation with Constance. "If I did tell someone, would that be a bad thing?"

Constance shoved her hands into her back pockets and shrugged. "I suppose it would depend on who you told."

"Like my mother."

"Exactly." She pressed her lips together tightly and gave him a tentative smile. "No offense, but I'm sure you've had your share of experiences with your mother's gossiping nature."

He grimaced. "No one knows better than me." James shook his head. "No. I haven't said anything to her. Though, I've been rather busy lately. From what I've heard, she's been more interested in other things as of late."

"Oh?"

James snickered. "You're not suggesting that you're interested in some town gossip, are you?"

She shrugged again; this time her smile broadened. "I suppose not. I'm too busy studying to worry about what's going on with other people in town."

"Somehow I doubt you would be interested in that sort of thing even if you weren't otherwise preoccupied."

Constance let out a heavy sigh. "You're probably right."

One more thing to add to his growing list of reasons Constance was a far better match for him than Brielle had been. It had gotten to a point where he'd started to wonder what he'd ever seen in the older Callahan sister.

Besides the excitement in the beginning from sneaking around and having the attention of a beautiful woman, she wasn't suited for him nearly as well as Constance appeared to be.

"What about you?"

She was now a few feet ahead of him and she lifted a brow when she glanced over her shoulder toward him. "What about me, what?"

"Have you told anyone about where you are tonight? Or rather, who you are with?"

Her body stiffened.

"Who would I have told?"

"Your sisters?" Of course she wouldn't have told her father. Perhaps she had a friend she might have told.

Constance shook her head. "No." Then she nodded. "Actually, I don't know why I said that. I did mention it."

His steps slowed as he stared at the back of her head. He willed her to turn around and make eye contact with him, to elaborate on who she told. But she didn't. "Do you want to talk about it?"

A sigh escaped her and she stopped. "Does it matter? I'd rather we enjoy our time together than talk about my family."

James closed the distance between them and reached for her hand. His fingers laced within hers and he squeezed reassuringly. "Sure. Whatever you want. How about you tell me something I don't know about you?"

"Yeah? Like what?"

Momentarily distracted by how good it felt to have her hand in his, James didn't respond right away.

"James?"

He shot a look at her. "I don't know. Like what your favorite food is. Or where you went the first time you left the state." He couldn't help himself. James chuckled as he wagged his eyebrows. "Or your first kiss." James had expected her to brush him off, at least on that last one. Instead, she surprised him.

"I love tacos. I've never left the state. And you were my first kiss."

He coughed, choking as he sucked in an unexpected breath. "You're kidding."

Constance laughed. "I like this game. Your turn."

He adjusted the basket in his hand. "I don't have a favorite food—not really. I'll eat about anything you put in front of me.

I crossed the border into Wyoming the first time I left the state. And my first kiss was B—" He coughed again, catching himself before he said the wrong thing. "Before I can remember."

She smirked at him. "You can't tell me that you kissed a girl when you were a child. You're not one of *those* kids, are you?"

"Would that be so bad?"

Another soft laugh filled the air, giving him a pleasant sensation of chills and warmth. She hadn't pulled her hand from his, giving the illusion that they were more than he knew them to be. "Should I be jealous?"

He tugged her to a stop, forcing her to turn around to face him. She gasped as his expression turned serious. "You will never have a reason to be jealous. I've only kissed you once and I can say with complete honesty that there is no one quite like you." She was the girl of his dreams. It was just too bad that it had taken actually kissing her to realize that. Each second that passed while being in her presence only solidified his opinion.

She rolled her eyes and laughed.

"Don't do that," he said, nudging her.

Constance sobered. "Don't do what?"

"Act like I'm just saying these things to get a reaction out of you. I'm not. Everything I'm saying is true." He searched her gaze, praying he might find anything that showed she believed him.

But there was nothing. Her confidence still needed support. His gaze dipped to her lips, and before he had a chance to slow down and really consider the consequences of what he wanted to do, he leaned forward and kissed her for the second time that evening.

She reacted beneath his touch. It was like she started out as a small ember but immediately grew into something bigger and brighter.

This kiss was unlike any other he'd experienced, that was

for certain. How had he gotten so lucky to find this kind of chemistry?

James pulled back from her, the corners of his lips quirking upward. "How about we make it to the clearing and set up that picnic? I'm famished." He didn't release her hand. Instead, he made sure to walk more carefully so as not to put any form of distance between them.

Finally, they arrived in a clearing near the top of the mountain. Evergreen trees mingled with maple and aspen trees. There were a few picnic tables on the outskirts of a large meadow that somehow hadn't become overgrown with foliage.

Constance's steps slowed until she came to a complete stop, and he had to face her to make sure she was ready to continue. Her eyes rounded like saucers and her mouth had dropped open. "How have I never been up here before?"

He chuckled. "It's a popular place for hikers. If you're more into riding, then I suppose you wouldn't have found this place."

She met his gaze once more before releasing his hand and moving forward toward the edge of the clearing.

16

Constance

 *S*he was on top of the world. It felt as though Constance could see the entire world around her. As far as the eye could see, there were lights coming on as the city continued to darken. Fall was quickly on its way and it was getting to be dusk sooner.

James's footsteps shuffled a little way off from where she stood at the edge of the mountain. There was a wooden fence blocking any sightseers from accidentally losing their footing. It was quiet. The only other sounds were that of bugs or small woodland creatures.

She had never felt so small in her entire life. This place was proof that in the grand scheme of things, the importance of certain topics was relative. The reasons she'd been upset earlier didn't really matter.

Why should she care if her sisters didn't want her out here with James? She knew he was a good man. Brielle was crazy if she didn't see that. They'd been friends once.

Unless the reason her older sister had warned her off was because of a falling-out.

Constance shook off that thought. She would have noticed if something had happened between Brielle and James to cause a rift. They'd just drifted apart. Brielle was probably jealous that James had moved away and followed his dream to become a veterinarian. That was her biggest judgment of him. She thought he was stuck up and full of himself. Brielle didn't know what she was talking about. Or maybe he'd changed since high school.

She glanced over her shoulder toward James who was setting out a blanket with the food. He'd pulled out a little electric lantern, and there was a single rose set out where she would be sitting.

Butterflies erupted inside her stomach. He was turning out to be such a romantic. She never would have guessed he had it in him. He was perfect.

Maybe too perfect?

The thought was laughable. How could there be such a thing as too perfect? Eventually she'd figure out that he had a bad habit or two or three. And it might drive her insane. But by then she might also be so utterly in love with the guy it wouldn't matter.

Perhaps she was already on her way there.

His eyes lifted and locked with hers as he placed the last container of food on the blanket.

She wandered toward him and settled onto her knees. "This is quite a spread you've got going. I would have thought that our first date would have been at a restaurant or bowling or something equally cliché."

He scoffed. "A picnic under the stars isn't cliché enough for you?"

She laughed. "No. It's everything I didn't know I needed on a first date."

James reached out and held her hand, trailing his thumb across the back of it. "I'm glad it makes you happy."

Constance settled into a more comfortable position. Her stomach growled as her eyes bounced from the fruit bowl to the chips and sandwiches he'd packed. "I can't believe you did all of this."

He shrugged, a proud smile pulling at his lips. "This is where I excel. It's sorta my thing."

As much as she tried to keep the thought at bay, a sliver of jealousy and doubt crept into her mind. He'd said he'd never brought someone up here with whom he'd shared a kiss like the one they'd experienced. But she'd be an idiot to think that he hadn't brought other girls up here. It wasn't necessarily a special evening he'd picked out just for her.

That negativity needed to go.

They were here together now. Just because she'd never dated anyone before didn't mean she could expect the same from him. He was older and didn't have the same restrictions she'd grown up with.

Constance picked up a grape and popped it in her mouth, forcing herself to be mature about this. Their experiences made them who they were. James might not have been such a perfect gentleman if he hadn't had the experiences that led him here tonight. The easiest way to do that was to pretend until it was real.

She tilted her head, chewing thoughtfully before swallowing the piece of fruit. "Tell me about the first one."

He frowned, confusion flittering across his face.

"Your first girlfriend?"

That was the wrong question to ask. Immediately the soft planes of his face sharpened. He released her hand and frowned. "Why do you want to know about that?"

She shrugged, attempting to act like the topic didn't scare her to death. "I'm curious."

"That's not the sort of thing you talk about on a first date, you realize that, right?"

Warmth flooded her cheeks and she let out a laugh that she hoped sounded more flirtatious than it did in her head. Her lashes fluttered and she shielded her eyes beneath them. "I don't think I need to point out that I don't have the experience you do. Maybe I'm just curious. What was young James like? Did he fumble through his dating years like a typical teenager?" She peered at him from beneath her lashes. "You don't have to talk about your past if you don't want to. It's not like we haven't talked a lot about ourselves while on the job. That subject is one of the only ones that hasn't come up."

James relaxed only slightly. He dragged a hand down his face and eyed her with what could only be read as suspicion.

She laughed. "I promise. I'm not trying to uncover some secret. Though if you have one, I warn you it will be unearthed eventually." She'd meant those words to be just as playful and light, but they seemed to hit him in a way she hadn't been prepared for. She didn't have any secrets except for knowing that Brielle had been the one to tell him to stay away. James hated secrets. He wouldn't have kept anything from her, and even if he had, she couldn't expect him to confess on the first date.

Maybe it was time to start preparing herself for the inevitable conversation with her father.

She looked up at James, finding him studying her once again. She shifted under his scrutiny. "Well? Are you going to lighten the mood with stories of your failed dates? Because I'll let you in on a little secret. I don't have any—unless this one turns out to be the first."

The corners of his mouth lifted into a hesitant grin. "I have never been on a date with a girl who was actually interested in hearing about my past exploits."

"Exploits, huh? Maybe I should walk away from this conversation while we both have our dignity."

This time he actually laughed, a sound that eased the growing ache of uncertainty within her. She grabbed another grape and bit down, letting the juice coat her mouth in a sweet and tangy layer.

"Okay, fine. But no names and only vague details."

"Deal."

He shifted, reclining on his side so he could prop his elbow against the blanket and rest his head in his hand. "I used to hike up here when I was in high school. Riding horses at my family's ranch always felt like a chore. I wanted something different, so I would come to places like this where I didn't have to take care of an animal."

She snickered. "You didn't like taking care of the horses at your ranch, so you got a job taking care of other people's horses."

James shrugged. "What can I say? I'm more complicated beneath the surface than I appear to be." He plucked a chip from a bowl and crunched it in his mouth as his gaze swept over their immediate surroundings. "This place was an escape. It's usually not occupied because most of the locals are like you and they want to ride their horses or they're too busy working. So I took full advantage of that and brought a few dates up here."

"How did that go? Did they find it as amazing as you did?"

He grimaced. "Honestly? No. Most of the girls I liked in high school weren't the hiking type. They weren't the working type either."

She made a face. "Geez, they sound like Brielle."

His brows creased and the frown returned to his face.

"Don't worry, I won't judge you for dating girls like that. I get it. Guys in high school were shallow." Her words didn't land the way she wanted them to.

He didn't appear to relax at all. Instead, he sat up and plucked at the little fuzzy balls on the blanket. "I had a huge crush on the first girl I brought here. But we only came the one time. She didn't like it—preferred to drive to the city. After her, I tried again twice more. They were laid back dates, nothing like this." His smile almost looked pained as he reached for her hand and held it tight. "Just because I brought other girls here doesn't mean it isn't special. I brought you here because this is one of my favorite places to go... Date or no date."

Tingles and chills assaulted her. The hairs on the back of her neck stood on end and the clear memory of their passionate kiss before they came here filled her thoughts. Her lips buzzed, as if asking for more. "Well, you've finally brought a girl here who can appreciate it."

Well, that was stupid to say. It was the only thing that popped into her head and it was ridiculous. She would be lucky if he didn't see her as the child she'd been when her crush started.

James leaned forward and grasped her chin with his finger and thumb. "Somehow I knew you would," he whispered before placing a kiss on her forehead.

How was it that he knew exactly what to say and how to say it?

Brielle was completely wrong regarding her opinions of James. It didn't matter how many guys she'd dated or spent time with. She wasn't going to be right about all of them.

The air had seemed to thin out all the tension that had once surrounded them. They each started eating their sandwiches and their chatter returned to subjects that weren't as taboo for a first date. James talked about his experiences in college. Their conversation shifted to his veterinary clinic and the plans he had for it in the future.

"Ideally, I'd like you to come work with me for the long haul."

She choked on some of the water she had in her mouth and her head ducked down as she attempted to clear her throat. "What?"

"You have to have known that." He shot her a boyish grin. "I've seen the way you pick up on things. I can tell you have a knack for this sort of stuff. I know your father would probably want you to stick around the ranch, and I'd be willing to share."

She bit back a laugh, not wanting a repeat of what had just happened. "You're not kidding."

"Of course not. I'm paying for your education—"

"Yeah, to help with training and to complete the contract we have."

"Yes," he drawled, "but that contract was just the beginning. I wasn't going to lock you into anything until we figured out how much you like it. Seriously, I could use another veterinarian for when things get really busy. What do you say?"

Constance wiped at her mouth with her napkin. There were so many other variables in making that kind of decision. What if their relationship didn't work out? They'd be stuck together but not wanting to see one another. A short-term job wouldn't be a problem; there would be an end in sight. But to commit to something for the long haul? "I'm going to have to think about it."

He nodded. "That's fair. I just wanted to get it out there so you know what my expectations—or hopes were."

"Thank you, James."

"For what?"

"All of it. For helping me pay for my education even though my father could have done it if he really wanted to. And teaching me—allowing me to shadow you. It's more than I could have ever dreamed."

17

James

Their date couldn't have gone better if he had spent years planning it. James was almost worried that she'd figured out he'd dated Brielle, the way she brought her sister up in the conversation. But everything worked out.

Constance hadn't even really seemed to mind about his past, which was an amazing win. To top it all off, she'd agreed to go on another date with him for the upcoming weekend. There was only one problem.

And she was charging right at him.

Brielle grabbed his wrist harder than he thought was humanly possible and all but dragged him into the barn.

"Geez, Brielle. What's your problem?"

She glowered at him and her voice lowered to a menacing hiss. "What do you think you're doing?"

"What do you mean?" He rubbed his wrist where she'd held him too tight. "You're going to have to be clearer if you're going to want me to help you out."

She let out a sound that was a growl and a groan combined. "You know perfectly well what I'm talking about." She blew a stray strand of hair from her face and the color in her cheeks deepened to match the red hue of her shirt.

If he'd still had a crush on her, he might have thought this little temper tantrum was adorable. But somewhere along the way, he'd lost that spark he'd carried for her all these years. James folded his arms and frowned at her. "I'm going to have to ask you to clarify what you're talking about."

She threw her hands into the air and paced in front of him. "Did you know that before Constance started to spend time with you, she had never broken any rules?"

James snorted. "I find that hard to believe. Constance is human. She's probably broken more rules than you realize— that is, if you're referring to your father's rules."

Brielle growled again. "*No*. I assure you I would know."

He shrugged. "Seems to me, you might not know her as well as you think you do."

She stormed toward him, closing the distance so quickly he nearly tripped back a few steps. "Constance was the epitome of perfection. Now, she's going out with you at all hours and lying about where she's been. It's only a matter of time before my father finds out, and then what do you think he's going to say about her keeping up with her schooling?"

James frowned. He actually hadn't thought about it that far. Would Zeke tear the opportunity she had away from his own daughter? No. He didn't seem the type for that. But he could refuse to let James set foot on the property if it meant keeping his daughter safe from a miscreant like the local veterinarian.

Brielle sneered. "*See*? There it is. You've finally realized that you're not only putting your new crush in jeopardy, but you're risking her education too." She poked him hard in the chest. "So what are you going to do about it?"

He brushed her finger away with the back of his hand and

glowered at her. "First of all, you could make this so much easier if you'd just find someone to marry like your sister did. Honestly, Brielle. You have all the power at this point and you're still refusing to help your younger sisters."

She gasped. "How dare you!"

"Secondly, Constance is an adult with a good head on her shoulders. If she wants to go on a few dates with me, that's her choice. And, as much as it looks like you want to, you don't get to have control over the situation."

Brielle's voice lowered; the sinister undertones were enough to raise the hairs on the back of his neck and turn his blood cold. "Didn't you break up with me because you couldn't handle the secrets I kept from my father?"

He stiffened and glanced around the barn, praying no one would overhear and share this tidbit of information with Constance. That secret Brielle had demanded he keep in the very beginning was probably the only one that made sense.

She pushed his shoulder hard, forcing him to meet her gaze once more. "Constance is doing the exact same thing." Her voice lifted an octave, and she mimicked his tone. "Honestly, James, you'd think you'd learn your lesson and go after the Callahan daughter who was actually available to date." Her brows lowered and her jaw tightened as she let her hurtful words sink in. "Unfortunately for you, it looks like you'd rather let history repeat itself." She shoved past him and headed for the door.

James spun around, itching to throw a retort at her, but she was too far away. Anything he said would most definitely be overheard by someone else. His hands clenched into fists, and he let out a growl of his own, then kicked at a bucket nearby.

The metal tin bounced around on the floor, making contact with a post and then rolling until it stopped against a stall door. How was it that Brielle still knew exactly where to poke to get the biggest reaction? They'd dated so long ago.

His chest was tight and it hurt to breathe.

The worst part was that she was right.

He'd broken up with her because he couldn't stand keeping their relationship in the shadows. It wasn't fair for him to have to hide where he was going or who he was out with from his parents. It wasn't fair that he couldn't take her to school dances or tell his best friends who he was kissing beneath the bleachers.

James had kept all those secrets for her, and in the end, he'd gotten nothing out of the relationship except for a broken heart and trust issues.

Constance *was* different. But she was dealing with the same family problems. Her only saving grace, according to him, was that she kept her secrets to maintain a peaceful home.

Brielle had kept her secrets because she was scared of the consequences of getting caught.

Blast it all! He was right back into a cycle he'd hated all those years before.

James stormed from the barn and headed for his truck. He needed to leave before he did or said anything that he'd regret. Their date was for later that night and Constance had run inside to get a drink. He would leave her a text message and tell her they were calling it a day early and he'd see her later at the clinic for their date.

Once he sent that message, he didn't waste any time waiting for her to respond. He needed to blow off some steam and the only person he could talk to was Shane. His friend was the only other person besides Constance, Brielle, and himself that was aware of the current situation—as far as he knew. Maybe Shane would have some advice to give.

The whole drive toward the country club, James stewed over the words Brielle had flung at him. He *had* thought that his relationship with Brielle had ended in a way that was amicable. But apparently he'd missed something. Why was Brielle so intent on keeping him away from her sister? It wasn't like he'd be the key to getting Zeke to agree to a change in the rules. He practically stomped all the way into Shane's office and proceeded to tell him everything that had just transpired.

"Maybe Brielle is still in love with you."

James let out a humorless bark of laughter. "You wouldn't say that if you had seen the way she looked at me. If you had heard her tone of voice, you probably would have assumed that the world was coming to an end."

Shane arched a brow. "There's no other explanation—not as far as I can tell. She's demanded that you not tell a soul about your past. She's threatened you for not leaving Constance alone. *And* she brought up that you might as well date her since she's the available one."

James sat up in his seat, his index finger out and ready to throw out a retort. He snapped his mouth shut and settled back. Shane made a good point. She was mad, but she'd never told him that she'd rather die than date him again.

He shook his head. "I don't know. Earlier she—"

"Women are confusing. It doesn't matter if she told you no before. For all you know, she might have been trying to make you jealous. And it worked. You turned around and started dating her sister. Now she's mad." Shane chuckled. "Man, you really don't know what you're doing, do you?"

"Of course I do. I'm going after the girl that is exactly what I want in a wife. Constance and I have this connection that I've never shared with anyone."

Shane sighed. "Now you're starting to sound like a sap."

"Is that a bad thing?"

Shane folded his arms and leaned back in his chair so he could rest his feet on his desk. "It is for you."

"How do you figure? I've finally found the person I want to spend my life with. There's nothing wrong about that."

"It's not the who that's the problem. It's the *who's* father." Shane made a clicking sound with his tongue. "I have only come in contact with Zeke Callahan a couple of times and let me tell you, if I were unlucky enough to fall for one of his daughters, I might just be convinced to fall for someone else instead."

James frowned. "Then that's not love."

Shane studied him for a few moments and his smug expression slipped away to be replaced by a more contemplative look. "You really love this girl?"

Constance's beautiful face filled James's thoughts. Her laugh, her graceful, caring nature, and her intelligence made her the perfect package. "Yeah, I think I do."

He rubbed his jaw with his hand, then let out a heavy sigh. "Then you're not going to like what I have to say."

James leaned forward. Whatever advice Shane might be able to give him was a better starting point than where he currently sat.

Shane chuckled. "You're pretty much up a creek, pal. There is no way you come out of this unscathed. Either you talk her into convincing her father that she's capable of making these kinds of decisions on her own, or you do it and find yourself on the other end of a shotgun."

"Do you seriously think that Zeke would—"

"Oh. He most definitely would. That man had to raise all his daughters on his own. He didn't have the gentle influence of his wife for most of those girls' lives. They are more precious to him than this whole place is to me, and that is saying something." Shane gestured around his office. "I don't know what to tell you, James. But if I were to guess, I'd say the easiest way to fix this whole mess would be to convince Brielle to find a beau of her own."

"It'd be easier to find a pig that could fly," James muttered. "Brielle isn't interested in finding a guy long-term. In fact, I'm fairly certain my relationship with her was probably the longest one she ever had."

"Well, what does she have against getting married?"

"Beats me."

"Come on, James. You dated her. What do you think it is?"

James stared at his hands in his lap and his thoughts raced through his mind. Each and every memory he had of Brielle—what made her tick. He could only come up with one reasonable explanation. "She doesn't like being told what to do. When she was younger, she didn't like being told she couldn't date, so she dated. Now she's being told to get married and she's being stubborn again."

"*Or*, she's upset she lost out on you and, if she can't have you, then no one can." Shane laughed.

James shook his head, still staring at his hands. "No, that's not it. I would be able to tell."

"Sounds like she needs to find someone so irresistible that she wouldn't be able to deny them."

James slowly lifted his gaze to meet Shane's. He was the most eligible bachelor in Copper Creek at the moment. Brielle would likely jump at the chance to go on a date with him.

His best friend lifted both hands and laughed. "Oh no, you don't. After hearing what you went through, I wouldn't touch her with a ten-foot pole."

"She's not that bad. The only reason we broke it off was because I wanted something more and she wasn't ready."

Shane shook his head once more. "I may not be ready for something serious, but I'm definitely not crazy enough to get close to that one."

James let out a sigh. "Then what do you think I should do?"

"I guess you could find someone who could distract her. Are there any other guys in the area that she might be interested in?" Shane picked up a file off his desk and flipped through it, his interest obviously spent.

James snorted. "I can't think of anyone who she hasn't already dated. She's probably exhausted all avenues for new love interests."

Shane arched a brow as he glanced over at James. "That's not possible. I mean, this town is small, but it's not that small. People are moving here all the time. Not to mention you guys breed like no one's business."

At James's disgruntled expression, Shane laughed.

"You can't possibly think it's normal to have families with more than three children. How many ranches have over five?" Shane asked.

"*My* parents only had two."

Shane waved his folder through the air dismissively. "But that's what I'm saying. There are a lot more men out here than you realize. She just needs to find one who can put up with her." He tapped the file on his right hand thoughtfully. "Isn't there a family out of town a little way that has like twelve kids? From what I heard, they don't venture out this way all that often —kinda keep to themselves. I'd bet Brielle hasn't dated any of them."

James got to his feet. "Thanks for the brainstorming, but somehow I don't think setting Brielle up with someone new is going to do the trick. She threatened me when she was currently in the throes of a relationship with someone else. No, this goes deeper than either one of us realizes."

"So, what are you going to do?"

He shrugged. "I don't know, but she's not going to scare me off. I'm falling harder for Constance every day. I'm not going to walk away from what I have with her just because her sister doesn't want me dating her."

A wicked smile crossed Shane's face. "Good luck. I've seen Brielle around. That woman might seem sweet on the surface, but I'd wager she's got some claws on her."

"You don't have to tell me. I dated her, remember?"

18

Constance

She shouldn't be nervous about tonight. It was a second date, not the first one. They had already decided that they liked each other enough to move forward. Constance frowned at her reflection in the mirror, a sense of déjà vu overcoming her. Last week she tried to talk herself off a ledge while battling with her feelings about Dianna betraying her.

But it wasn't Dianna she had to be worried about anymore.

How had Brielle done it all these years? Two weeks of keeping this secret and already she wanted to go running to her father and just tell him what was going on. While she told herself that she was keeping her relationship a secret because she didn't want to hurt him, there was more to it than that.

A part of her wanted to keep it a secret for fear that if it came out, she would lose the excitement of this little forbidden romance. Another part of her worried that it would become too real, too fast.

What if her father's rules were there for reasons more than just to keep tabs on her sisters? Maybe she wasn't ready for this stage of her life.

A darkness that clouded her thoughts threatened to continue filling her head and she shoved them aside. She was overthinking this. She shouldn't care if Brielle didn't approve. The only people who mattered were the two people in this relationship.

Constance opened her door and a yelp tore from her throat. Her hand flew to her chest, covering her pounding heart as if the action alone would slow it down.

Brielle blocked the doorway, her hands on her hips and her eyes narrowed. "Where are *you* going?"

"Leave me alone, Bri." Constance scowled as she attempted to brush past her sister. "It's none of your business where I'm going."

"That's where you're wrong. Adeline isn't the oldest in the house anymore, I am. So I have to keep track of you."

Constance let out a laugh that almost sounded like she should be committed. "Do you even hear the words that come out of your mouth these days? I don't know what happened to you to make you act like this, but it's not a pretty color on you. Now, if you'll excuse me, I have a date to go on." Once again, she moved to push through the doorway but Brielle's hand shot out, slamming against the doorjamb and blocking her escape.

Brielle's features softened and she pressed her lips together. The change was sudden and far more unexpected than everything Brielle had been doing previously.

Hesitation flooded Constance's insides. Her instincts sent up a red flag, warning her that if she didn't at least ask Brielle what the matter was, she'd regret it.

Then again, she might regret asking anyway.

Constance let out a sigh and folded her arms. "What?"

Brielle didn't move right away. She didn't speak or show any indication she was willing to share what was upsetting her. Then she blew out a breath through pursed lips. "Why do you want to do this?"

"Why do I want to do what? Go on a date with James? To finally get the guy I've been drooling over since I was in high school? Gee. I don't know, Bri. I guess it's because deep down I know that this is what will make me happy."

Brielle flinched at Constance's sharp tone. "Guys don't bring happiness, you know that, right?"

Constance huffed. "Once again, you're saying the one thing that goes against everything you've demonstrated in the past. Why did you date all those guys? Because it sure seemed like it was making you happy."

Her sister shook her head. "You don't know anything. My reasons for dating guys are my own. You can date a million of them, but if you don't find the right one, then it doesn't matter."

"Well, maybe James is the right one for me. Have you considered that?"

Brielle's face briefly took on a pained expression. "How much do you even know about the guy? You've never dated before. What makes you think that you can trust him? Guys will say anything—do anything—to get what *they* want."

"Yeah? Well, what would you call what you do to guys?"

She grimaced. "I don't have to answer to you. But I do want to give you some advice."

"What? *Don't* date? Yeah. I got that. No offense, but I'm not interested in taking that advice." She took a step forward, then stopped herself short and glowered at her sister. "Do you mind? I don't want to be late."

Brielle sighed. "Just think about what I said, okay? If he's not being one hundred percent upfront and honest with you, then he's not worth the risk. What do you think Dad would do if he found out you were dating James?"

She'd thought about it a lot, actually. "I'd like to think that he'd say he wanted me to be happy."

"Don't you think he'd follow through with his threats and kick you out of the house?"

"I don't know. That's why I'm steering clear of him until I can figure out a way to tell him. If Adeline was able to get Dad on board with Sean Baker, then I think James would be a piece of cake. He already likes James. He just needs to view him as the potential to be something more." This time Constance was able to slip between the doorjamb and her sister and finally make it out into the hallway.

Brielle's hand shot out and wrapped around Constance's wrist, causing her to freeze and stare at where her sister held onto her.

"You can let go now."

"Just—be careful. Don't give him your heart just because he's the first guy who gives you attention. There could be better men out there."

"Not for me," Constance bit out through gritted teeth. Her sister's words had caused her enough pain for the evening. She didn't need the doubt or self-loathing that her statements had also caused.

She needed to get to the clinic and throw her arms around James for a much-needed hug.

Perhaps something more.

THE SECOND she walked into the clinic, she felt like she was coming home. There were no sisters judging her for mistakes they themselves made. There was no threat hanging over her head if she were to get caught breaking her family's one cardinal rule.

There was just the smell of a freshly mopped floor, the cool crisp air from when the AC kicked on, and the sound of Chloe's fingers on the keyboard. She glanced up from the reception desk and smiled warmly at Constance.

"How are you this evening?"

"I'm doing good."

Chloe's gaze swept over Constance's dress, nice cowboy boots, and purse. "You going out with James again?"

She nodded. "I think we're getting dinner, but I'm not sure." Constance nodded toward the back office. "Is he in there?"

Chloe nodded and waved her back. "Go ahead. I'm sure he's expecting you."

Constance moved around the reception desk and pushed open the door to James's office. He stood near a window, the phone to his ear. "Yes. That's exactly what you needed to do. Don't worry, I'll be over there in ten minutes."

James turned around as he hung up the phone and jumped when his eyes landed on Constance. He pulled up his wrist and checked his watch. "Oh no, I lost track of time."

"What's the matter? Do we need to postpone?"

He moved toward a cabinet and pulled out a hefty clinical-looking bag. "I'm afraid so. I don't have anyone who can handle this tonight. There's a ranch just on the outskirts of town. Keagans, I believe. I've never been out there, but they have a horse that's having trouble giving birth."

Without hesitation, Constance dug through her purse and retrieved an elastic. She was in the middle of pulling her hair back when James stopped what he was doing to stare at her.

"What? I'm coming with you," she said.

He strode toward her, a small smile on his face. "You don't have to do that. I'm sure we can reschedule our reservation for tomorrow. You'd probably prefer to stay home instead of working on your night off."

She shook her head. "You of all people should know better than that. I'm not going to let you go to another birthing and have all the fun without me. Besides, you need me."

The way his bright eyes swept over her from her hair down to her boots and back to her face gave her pleasant chills. Her skin tingled with nervous energy and all the dismal thoughts that had weighed her down from before had disappeared.

She closed the distance between them and wrapped her arms around his neck. "This is what makes us perfect for each other, you know."

"What's that?" he murmured.

Constance lifted a shoulder and her grin widened. "It's our second date and you had to cancel because of an animal emergency."

His happiness faded. "I'm sorry."

"No. That's not the good part. What makes us great together is the fact that I'm perfectly content to have our second date in some musty barn helping a horse have her baby." She stood up on her toes with the intention of kissing his nose, but he blocked her, capturing her lips with his own.

His arms slipped around her waist, pulling her close, allowing for their kiss to go on a little longer than expected.

The flicker of happiness in her chest exploded into something far hotter and more dangerous than she'd encountered before. She moaned softly and deepened their kiss, only to tear herself away from him when they heard Chloe clear her throat from the doorway.

Constance ducked her head and folded her arms, pressing her sensitive lips together. The heat from her chest had expanded to her skin, covering what felt like her whole body in a blush.

James chuckled and retrieved the document Chloe had in her hand. "What's this?"

"It's an official contract between you and Shane Owens's equine therapy business. He sent it over this afternoon. Once you sign this, everything will be official." Her gaze drifted toward the clock on the wall. "You better start heading out if you're going to get to the Keagan's ranch on time."

"Right," James faced Constance. "Are you sure you want to come—"

"Of course. This is why I started taking classes in the first place."

James gathered everything he required, and this time Chloe wasn't needed. It would be just the two of them like it had been for the last couple of weeks.

Even though she'd been through this with Calliope and Clio, she was a bundle of nerves. So many things could go wrong when it came to labor and delivery. Her legs bounced and she stared out the window at the darkening sky.

James placed a hand on her knee and she jumped. He chuckled. "It'll be fine. I've seen enough of these to know that it'll all work out."

"Sometimes it doesn't."

"True. But this won't be one of those times." He offered her a reassuring smile.

"How can you be so certain?"

"I can't. But I find that arriving at a birth with the mindset that it's going to go wrong won't help me at all."

Mindset. It was a powerful thing. "What's the matter with her—the Keagan's mare?"

James reached for her hand and laced her fingers within his own, then immediately dove into all the technical terms and descriptions. She stared at him blankly, only catching about half of what he'd said.

His lips twitched and he grinned. "It's nothing serious. The horse has just been in labor for longer than we'd like. If she doesn't give birth after a certain amount of time, the foal could suffocate. Worst case scenario, I'll have to reach in there and help guide it out."

When they pulled up to the ranch, Constance peered out the window at the old house and barn. The place looked like it hadn't been inhabited for years, though she'd heard of the Keagan name before. The buildings were dilapidated, paint peeling from the wooden siding. One window was boarded up and there was a workbench out on the porch.

She met James's eyes. "How are they able to live here?"

He shrugged. "People make do with what they have. It's not our place to judge."

"I'm not judging. I just..." She shook her head. Seeing this place made her realize how lucky she'd been to grow up with the stability she'd had. "Maybe I could convince my father to help out."

"I wouldn't."

Constance frowned at him, disappointment slithering around in her stomach. "Why? Don't you think they could use it?"

James reached for his bag from the back seat, then glanced at the house. "Of course they could use it. But based on the conversation I had with Wade Keagan, there is no way he's going to accept any kind of charity. I don't have to meet the guy in person to know he's a proud man. But it's sweet of you to want to help." He pushed open his door and climbed out.

She followed suit and together they made their way toward the house. Someone hollered at them and they stopped, turning toward the barn. A teenager who looked to be about seventeen waved his arms back and forth. "Over here."

They headed toward the kid, their steps a little quicker. James placed his hand on the small of Constance's back, his touch warm and comforting. Just being with him was enough. She didn't have to go to a fancy restaurant or be treated to flowers or chocolates.

She was just happy to be with him and doing what she loved.

The only problem with that was her father's silly rule.

Perhaps James had a point. She needed to start making a plan on how she would tell her father that she wanted permission to officially date James. With Adeline married, maybe his stance had softened. She could only hope that he liked James as much as he was letting on. That would be her only saving grace. Because regardless of what Brielle thought, James was a good guy.

19

James

James pulled his gloves from his hands and tossed them into a nearby bucket. The oddly comforting smell of fresh cut straw and manure wafted through the barn. Constance was over by the mare, speaking softly to her as she trailed her hands up and down the horse's back.

The mare's ears flicked to the sides, and she chewed lazily. Her whole demeanor was relaxed and happy. It was moments like this that he loved his job. When everything finally settled and there wasn't anything to worry about.

The kid who'd led them to the barn stood just outside the stall, his arms folded over the top as he stared with interest at the new foal. He fired off question after question at Constance who answered every single one without missing a beat.

"Shouldn't she be trying to stand up already?" Liam asked.

Constance glanced at James with amusement. "If she's not walking within three hours then there's a problem."

His brows lifted. "Three hours? I guess it's been a while since I've seen the birth of a foal."

She tilted her head, moving away from the mare and leaning against the stall wall. "How long have you been living here?"

"My whole life."

She shot James a concerned look and he gave a sharp shake of his head. She shouldn't go there. These folks weren't her charity case.

Of course she'd ignore him.

"Where are your folks? Is Wade—"

Liam laughed. "*Wade*? No. He's my brother. My folks are dead."

Constance paled and dragged her gaze over to James once more. Great. At this rate there would be no convincing her that they needed to leave well enough alone. He nodded toward their supplies. "Constance, why don't you gather up our things?"

She faced Liam. "So Wade's your brother, and he's taking care of you? How many brothers and sisters do you have?"

Liam shifted his focus back to the foal. "Look. She's trying to stand."

"Constance," James's warning tone did nothing.

"Liam, how many siblings do you have?"

He glanced at her. "What? Oh. There's twelve of us."

She gave James a pointed look and mouthed the word *twelve*.

"Yeah. There's Wade, Annabel, Elijah, Lucas, Henry, Daniel, Mason, Hudson, me, Carter, Caleb, and Charlie."

"Wow. Eleven boys and one girl. I bet Annabel doesn't know what to do with you, huh?"

He shook his head. "Charlie's a girl." Liam pointed to the horse. "Can I come in and pet her? Or will her mom get mad?"

Constance reached for the stall door. "She's settled down. Just be careful."

James let out an exaggerated sigh and opened his eyes wide, hoping the strange look on his face would prompt her to come over to him. He cleared his throat and jerked his chin toward the supplies.

Constance motioned toward Liam as if that was enough to get him off her back. Nope. She needed to butt out before Wade got back with the towels he'd said he'd get.

James marched over to her and took her hands in his. "I understand that you want to help these folks, but you really can't."

"Why not? They clearly need it. They don't have any parents—"

"What makes you think their parents did much of anything in the first place? I'd love to help them as much as the next guy, but the truth is I can't. If Wade wanted help, he'd ask for it. So do us both a favor and let's not get fired."

He felt the hurt and frustration she wore on her face acutely. He could empathize, but he'd learned a long time ago that there were just some things he couldn't change. "Look, we're not going to charge them for our services today. We'll keep an eye on them and make sure the animals stay healthy."

"I thought you said that Wade doesn't accept handouts?" she said.

"I'm sure we'll come up with some kind of arrangement that he will find acceptable. For now, just *please*, stay out of their business." He squeezed her hand and pulled her a little closer so he could press a kiss to her temple. "I think we can still make it out to the country club for a little dancing if you want."

She gestured toward her dress which was now covered in straw and probably some fluids from helping him with the foaling process, then shook her head. "Somehow, I don't think Shane would find my attire all that appropriate."

"It's not Shane's opinion that matters." He nuzzled her ear with his nose, loving the way she leaned into him with a soft exhale. "Let me take you dancing. It'll be fun."

"On one condition," she crooned.

"What's that?"

"We stay outside and away from the other guests. I don't care what you say, Shane is still the owner of that establishment and I'm sure he'd have no qualms about asking us to leave."

James chuckled. "As long as I can have you in my arms for the night, I'll be happy."

Footsteps echoed down the concrete ground toward them, and Wade's stern face appeared. "I was only able to find a couple towels. We're a little behind in our laundry." His gaze shifted toward Constance, then to Liam. "Time for you to go inside and finish your chores. The horse will wait until tomorrow."

Liam frowned. "But—"

"If you're going to live under my roof, you're going to follow the rules. Each of us has weight to pull and until you can handle the bigger stuff, you're gonna take care of the dishes."

"Can't Charlie do them?"

Wade's expression tightened as he glanced once more toward Constance. "Charlie is doing the laundry with Caleb. I'm not going to ask you again. It's either you help out around the house or you get a job in town. Which is it?"

"Fine," Liam muttered. He slipped out of the stall without another word, muttering something about dishes being harder than anything else because of how many people ate supper.

Constance shifted beside James and he gripped her hand a little tighter, praying she'd understand the warning he was giving her. Thankfully, she didn't end up saying anything.

Wade tossed the towels over the stall door. Constance grabbed them with a small smile before heading over to the animals. They both watched as she dipped the end of a towel in a bucket of water and set to work cleaning the mare of any bacteria the foal might come in contact with.

Wade reached into his back pocket and pulled out his wallet. "I don't know what you charge for house visits—"

James held up a hand. "It's fine. I'm not going to charge you for this one."

As expected, Wade's jaw tightened and his eyes narrowed. "I don't need a hand-out. I'm perfectly capable of paying—"

"That's not what I'm suggesting. What do you think about having Liam come out to the clinic a couple times a week to do some cleaning? He could mop floors and stock shelves."

Wade returned his wallet to his pocket and rubbed the back of his neck. "I don't know. I suppose I could talk to him about it."

James clapped Wade on the shoulder. "You let me know what you guys decide. And if that doesn't work, we'll figure out a different payment arrangement."

He nodded. "Thanks, Dr. Pratt." His focus shifted to the foal who was now standing on wobbly legs but not quite ready to walk. "How is she?"

"She's perfect—a real fighter. I wouldn't be surprised if she ends up giving you a run for your money, full of spirit and energy." James chuckled, then moved toward the supplies and started the process of gathering everything they'd brought. Constance finished her work and left the towels hanging over the side of the stall.

By the time they were on the road, James could sense that Constance was more than a little frustrated. She continued to sigh and shift in her seat.

"They'll be fine, Connie. They've been figuring things out for a lot longer than either one of us has been aware."

"That's just it, though." She frowned at him. "They've been dealing with those living conditions all on their own. Where's the sense of community we share here in Copper Creek? I can't believe they've been dealing with that under our noses all this time."

"I offered Liam a job. That should help with some of it."

She stilled, then swung her head around to stare at him. "You did?"

"Yeah—but to be fair, I offered it as a way to pay for our services tonight.

Her scowl returned. "Why do guys have to be so stubborn about things like this? Can't Wade see that he's not doing anyone any favors by—"

"Hey, now. That's not fair. Just because you grew up on Slate Rock Ranch with everything you could ever ask for, doesn't mean you had it good either. I'd wager that people comment on your upbringing just as much as you're fixating about the Keagans."

She gasped. "What's that supposed to mean?"

He ran a hand through his hair and shut his eyes briefly. "Nothing. I didn't mean anything."

"No. You definitely meant something. What was so wrong about my upbringing that had people worried for my wellbeing?"

"Do you really want to get into this?"

"I think we should."

He sighed. "Well, your father's rules, for one. He doesn't seem to understand that in modern times women are not property." He grimaced. "That didn't come out the way I wanted it to."

"Really James!? Then just how *did* you want to say what you just said?" She folded her arms and glared at him.

James sighed. "All I meant by it was that no one is perfect. No one has the same needs. That family needed each other, and Wade was able to make that happen. It doesn't matter that the house needs repairs. He's doing his best." James gave

Constance a sideways glance. "And when your mother passed away, you and your sisters needed your own form of stability. Isn't that what you were trying to convince me of before? That your dad has his reasons, and even if I don't agree with them, I should still respect them."

The fury in her eyes melted and she slumped into her seat. "That's a good point."

"So just because the Keagans weren't as blessed as you financially, they were able to thrive with what they had."

"I still think we should do something to fix up their place and get them started on the right path. Twelve kids? And no parents? That had to be so hard."

"I'm sure it was," he murmured. Constance's heart of gold and the soap box she stood on was enough to push James forward. He didn't have the finances to be able to help that family, but he knew someone who might.

James pulled up to the country club and Constance groaned. "Oh yeah. I agreed to this, didn't I? Can't we just go over to Sal's and get some pie to go? I really don't want anyone seeing me like this."

"Seeing you? Or seeing me?"

She shot him a warning look.

Right.

Constance didn't want any of that being pointed out.

He turned to face her. "Okay. We don't have to go in. I'll even take you to get some pie. But I'm going to run inside and have a quick word with Shane for a minute. You wait here?"

Her face split into a wide smile and she nodded. He leaned over the armrest and kissed her quickly, then climbed out of the car and hurried inside.

Loud music flowed from the dance room down the hallway toward Shane's office. Laughter, conversation, clinking glasses —all the sounds he'd expect to hear on a Friday night. The noises grew quiet as he made it to the door and knocked.

"Come in."

James pushed the door open and poked his head inside.

Shane glanced up at him, then did a double take. "Aren't you supposed to be on a date tonight?"

"Long story." He moved into the office and shut the door quietly behind him. "I have a question for you."

His friend gestured toward the chair and closed the file he had on his desk. "What's up?"

"Have you met any of the Keagans?"

"That big family we talked about? No, why?"

James settled onto the edge of the chair and clasped his hands together. He shifted, attempting to get comfortable but wasn't very successful. "Constance and I went out to their property to help one of their mares give birth." Suddenly James wasn't so sure he should be telling Shane any of this. But Constance sat in the car out in the parking lot, and he hated seeing her heart so heavy.

Shane gave his undivided attention, making it even more difficult to come up with the words James needed.

"Their property is run down and in need of a great deal of repair. They have a lot of land that could be used for crops or raising animals." He blew out a breath through pursed lips. "I thought I'd see if there was something you could do to help them."

Shane's gaze didn't leave James's face and the longer he stared, the more James fidgeted.

"Obviously, if you don't have the means to do anything—" James started to say.

He held up his hand. "I have certain funds set aside for charitable opportunities. What exactly are you thinking?"

All reasonable thoughts left James's mind. He hadn't expected Shane to agree so quickly. Best case scenario, he might say he'd think about it. "I'm not sure. I'd say they need to fix up their living arrangements and maybe get a few pieces of equipment."

"I think that sounds reasonable. What do the Keagan's think of this plan of yours?"

James made a face. "They don't exactly know. In fact, that might be the one thing that causes a problem."

Shane arched a brow. "How do you mean? I don't understand. Why would you come to me before speaking with them first?"

He swallowed hard. "Think about it, Shane. If you were in a tight spot, would you be okay with someone barging in and forcing you to take charity?"

"I see what you mean." Shane rubbed his chin. They sat in silence for a few minutes.

There had to be a reasonable solution, but James couldn't see it.

Shane nodded once. "Let me think about it and I'll let you know what I come up with. But we'll figure something out."

James smiled. "Thank you. And if there's any way I can help, please call me."

"Of course." Shane turned to his computer. "I'll contact my CPA and see how many funds we can allocate to this project. Then I'll check with my assistant and maybe we can come up with a way for the Keagans to accept our offer without feeling like a charity case."

James rose to his feet and held out his hand. "Thanks again."

Shane glanced up at him, then got to his feet as he accepted James's hand.

He wouldn't be able to tell Constance about his plan, at least not yet. Especially when he didn't quite have the whole plan yet. But when everything got figured out, he'd make sure she was the first to know.

20

Constance

 eeks turned into months and Constance continued to fall more deeply in love with James. When he'd hired Liam to help out at the clinic, it had melted her heart. There were still little bumps in the road. Plus, there was the big issue that continued to hang over her head.

She still hadn't gotten up the courage to tell her father about James. Brielle continued to shoot judgmental looks in her direction across the dinner table or when they crossed paths while getting work done on the ranch. But she was the only one out of those who were aware of her secret relationship who even seemed to care.

Dianna might not approve of Constance's relationship, but she seemed content to let Constance make her own mistakes. And Adeline was completely in her corner. Everyone else, including Sarah, Dax and the other ranch hands, were completely in the dark. At least Constance was pretty sure they were.

The hardest part about her relationship was that the closer they got, the harder it became to want to keep it a secret. James made her happy. He was kind and generous, and all it took was one look to make her feel like the most beautiful girl in the entire world.

She should want to be able to share what she found with other people.

Her father included.

Constance sat at the kitchen table before everyone had come down for breakfast. It was about two months to the day that she'd gone out to the Keagan's property with James. She stared at the contents of her steaming mug, getting lost in her thoughts.

She'd just completed one overloaded semester and was getting closer to becoming a veterinary technician. After that, she'd have a couple more years of coursework and she'd be on her own.

Fear was becoming a thing of the past. With a degree like this, she wasn't as worried about her father kicking her out of their home. The closer she got to it, the more she realized that maybe she'd assumed the worst of her father.

What man would kick out his daughter for wanting to get married? Sure, he'd threatened it when they were teenagers, but now? The thought seemed preposterous.

Zeke entered the kitchen and headed straight for the coffee maker. He opened the cupboard that was over the machine and retrieved a mug. His eyes met Constance's briefly and they exchanged small smiles. He set to work dumping some sweetener and a little cream into his cup, then stirred it before he strode toward the kitchen table.

He sat down with a grunt and reached for the morning paper that sat unfolded on one side of the table. His grey eyes shifted to her before he started reading. "You have always been an early riser, but even this seems a bit early for you."

She smiled, more to herself than to him. "I've got a lot on my mind."

Zeke's gaze cut to hers for just a moment, then he flicked the paper and continued scanning it. "Anything I should be worried about?"

Constance turned her mug between her hands, attempting to come up with the words that had been begging to be let loose the second James had asked her on that first date. She opened her mouth, then shut it.

As much as she'd like to think there was an easy way to bring up the topic, she knew better. This was the one rule that even Adeline hadn't been able to convince their father to drop. Why did she think she was any better?

No one else had stood up to him before, that's why.

Constance chewed on the inside of her cheek. "I was thinking about the rule you have about getting married."

The paper fluttered to the table and Zeke's features tightened. He didn't say anything, but he didn't have to. His dark eyes seemed to grow cloudier and his jaw was so rigid that it could probably cut a diamond.

She ducked her head and lifted her mug to her lips. The scalding liquid burned the sensitive skin there and she winced. "Not that I want to get married right now, but I was wondering if I were to meet a man who you approved of... would I be given the chance to—you know—date him?"

"Is this about Dr. Pratt?"

Her eyes rounded and she shook her head vehemently. "No, it's not about him. I mean it isn't about anyone in particular." Inwardly she cringed at the lies that continued to spew from her lips. When had telling lies become so second nature to her?

Constance's stomach churned and suddenly she'd lost her appetite. She didn't even want to hear her father's response. Already she knew she'd hate it. If she could somehow make herself invisible and slip out of that room unnoticed, she would.

She just wasn't that lucky.

"In answer to your question."

Constance flinched, unwilling to meet her father's shrewd gaze.

"No. I don't see the purpose for any of you girls getting married before it's your turn." His voice was gruff and unwavering. He'd made his decision and she'd be forced to follow his rules.

"But Brielle isn't—" she started.

"Brielle will decide when she's good and ready. You don't need to go off and marry the first man who gives you attention. That's where you get into trouble. You need to find someone who is willing to wait for you." He probably meant for his words to be inspiring or at least moderately romantic, but all she heard was the clanging sound of a cage being built around her.

She shot out of her chair and strode out of the room without another word. She'd heard that tone of voice before. She knew it like she knew every line, every wrinkle in her father's face. He wasn't going to change his mind for anything. The only way she'd get what she wanted was to break the rules and move out.

If she did that, she'd not only lose her home and her inheritance, she could possibly lose the relationships she had with her family. That was something she wasn't prepared for.

Constance charged out the back door and toward the barn. Her father wouldn't even consider listening to her side of things. Why did he have to be so stubborn? She wasn't one of those girls who threw themselves at every guy they met.

A snort escaped her throat. Brielle fit that bill more than she did. As Constance continued her angry pace, her whole body was electrified by the fury she felt over not being heard.

But it wasn't just the fact her father had shut her down. She hated that she'd felt the need to even ask.

The more time they spent together, the more James brought it up. He might not say it in so many words, but he didn't seem to mind hinting at it. She could practically read his mind on the subject. He wanted her to talk to her father so that they could be more out in the open. He wanted to hold her hand or kiss her without being worried that someone was watching or judging.

He'd do all of that and more if she didn't put parameters around their relationship. She shouldn't even have to make excuses. If James cared about her, he should be willing to accept what little she could offer right now. Was her dad right? Should James be willing to wait for her? It was all so confusing.

Constance stormed into the barn and saddled her horse as quickly as humanly possible. For once, she didn't want to be here when James showed up. She couldn't look him in the eye and tell him about her father without bursting into a puddle of tears.

Her options from this point forward were limited.

She could follow her father's rules and pray that Brielle would come to her senses and pick a guy already. Or she could stand up to Zeke, accept all ridiculous consequences and inevitably be kicked out of her home.

Oh, the gossiping people in town would just love that.

Neither option was something she wanted to accept. She was completely and utterly stuck with no feasible escape from the mess she was in.

James was right. She didn't have the charmed life she thought she had. While she'd grown up with a roof over her head, she'd been confined to a small little box with no room to spread her wings.

In fact, it had taken James's intervention to help her father see that her education was something of value. And every single one of her younger sisters were doomed to the same cage.

Constance shoved the toe of her boot into the stirrup and climbed into the saddle just as Sarah wandered into the barn. Her eyes widened briefly and she smiled. "Hey, Connie. I didn't know you were up." She moved toward a stall and got to work saddling the horse she was in the process of training. "Where are you going? Isn't Dr. Pratt coming by today?"

With ropes coiled tightly around her hands, Constance tugged just firmly enough to keep her restless steed secure. "I'm taking the day off."

Sarah glanced in her direction but didn't say anything.

"I thought I'd go for a ride to clear my head," Constance added.

Her friend's smile widened. "Those are the best ones. Mind if I tag along?" She cinched the belt tight and climbed into the saddle.

"If you can keep up."

Sarah chuckled. "I think we can manage that."

Constance burst from the stable and urged her horse faster and faster. The wind whipped her hair around her face, the ends stinging her skin. She didn't know where she was going; she only knew she needed to ride until she could figure this out.

Sarah stayed fairly close, not having any difficulty as they wove through various paths toward the wooded area on the far side of their property. She'd found her stride in riding and her skills now rivaled those of Constance's younger sisters. Though she'd been more of a stranger the year before, Sarah was now like an adoptive sister, and Constance found herself glad to have her company.

They ended their sprint a few miles into the wooded area, stopping by a brook with gurgling water. Light shone through the boughs of trees overhead and dust glittered through the streams of light. The only sounds were the pawing hooves of their horses and the occasional bird chirping.

Sarah leaned over her saddle horn and sighed. "This place is so beautiful. You don't get views like this in the city where I'm from." She peeked at Constance. "You're pretty lucky you grew up here."

Constance's chest tightened and her stomach roiled. "No, I'm not."

Her friend arched a brow. "You might be able to convince someone else of that, but not me. This place is a paradise."

Constance climbed down from her saddle and wandered toward the little stream. "I'm not discounting that this place is beautiful. Yeah, it's peaceful, and it's a great place to enjoy nature. I'm talking about the circumstances that I grew up in."

Confusion marred Sarah's features but then, all too quickly, understanding flitted across her face. "Yeah. I wouldn't trade what I had for what you have to deal with."

Her grip on the reins tightened and Constance turned away. She focused on taking deep breaths and letting them out slowly. "What should I do?"

"About what? Your dad's rules?"

Constance glanced over her shoulder and gave Sarah an irritated look. "Of course that's what I'm talking about. What am I supposed to do when I finally find someone I'm ready to settle down with but it's not 'my turn' to get married?"

Sarah glanced down at the ground and dug her booted toe into the soft earth. She twisted it around a little before lifting her focus to Constance. "You don't want to ask me that. You won't like the answer."

"You can tell me. That's why I asked."

She moved closer to Constance, empathy and a little sadness on her face. "Tell me something first. What do you think would happen if you were to defy your father's wishes and just do what you wanted?"

Constance huffed. "Based on our conversation this morning, he'd probably have no problem kicking me out of the house and telling me to find my own way."

"Really? Because I think he's set these rules up so you *don't* end up out there on your own. He's not thinking clearly, Connie. He's a man who was hurt when his wife passed away, and he's holding onto any thread he can to make sure that doesn't happen to any of his daughters."

Constance frowned. "So you're saying the likelihood that he'd disown me is—"

"Improbable. He'd be more likely to ruin the life of whoever you wanted to marry before you have a chance to say 'I do.'"

Her head spun. She hadn't considered that her father would go after the person she loved.

"You see it, now, too. Your father has a lot of reach in the community. He's partnered with the Baker's ranch. He's got money and land, and he's not afraid to use force if he has to. He loves each of you so much, that he probably wouldn't care if he destroyed the lives of anyone in town."

Constance shook her head. "He's never mentioned that kind of threat, though."

"Think about it. If he keeps you from even thinking that romance is a possibility, he doesn't have to tell you what his real plans would be. With his reach, I would wager that he could even get Shane Owens on board."

Constance shook her head. "Shane is James's best friend. He'd never do anything that would hurt James or his reputation."

Sarah shrugged. "Your brother-in-law is the one training his horses. Your ranch and the Baker's ranch provide horses. Shane's business would probably survive, but it would be a headache to deal with if your father cut off access to those things." She frowned, reaching out to touch Constance's arm. "I could be wrong. I don't know your father like you do. But I have seen how much he loves you and I know he wouldn't give you up without a fight. So it's not you who would lose everything you held dear. It'd be—"

"James."

Sarah nodded.

He could lose clients, his business—and probably more than she could comprehend. Constance might not even have a choice in the matter. If James felt like he was drowning, he'd cut ties with the one thing dragging him down.

James would be the one to break up with her.

The realization made her even sicker to her stomach than before. That was it then. She couldn't fight for the love she'd found—but it wasn't for her own good, it was for James's.

.

21

James

James sat back in his office chair bright and early before anyone had arrived and just reveled in the current state of his life. He set his legs on his desk and crossed them at the ankles, then let out a contented sigh.

His life couldn't be more perfect than it was at this moment. James had the girl, he was training one heck of a veterinarian, his business was thriving, and he couldn't think of anything else he wanted in his life.

Okay, there was *one* thing.

He'd been dating Constance for several months now and there was still no sign that she was willing to stick up for herself and tell her father what she really wanted. How was he supposed to even confess how deep his feelings ran if she wasn't willing to risk making her father angry in order to be with him.

James was painfully aware that neither one of them had admitted they were in love. It was the hardest thing he had to fight against. When he was younger, those words came so much easier.

With Constance, they meant more. And he wasn't sure he could tell her how he felt when he didn't know if they would stay together.

It was ridiculous. They were just three small words. They shouldn't have the power over him that they did.

Maybe it had been the relationship with Brielle. He'd told her he loved her when they'd been together for a couple weeks. Why couldn't he get up the courage to tell the woman he wanted to spend the rest of his life with that what he felt for her surpassed anything he had felt for anyone else?

Because he was a coward.

What if she was waiting on telling her father about their relationship until she knew what they had was stable? He might be the one who had pulled this relationship train to a screeching halt. If he wanted this relationship to work as much as he thought he did, he needed to do something to show it.

It was almost too simple.

His feet dropped to the ground. How could he have been such an idiot? He kept expecting Constance to do something when he needed to take the initiative.

The front door to the clinic opened and swung shut, jostling the bell overhead. He jumped to his feet and hurried toward the doorway.

Chloe gasped, her hand flying to her chest. "What are you doing here so early? Don't you have rounds to make?"

He shook his head. "The final checkups for the Callahan account and the Owens account happened on Friday. There will be follow-up visits, but those will be here."

She glanced around the clinic. "Where's your little protégé?"

"Constance will be coming in when we open. She had some

exams for the end of the semester." He waved his hands through the air. "I need your help with something."

"Sure, what do you need?" She moved around the reception desk and deposited her purse on the counter before she pulled her chair out and sat down. When she turned around to face him, he was still hovering in the doorway of his office. Her lips quirked into a smile. "What do you need, James?"

Shoot, he hadn't thought this through before he'd asked for her help. No one knew about their relationship except her sisters. His chest tightened. Chloe was trustworthy; she wouldn't tell anyone. At least he didn't think she would. And besides, she did walk in on their kiss.

James shifted, folding his arms as he leaned against the doorjamb. "But before I ask you, I need to clarify something."

She snickered. "Geez, James. The way you're acting, I'm beginning to think that something is wrong."

He shook his head. "Nothing is wrong, but what I'm about to tell you isn't something I want spread around."

Chloe sobered. "You're not lumping me into the gossiping women in town, are you? Because I'm not interested in that kind—"

"Of course not. But I have to make it clear that you can't breathe a word to anyone."

She sighed and turned in her seat to face her computer. "Now you're just being ridiculous."

He moved toward her and leaned back against the counter so that he could see her face. "You wouldn't say that if you knew what I'm dealing with."

"Just say what you're going to say. I've got a long list of things to do today." She placed her hand on the computer mouse and the computer screen in front of her lit up. Right away, she started clicking and typing.

"I need to know the best restaurant to take a woman to for a special occasion."

Chloe froze and slowly lifted her face so she met his gaze. "You're kidding."

He shook his head.

"If this is about Constance, you have to be joking."

James stilled. "What?"

She rolled her eyes. "Come on, James, I'm not *blind*. The first time she came around, I wasn't *positive*, but when she came dressed up for—"

"A *business* dinner."

Chloe snorted. "Anyone with eyes could see that you two were going steady."

"Do people even call it that anymore?"

She shrugged, her smile returning. "Then the time that I caught you guys kissing. Seriously, if that's your big secret, then you might have bigger problems."

His brows furrowed. What she said made sense. But to be fair, he hadn't really worked that hard to keep his interest in Constance quiet. "Fine. Yes, that's the secret I was talking about. You haven't told anyone, have you?"

Chloe snickered. "Like I said, I don't have any interest in sharing secrets that aren't mine to tell. You said you wanted to know a good place to take her?" Her eyes widened and she sucked in sharply. "You're not proposing to her, are you?"

"What? No. Of course not! Her father would chase me out of town before I could get all four words out. But I do want to tell her how much I care about her and that in the future, I can see us together."

She lifted one brow. "Have you seriously not said any of that up until now? For heaven's sake, James. What has it been? Three months? All that sneaking around and she doesn't know how you really feel?"

Heat crawled up his neck and he propelled himself from where he stood and strode toward his office. "Forget it. I'll come up with something on my own."

Chloe laughed and turned around in her seat. "Oh, don't be like that. Come back here. I'll help you figure something out."

He paused in the doorway and glanced over his shoulder toward her. "I just need to find a place that would wow her. I can't take her to Sal's, and I don't know if we can make it all the way to the city without someone noticing."

She tapped her chin a few times, then her eyes brightened. "Didn't you once tell me you learned how to cook?"

"I seem to recall that I told you I learned how to cook *one* meal."

"Then do that. Take her to your place, cook her a meal—"

He frowned. "That hardly sounds romantic. What I need is something that will really make an impression."

She folded her arms and gave him a pointed look. "There are only a few things in this world that are truly irresistible to a woman like Constance."

Her words finally did what they were meant to, they captured his attention and he'd latched on like a fish on a hook.

"They want someone strong, considerate, and well-rounded."

"That doesn't help me at all."

"I wasn't done," she grumbled. "Women love men who know how to fix things, are good with kids, and can cook."

He frowned. It couldn't be that easy. And even if it was, he'd been telling her the truth when he said he could only cook one decent meal. Everything else he knew how to prepare ranged from frozen meals to hoagie sandwiches.

"I can tell you don't believe me. But just think about it. If you can cook for her and give her a thoughtful gift, she's going to be all over it."

"And you think this idea of yours is foolproof?"

Chloe turned back to her computer and shrugged. "It would work on me. If a guy went through the trouble to cook me a meal and make me feel special, I'd be all in." She placed her hands on the keyboard and the sound of the soft clicks took the place of their voices.

If she was right, then tonight would be simpler than he'd expected. He'd make fettucine alfredo, get her some flowers, and then he'd tell her he loved her. If everything went well, then afterward, they could discuss how they wanted to move forward.

JAMES HUSTLED through his small apartment kitchen with a tray of rolls. He didn't have an official dining room, so he'd set up his table in the living room with candles and the fireplace on. The days were getting shorter and the air was crisper in the mornings, so the fire gave the evening just the right touch.

The pasta was done cooking and he left the sauce simmering. James placed the garlic rolls on each of their plates and then returned to the kitchen for the pitcher of ice water. Everything was perfect, from the food to the atmosphere.

Excitement and nerves swirled within him, crashing the party his confidence was trying to throw. Constance would be arriving any minute.

As if in agreement with his thoughts, the doorbell rang. He jumped, nearly dropping the pitcher. Never had he felt so worried over one evening. Even when he'd realized that his relationship with Brielle wasn't going anywhere, he had known he was making the right decision.

The one he'd made tonight was definitely the right one; he just didn't know if Constance realized it.

James returned the pitcher to the kitchen and wiped his hands on a dishtowel that hung from the oven. He tossed the rag on his shoulder and made it to the door just before Constance's hand made contact with the wood.

All it took was seeing her to quell the worries that had been wrapping tighter and tighter around his throat. She wore a blouse and a pair of dress pants, probably what she'd worn to her exam earlier today. She'd opted to skip coming into the clinic due to her schedule and he'd missed their usual inter-actions.

Without warning her, he pulled her close and pressed a firm kiss against her lips. Her sweet taste and soft curves were heaven. He couldn't even remember why he'd been so upset in the first place. Constance had a way of calming him that he'd never experienced with anyone before.

She relaxed against him, wrapping her arms around his neck and pulling him in tighter for a deeper kiss.

His heart exploded and his stomach seemed to have forgotten that gravity existed. Keeping her in his arms, James backed up a few steps and kicked the door shut. He pressed her against it, his breathing ragged and out of control. "I've missed you," he murmured against her lips.

Her hands slipped down to his shoulders, and she pushed him away a few inches so her gaze could meet his. "I've missed you, too." There was a tightness in her voice that sent a warning note to his brain. It was far too easy to immediately go to a dark place. What was wrong? Had something bad happened? Or was it about to?

No, that wasn't it. He was imagining things. She'd had a long day and all she needed was to put her feet up and enjoy a good meal to feel better.

"How did your tests go?" James placed his hand on the small of her back, feeling a slight resistance as he guided her through his apartment and toward the table in the living room. He pulled out her chair and she turned toward him.

"James, there's something—"

The timer on the stove went off and he shifted his focus to the kitchen. Holding up his finger, he shot her a smile. "Hold that thought." He hurried toward the oven and turned off the timer, then gathered the salad bowl and dressing before returning to the table.

Constance was seated, her fingers tracing the designs in the flatware. He placed the bowl in front of her and when she looked up, he gave her another warm smile.

"I might only be good at cooking one thing, but I know it tastes delicious. I'll be right back." He reached for their plates and returned to the stove. In no time he'd drained the pasta and served it up. The smell of the alfredo sauce filled the whole apartment and his stomach grumbled. He returned her plate to the spot in front of her, then put his own plate down on the table and finally took a seat.

"It all looks great," she murmured. Her eyes lifted to meet his, and once again, he got that feeling that something bad was about to happen.

His brows furrowed as he picked up his fork. "Is everything okay?"

Constance pressed her lips together. She moved her food around her plate with the fork and didn't meet his gaze.

"Did your test go okay?"

She nodded but still didn't say anything.

"There was something I wanted to talk to you about," he hedged, now not quite sure whether he should mention his feelings anymore. Then again, if she had a tough day, perhaps it would make things better.

"I think there's something I should talk to you about, too," she murmured softly.

She didn't sound nearly as excited as he did. Maybe she didn't want to work with him anymore? That would be fine. He'd manage, and she wouldn't have to worry about ending their contract a little early. James nodded and let out a slow breath. Here went nothing. "I love you."

"I think we should break up," she murmured at the same

time. James wasn't even sure she heard what he said. But now he wasn't so sure he wanted her to.

His mouth dropped open and the blood in his face drained, causing him to feel lightheaded. James placed his fork down as they stared at each other. Then he let out a soft chuckle. "I'm sorry, what? It sounded like you want to break up."

She looked away, putting her fork aside and placing her hands in her lap. "I do."

He blinked, feeling cold and hot all at once. This wasn't happening. It couldn't be. There had to be a reasonable explanation for what she was saying, but all he could do was stare at her blankly, praying she would tell him where he'd gone wrong.

22

Constance

*C*onstance had repeated everything she was going to say in her head a thousand times. She knew this was the right choice—for now. She just hoped that James would see it that way, too. After having that talk with Sarah and knowing exactly where Brielle stood on the subject, Constance could see no other way.

Even if she left home and started working for James, she didn't know what her father might do to sabotage James's business or his reputation.

She took in a deep, heart-wrenching breath and forced herself to look at him. "Before you say anything, this isn't about you."

He huffed out a sharp indignant sound. His mouth opened then shut and he shook his head. James slumped back against his chair and just stared at her. He didn't utter a word, and the silence hurt more than anything he might have said to her. She almost wanted to shout at him to say something even though she'd already cut him off from doing just that.

Constance's eyes dropped to her plate; her appetite completely gone. "I've been thinking about it a lot. And I've realized you were right."

She could sense more than see him stiffen. The air had grown thin and cold. All she wanted to do was stand up and escape from his apartment. This was exactly what she'd been worried about. Agreeing to date him when he was also her boss was a bad idea, and she'd known it from the start.

When she lifted her gaze, she froze. His eyes had darkened and swirled with a pain that she felt internally, as if just by looking at him he could shift all his emotions to her. Constance swallowed hard. "That is to say, you were right when you said our relationship couldn't work if I wasn't upfront with my father about it."

His brow lifted, but that was the only reaction she could see.

"I can't," she murmured.

James leaned forward in his seat and his eyes narrowed. "You can't *what*?"

"I can't tell my father that I want to date you."

His frown deepened. "Can I ask why?"

She let out a shaky breath. "Because I know it will hurt him. And I don't want to do that. We'll have to wait until Brielle finds someone. It'll be easier that way."

He pressed his lips together tightly and breathed out slowly through his nose. "You realize this isn't about your father, right?"

She stared at him dumbfounded. Of course it was about her father. "He lost my mother. He doesn't want to lose me—"

James snorted derisively. "How exactly is he losing you? It's not like I'm asking you to move across the country. Getting

married would actually mean you would have a higher likelihood of staying in town for the rest of our lives."

Chills ripped through her chest. *Marriage?* Throughout
their relationship they had been very cautious. James had only
just told her he loved her for the first time. Granted, she
assumed he did. It hadn't been a surprise when he'd told her.
She felt the same. Which was why none of this was fair. She
wanted to tell him she loved him back and throw her arms
around his neck and tell him they'd make it work.

But if she did that, there was no telling what the consequences would be. She'd finally come full circle. At first, she
was willing to risk anything to have James's attention. But now
she'd give anything to be Brielle—to have more control over
her future.

It might sound crazy to James or to the people in town, but
she didn't think she could follow through with her desire to fall
in love with him and ride off into the sunset. Her stomach
churned and she rubbed her nose with the back of her hand.
"We both knew that when we started getting closer that it
might not work out."

He shook his head. "This isn't about something 'not
working out.'" James pointed at her. "This is about you being
too scared to fight for something that makes you happy. If you
hadn't listened to me about becoming a veterinarian, then you
would still be at home dwelling in your quiet unhappiness."

Constance shot up out of her seat and headed toward the
door. She had expected him to be upset. But she hadn't
expected him to lash out at her—to *blame* her. He'd been so
sweet up until now, offering to be patient as she worked some
things out.

Well, she blamed herself enough for both of them.

He didn't have to add to the pain she was dealing with. He
rose, his features crumpling. "Where are you going?"

She slung her purse on her shoulder and shook her head as the first hot tear skittered down her cheek.

James took a step toward her. "Constance, I'm—"

"*No.* I'm sorry, James. I should have known better than to let myself get involved with you. I'm going home. I'm sorry about dinner."

"Constance, *wait*," he pleaded.

She stopped, her hand on the doorknob. Squeezing her eyes shut, more tears fell from her lashes. This was best for both of them. She didn't know when Brielle would get engaged. It could be next year, or it could be in five years, or it could be never. There was a slim chance her father would acquiesce to the idea that her sisters deserved to find their own loves, but she couldn't put all her eggs in that basket. She'd gotten her career and that would have to be enough.

Taking a deep breath, she released it as she turned the knob. He wasn't speaking. Deep down she knew if she turned around to look at him, she wouldn't be able to leave. "By the way, I love you too, James. And one day there might be a chance for us. But right now, you could lose more than you might realize. I'm not going to ask you to wait for me. Trust me when I say that this is the best option for both of us." With that, she pulled the door open and slipped out into the night.

Her quick steps propelled her toward her truck and she climbed in before she could change her mind. She'd given him a good enough reason. He didn't need to know every little detail. If he did, he'd only argue with her. Or worse—he might confront her father.

Constance rested her head on the top of the steering wheel and took several deep breaths, then started her truck and drove away.

~

"Hey, Constance. Where were—what on earth happened to you?" Brielle darted in front of Constance as she moved through the house as quick as she could to avoid making contact with anyone—most specifically her father.

Unfortunately, Brielle was in her path and she didn't seem willing to step aside.

Constance brushed at her cheeks, but they were dry and her skin was stretched tight from the salt in her tears. "I'm fine," she muttered as she attempted once more to move past her sister.

Brielle shifted with her, blocking the way to the stairs. "No, you're not. What happened? Did James—"

Constance's sharp gaze cut to Brielle's. "Don't say a single word about him. He didn't do anything. It was all me." This time she shouldered her way past her sister and made it to the stairs, where she could finally sprint away from the one person who would be able to cause the tears to return.

Brielle's shuffling behind her made it clear she didn't think the conversation was over. When Constance made it to her room, Brielle managed to slip inside before Constance could lock her out.

Dianna was curled up in a chair in the corner of the room, a book in her hand. She lifted her eyes to where Constance threw her hands into the air. "Fine. Stay. I'm not talking to you."

"Oh yes, you are." Brielle shut the door behind her and leaned against the door. "I told James to stay away from you. But did he listen? Of course not. Why would he listen to me? He only wants what he wants and doesn't care about the consequences," she said bitterly.

Constance shot a confused look in Brielle's direction, then dragged her attention to her dresser where she placed her purse. She yanked open the drawer that contained her pajamas and attempted to tune out her sister's incessant "I told you so" lecture.

"*Bri*," Dianna snapped, successfully stopping their sister's tirade. "This isn't about you."

Constance could feel the exact moment when both Dianna and Brielle were staring at her—expecting her to finally tell them what happened. They'd be sorely disappointed if they thought she'd share anything that had happened between herself and James tonight.

What was she supposed to tell them? That *she* broke up with him after she'd been so insistent over being able to date?

Ha.

That wasn't going to happen.

Constance's hand gripped her pajamas tightly in a fist and she spun around. "I'm going to go change."

Brielle folded her arms, still leaning against the door. "Not until you tell me what happened."

"I don't see why that matters. You got what you wanted."

"What is *that* supposed to mean?"

"I'm not in a relationship with James anymore. That's what you wanted, right?"

Brielle's gaze bounced to Dianna and then back to Constance. She didn't deny it, which caused a huff to burst from Constance's lips. "See? I knew you didn't approve of him. Though I can't figure out if you don't approve of him specifically or if it would have bothered you had I dated anyone."

"That's not fair."

"Isn't it?" Constance spat at her. "You never liked him. So now you're the only one who gets to go on dates." She motioned toward the door. "Now, can I go?"

Brielle sighed. "It's not what you think. I don't care if you want to find and fall in love with someone—"

"Just not *James*."

At some point, Dianna had gotten up from her seat and moved across the room. From the sound of it, she stood about a foot behind Constance.

Brielle shifted her weight from one foot to the other. She gnawed on her lower lip as if the conversation had made her uncomfortable. She'd been caught being selfish, and Constance didn't have the heart to coddle her.

The only person who had a broken heart right now was Constance. And right now, all she wanted to do was lick her wounds and try to prepare for the next time she had to come face to face with the only other person who might feel the same as she did.

"Please, Bri. Can we just drop this? None of it matters anymore."

Brielle took a step forward. "But it does matter. As much as I thought James wasn't a good fit for you, I still don't want to see you hurting." She sighed. "You deserve to be happy—"

"If you really felt that way, there are so many things you could have done to prevent this." Constance shook her head. "You know what? Nevermind. I'm not going to get into this with you."

Brielle moved forward again. "What do you want me to do?"

Constance pushed past Brielle, her escape finally unguarded. She pulled open the door and hurried down the hall before Brielle could stop her again. She took her time changing, brushing her hair and cleaning the mascara from her cheeks. After a splash of cool water, she felt more prepared to return to her room.

Brielle was probably lying in wait—ready to bombard her with more questions or to give her false statements of empathy.

Her steps slowed as she approached her room, her ears straining for any sound to indicate that Brielle was still in there with Dianna. And she wasn't disappointed.

"Do you think she knows?" Dianna murmured.

"It doesn't matter anymore. She broke up with him," Brielle's quiet voice snapped back.

Constance froze, her hand reaching for the door. Her ears burned. What was Dianna talking about? Was there some kind of secret that James had kept from her? And how would Brielle know?

"You're going to have to tell her at some point. You know that, right?"

Brielle sighed. "I thought I might. But maybe not."

"*Bri—*"

"Shh. She's just down the hall."

Constance's face burned and she stepped back, leaning against the wall. Until this point she didn't think things could get any worse. Now she had lost the man she loved and the security she'd had.

"If you don't tell her, I will. She's already broken up with him."

"Exactly. She's already upset. Why would I want to make everything worse by telling her that I dated James?"

If Constance thought that she'd hit rock bottom, she was wrong. It was like the air had been knocked out of her lungs. She clutched at her heart and her head thumped against the wall. Everything suddenly made so much more sense.

The way James had stared at Brielle before Constance had gone on a date with him. Brielle's distaste for him and her insistence that Constance shouldn't date him. There was history there.

Thoughts spiraled out of control with each passing second. What if he'd dated her to get over Brielle? How long ago had they been together? Was he still hung up on her even now?

She felt sick to her stomach and dizzy at the same time.

Constance's hands clenched into fists and she charged into her room. Both of her sisters jumped and stared at her with wide eyes. Constance pushed past Brielle, their shoulders colliding.

Brielle grunted.

"Get out," Constance muttered.

"What? Why?"

"Bri—" Dianna warned.

Constance grabbed a pillow and launched it at Brielle's head. "I said get out."

Brielle ducked, her eyes narrowing. "Are you going to tell me what's gotten into you?"

Glowering at her older sister, Constance reached for another pillow. She took aim until Dianna's voice stopped her.

"Connie. That's enough."

Constance shifted her focus to her younger sister and muttered, "You're no better than she is."

Dianna glanced away. At least she had some semblance of shame.

"When were you going to tell me that you had dated my boyfriend?" Constance spat.

Brielle finally dropped her gaze to the ground. "Oh."

"Yeah. *Oh.* Lucky for you, I wasn't paying much attention to the guys you used to sneak around with. I guess everyone got a good laugh watching me get your sloppy seconds when James was still infatuated with you."

Brielle's head snapped up and her face paled. "What? Of course not. That wasn't how it was at all."

"Whatever. Just—please, just go." Constance's voice had softened but more due to the energy that had been zapped from her body by having to discuss all of this with the one person she knew she'd inevitably forgive.

But James was different. He had kept this from her deliberately. If she hadn't already broken up with him to save them each some heartache, she might have had to go over to his apartment again so she could put him in his place and end things based on principle.

"Connie, I—"

Constance held up a hand and turned around so she could sit on the bed with her back to her sisters.

"I think you should go, Bri," Dianna whispered. "Just let her be."

"I really am sorry," Brielle murmured.

23

James

$\mathcal{N}$umb.

Nothing registered in James's whole body except the blinding numbness. He couldn't tell if he was hot or cold. Maybe he was a little bit of both. He was still shaken over the whole thing. When the night had started, he'd been thrilled to be able to tell Constance that he was so in love with her that he wanted her to be in his life for the long haul.

He'd even let it slip that he wanted her to be his wife. That thought had come out of nowhere, but the second he'd said it, he hadn't regretted it whatsoever.

Constance was the woman he wanted to spend the rest of his life with.

How was he supposed to work with her and not acknowledge the feelings he had for her? It was impossible.

James still sat at the table in his living room, staring forlornly at the table setting. He'd been like that for thirty minutes and couldn't recall a single time in his life when he'd felt this upset—not even when he'd ended things with Brielle.

That was one realization he would have been excited to figure out, except now he was once again alone.

He itched to swipe his arms across the table to fling everything on the floor and listen to the shatter of the dishes against the tile. But he didn't have the energy to do so.

It wasn't until Constance had severed their relationship that he'd finally come to the understanding that she was the reason he'd been so happy lately. She was what he looked forward to every single day.

James placed his elbows on the table and rested his head in his hands. Already he was trying to figure out how to go about ending their contract. He wouldn't make her pay back the tuition he'd supplemented. And if she wanted to continue working for him, he'd accept that. He could be professional.

Something pounded on the door and his head whipped around to stare in that direction. It couldn't be. Constance wouldn't come back, would she?

A glimmer of hope flooded his chest and he rose to his feet. Then again, he might be hallucinating things. The way she'd left things had felt so final.

Another knock.

James jumped and surged forward. He crossed the floor faster than he ever had. Without looking through the spy hole, he turned the knob and jerked the door open only to be nearly brought to his knees by the last person he'd expected to see.

Brielle stood in front of him, her arms folded and one foot out to the side as she put all her weight on the other. She glowered at him, eyes flashing with a venom he had only glimpsed a handful of times in his life.

His jaw tightened and he nearly shut the door in her face. Instead, he gestured for her to enter.

She pushed past him like she had several times before.

When he had the door shut and was leaning against it, she spun around. If it was possible, she looked even angrier. Sparks shot from her eyes as she strode toward him. "What did you do?"

His head reared back. "Me? You're going to have to elaborate."

"Don't play games with me. I know you did something."

"Me?" James repeated. "I didn't do anything to her. No, that's not right. I told her I loved her. That's what I did. And Constance opted to break up with me. I guess I overestimated how much she cares for me."

The steam he could almost see rising off Brielle's shoulders dissipated and her mouth fell open. "What?"

"Yeah. It didn't make much sense when you barged in here like I'm the bad guy. She was obviously done toying with me and was ready to send me off to pasture." He didn't even care how bitter he sounded at this point. He'd tried to win the heart of two Callahan daughters and each one ended in disaster.

Brielle blinked. "You love her?"

"Of course I love her. Why do you think I've been willing to date her for so long in spite of her refusing to ask her father if she can cut in line for betrothal?" He let out a derisive laugh. "Ironic, isn't it? I loved you when you were second in line. Now it's Constance. I can't seem to catch a break." He moved toward the table and gathered his plate and the one Constance had been using. Might as well start cleaning up the evidence of his botched evening. He knew the Callahans too well to think that Constance would change her mind. There was no point in chasing after her and demanding that she give them a chance.

"There's a difference," she murmured.

He stilled, not turning to face her. "What are you talking about?"

She didn't respond right away. The silence stretched long enough that he wouldn't have been surprised if she'd slipped out the door. When she finally spoke up, she said the one thing he hadn't expected. "I wasn't in love with you, James."

He nearly dropped the dishes in his hands. Before that happened, he placed them back on the table, then turned to face her. "You weren't?"

Brielle shook her head.

"Why—" He raked a hand through his hair and searched through the memories of his time with her. He couldn't recall once when Brielle had said she loved him. A vague memory tickled the back of his mind—something about the word being used too frequently and losing its effectiveness. He'd just assumed that she did love him and would say it when she was ready. James shook his head. "Why would you stay with me for so long?"

Brielle shrugged, looking away. "I don't know. We were having fun. You were sweet and were fun to spend time with. I guess I thought maybe one day..." She let out a heavy sigh. "It doesn't matter. But I never felt what I think Constance probably feels for you."

He snorted. "If she cares about me so much, then why would she break up with me? It doesn't make any sense."

She threw her hands into the air. "I don't know. I thought for sure she was well on her way to being the first one to outright defy our father's rules." Her voice softened. "I've never seen her so upset. That's the reason I came over. I thought for sure you gave her the same ultimatum you gave me—when you ended things."

James grimaced. The ultimatum. That was the first decision that had set his life on this course. If he hadn't broken it off with Brielle, then he wouldn't have had the chance to date Constance. Could he really be upset about those past decisions? This time around, Constance had been the one to break it off.

Based on what Brielle had said, maybe he could get

Constance back. If she was actually in love with him, it shouldn't be too hard.

He met Brielle's gaze. "So you weren't in love with me, but you still hated me enough to tell Constance that we shouldn't date. Why would you do that?"

"It wasn't that I hated you. I mean, you sorta bruised my ego when you broke up with me. No one had ever done that before. But it's more than that. Constance doesn't take big risks. If you told her to stand up to our father or you would break up with her, I knew she wouldn't do it and you'd end up breaking her heart."

"Oh." His chest tightened. "But that's all? You didn't want me to be with her because you were worried I'd hurt her." He forced himself to relax. This might mean that Brielle was in his corner. Maybe he could get her to talk to Constance on his behalf.

She nodded. "And…"

He stiffened again. "And what?"

Brielle folded her arms. "And that little detail about us dating first."

"Why would that matter? It was in the past."

"I wasn't sure it would matter. But I didn't want to risk it. I could tell she liked you so much. And she knew how many guys I've dated over the years. I just—didn't want her to think of herself as second place."

His brows creased. "But I broke up with you."

She shrugged again. "It doesn't matter anyway. I was right."

James moved toward her. "What do you mean you were right?"

"She overheard me talking to Dianna about us."

Every last bit of hope he'd been feeling crashed to the ground and shattered at his feet. "And she wasn't happy."

Brielle shook her head. "She threw pillows at me and told

me to leave. She said that we must have been laughing at her about all of it."

He pulled out a chair and collapsed onto it. "So that's it then. She's not even going to hear me out and let me explain. And I can't ask you to vouch for me because she'd just read into that."

"Probably."

He dragged a hand down his face. "I can't believe I lost her."

"Not for good. I mean... you might be able to win her back after she lets things settle."

James shook his head. "You forget that I know just how stubborn you Callahans can be. I know she's not going to do anything until it's her turn to get married. So, unless you have a secret fiancé in your back pocket..."

She made a face.

Right. Brielle wasn't ready for a long-term relationship or she was too scared for one. Either way, she was the wall that stood between Constance being willing to date him or anyone for that matter.

"But you never know. Constance is one of the most forgiving people I know. It might take some time but..."

"But I don't want to wait that long."

She pressed her lips into a thin frown. "I know. I'm sorry." She moved closer to the door. "I should probably go now."

He nodded. Then his head snapped up. "Bri?"

She paused and glanced in his direction.

"Do you think that maybe you and your older sister could talk to your dad? I plan on trying to win her back, but if Zeke is still in the way, I don't think she'll listen to me." It was a long shot. He didn't even dare hope that Brielle would be up for it.

The frown on her face was enough to give him his answer. "I can't do that."

James almost asked her why she wouldn't even consider it, but she answered his question before it left his lips.

"My dad has those rules for a reason, however misguided. Yes, my sisters will probably suffer because of how I am. But I'm not willing to settle for someone who won't make me happy. Hopefully, the guy who's meant for me will come into my life sooner rather than later."

He couldn't help it. Hearing those words coming from her turned his stomach a little. Brielle was the second out of seven. He couldn't imagine Constance being nearly so selfish.

Jaw tightening, he gave her a sharp nod. It was too much to ask Brielle to stick her neck out for her family. He'd have to come up with something else.

Brielle didn't say anything else before she turned once more toward the door and let herself out.

James retrieved the dishes and headed for the kitchen. For now, he needed to regroup. The only good thing that came from Brielle's visit was that he had more information. Constance knew about his past relationship with Brielle and wasn't happy about it. She broke up with him due to the situation with her father. He might be able to work with that.

ONE WEEK PASSED with no contact from Constance. He hadn't really expected her to reach out to him, but he'd hoped she would at least message him back. Constance hadn't come into work since the night of their dinner. She'd called Chloe to take some personal days.

It was getting to the point where he was about to go over to her property and ask her to just talk to him.

But Chloe insisted that was a bad idea.

Now, he sat in his office, staring blankly at the health records for the horses that Shane owned. There were a few he should probably visit, but he didn't have the energy to head out to where he might see Sean or Adeline.

They no doubt had heard about what was going on. He didn't need their pity.

There was a knock on his office door that hung slightly open. Chloe poked her head in and smiled. "Do you have plans this weekend?"

He tossed the file on the desk and shook his head. "I don't feel like doing much of anything after..."

Chloe nodded. "I get it." She edged inside and shut the door with a soft click. "Do you remember when I was dating that guy from the city?"

"No offense, Chloe, but I don't need a pep talk." He sighed and got up from his seat to gather his things.

She scoffed. "This isn't a pep talk."

"Well, whatever it is, I don't need it. I'm dealing with this the best way that works for me."

"You mean by staying locked up in your office?"

He scowled at her. "You're not my mother."

"How is your dear mother doing? Is she aware of everything that has happened?"

James snorted. "Do you know what my mother would do with that information?" That was a stupid question. Of course she knew. At one point, Daphne Pratt had assumed that Chloe was going to be his next love interest. Before he knew what was happening, the whole town had started believing they were involved in a secret love affair.

Luckily, they were both single at the time and no one was hurt—unless one were to ask his mother. She claimed she was heartbroken when the town finally realized she was wrong. If she'd had it her way, James would have started to date Chloe just to help save her reputation from being known as one of the county's most notorious gossips.

"Anyway," Chloe continued, "when Scott broke up with me, you told me that I needed to get him out of my head and start thinking about the future."

That advice wasn't going to work for him. He already knew that Constance was his future. Somehow, he thought he knew it from the time Clio was born.

"You need to get out and start living your life again," Chloe's voice broke through his reverie. "Before you get all hot and bothered, thinking that I'm telling you to get over her, hear me out. You don't need to give up on her. But you're not going to be any good to yourself or her if you don't take care of your mind. You don't want to let the pain fester until you see her and end up saying something stupid because you haven't forgiven her."

His head snapped back in her direction. "Who said that I was angry with her?"

Chloe held up both hands. "No one said any such thing. But you never know what kind of things you harbor toward people you love. Just trust me. Come out with me. We can go dancing at the country club, and while we're there, you can check on those two horses that Shane wanted you to see."

James's focus bounced toward the files on his desk. She made a good point.

And she was a good friend. He let out a sigh as he rubbed his chin. "Fine. Let's go dancing."

24

Constance

Constance's vision blurred as she stared at her computer screen. The words went out of focus in front of her. She needed to sign up to receive her certification so she could continue on to the next phase of becoming a veterinarian.

Even though her relationship didn't work out with James—for more reasons than one—she wasn't going to lose everything she'd worked for to get where she was in her career.

There was only one problem.

Her heart didn't agree.

Part of her was still holding onto the hope that she'd be able to have it all, even though she knew deep down that it wasn't possible. There was a conflict warring within her. James and Brielle had lied to her—through omission—but it was still a lie. Every single excuse Brielle had made when it came to James only added to that lie.

Constance was still kicking herself for not realizing that James had something more than a little crush on Brielle back before she'd started dating him. Shoving those thoughts as far down as she could, Constance forced herself to focus on the computer screen again.

This used to be so much more exciting when she was doing it with James. Constance pushed away from the computer desk with a groan and got up.

"You know what we should do tonight?" Dianna's voice filled the quiet room.

"Don't you dare say we should go out—"

"We should go out."

Constance shot Dianna a dark look.

"What? You've spent the last several months hanging out with James, and this is the first Friday where you can actually go out and have some fun."

"I don't need to have any fun. I need to figure out my schedule and how I'm going to survive work next week." Constance fell back onto her bed and stared at the ceiling.

"You never went into work this week?"

Constance didn't answer. Her sister already knew well enough that she hadn't gone to work. She'd sulked in her room over the situation she'd brought on herself. It was ridiculous and stupid, but she hadn't wanted to see James's face at all, and she didn't think she would be able to focus if they shared the same space.

Dianna moved on her bed, the shuffling sound the only thing Constance could hear until she settled on the edge of Constance's bed. "Come on, Connie. You need to get out. I know you're mad at Bri and all. And you don't want to have to see James, but maybe after a cute cowboy swings you around the room a little, you'll change your mind about your current predicament."

Constance rolled her eyes. "I hardly think replacing James

with someone different is going to fix my *situation*." A lump formed in her throat. She hadn't told Dianna about the one thing that had weighed on her heart.

James had confessed that he loved her.

He was the only one who had ever told her that.

And now her heart was broken because she had to tell him she didn't love him *enough* to fight for him.

The worst part was that if he knew her *real* reasons for the breakup, there wasn't a doubt in her mind that he wouldn't have let her leave. James was like that. He was the kind of guy who fought for what he wanted if he saw a glimmer of hope that he might get it.

Dianna scooted closer to Constance and nudged her playfully. "You know you don't want to stay here all alone."

"I won't be *alone*," she muttered. "Did you forget that we have younger sisters?"

"But they won't help keep your mind off of—you know who."

Constance groaned. "Are you seriously going to make this a big deal? Because it isn't. It's been a week. I'm over it." She chanced a look in Dianna's direction which was a big mistake. Her younger sister's expression was one of disdain. "Stop looking at me like that."

"For the record, no one expects you to be over him. He was your first love."

Constance huffed. "How could he be considered my first love if I never told him I loved him?" She grimaced and hoped her sister didn't catch her in her lie. She *had* admitted to loving him, but she'd said it just as she left and when she'd cut ties with him. Did it even count?

Dianna nudged her again. "It doesn't matter what you said or didn't say. Just come with me to the country club and keep me company."

She shut her eyes tight and let out a sigh. What were the

chances that James would be there? Shane was his friend. He could be visiting for that reason alone. But knowing James, he would be in the clinic catching up on work. It wasn't hard to convince him not to take her there. They both seemed to prefer the company of each other out in nature.

Her heart twisted inside out and she let out another groan. "How long are you going to want to stay?"

"I dunno. How about we get out there and then decide. You might find out that there's someone who is more interesting to visit with."

Constance opened her eyes and craned her neck around to glance up at her sister. "I doubt that. I don't need someone *new*. The only thing you said that made sense was that I needed to get my mind off things. So I guess I'll tag along for a little bit. But the second—and I mean the second—someone hits on me, I'm leaving. You can come with me, or you can get a ride home with someone else."

Her sister snickered. "Don't be ridiculous. If someone hits on you, I'm going to be right there to tell you to go for it."

"Dianna! I don't—"

"What will one kiss hurt? Seriously, I don't understand why you're so against moving on."

Constance's eyes narrowed. "Weren't you the one who said that dating was a bad idea? I seem to recall something about not wanting to break Daddy's rules."

"*Dating*, yes. But an innocent kiss?" She shrugged. "I've gotten a kiss or two at the end of the dates I've been on. But I won't be caught in a serious relationship. Those just cause trouble."

Eyes growing wide, Constance let out the first small laugh she could remember uttering since she'd last seen James. "Dianna! You're joking, right?"

She shrugged and gave Constance a wry smile. "There are

some things I prefer to keep to myself." Dianna scooted off the edge of the bed and turned around to hold out her hands toward Constance. "Let's go. It'll be fun."

Constance sat up on her elbows and stared at her sister with a wry grin. "I highly doubt that."

THE MUSIC in the country club flowed through the people dancing and visiting within the whole building. Constance found a sofa to sit on and held her glass of Coke in both of her hands. She didn't focus on anyone in particular, and Dianna had split the second they'd arrived.

It was nice to be out of the house, but being at one of the places where Constance spent more time with James while working wasn't actually helping her mental state.

She curled her legs up beneath her and pulled out her phone, praying the gesture would be enough to keep anyone from coming over and talking to her. Music could flood her senses enough to drown out the people and she could just get some peace from her overactive brain.

About thirty minutes later, the cushion beside her compressed as Dianna settled onto the sofa next to her. "Why aren't you out there dancing? I thought you said you'd come to have fun."

Constance waved her phone around and forced a grin. "I'm having the perfect amount of fun right now. I promise."

Dianna's cheeks were flushed from the amount of dancing she'd already participated in. Most of the songs had been upbeat—not the kind she'd spend with a partner. Currently the slow song had forced people to couple up and get close. Constance's eyes narrowed and her grin widened.

"You know what I think?"

"What's that?" Dianna's gaze swept through the room as she settled back against the couch.

"I think that you're full of hot air."

Dianna laughed and fanned her face with her hand. "I do feel a little over-heated. Do you want to go outside and get some fresh air?"

"No. I mean you're a liar."

This time Dianna glanced in Constance's direction. "That's not a very nice thing to say. Besides, I'm not the one who was lying about my relationship." Her tone remained lighthearted and the smile behind her eyes confirmed she wasn't offended in the slightest.

"What I mean is that I don't think you've ever kissed a guy."

Dianna tossed her head back and laughed. "Okay. You got me."

Constance let out a loud laugh, drawing the attention of some of the closer couples. "I knew it wasn't in your character to go kissing random guys. You're too much of a rule follower and too much of a romantic."

Her younger sister shrugged. "I had to get you out here somehow. I didn't think you'd come if I told you that I just wanted to dance." She elbowed Constance in the side. "The next song, you should come out with me."

She held up her phone once more. "I'm perfectly happy reading the books I have on my app."

"But you said you'd come for me." Dianna pouted with exaggeration.

Constance laughed again. "What? Do you want to go out there and dance with me right now? I hardly think this song would be appropriate for the two of us, but I guess I can't be certain."

Dianna glanced at the dance floor, then swung her focus back to Constance. "Sure, why not?" She grabbed Constance's hand and got to her feet.

A gasp tore from her throat as Constance tugged back. "I didn't mean it. I was joking."

"So? I think it would be fun to dance with my sister. And you're right. I don't have any interest in the guys here because I don't have any interest in falling in love any time soon."

Constance pressed her lips together. She really wasn't worried that people would talk. They were a close family as it was. Her hesitancy came from being around other couples in love and the tendency for her thoughts to go rogue. She didn't want to think about James and what she had willingly lost. "Fine. One dance. That's all." She allowed Dianna to pull her to her feet and they moved onto the dance floor.

The slow country song was one she hadn't heard before. It told the typical story of a cowboy losing his love and wanting to get her back. Constance's heart ached, not just for herself but for James, too.

It wasn't the first time she'd thought of him and wondered if she'd made the wrong decision. She hadn't exactly stood up to her father to find out what would happen if she told him she was in love.

There were worse things.

She squeezed her eyes shut momentarily. Her father was no longer the only thing that stood in her way. James had a lot to explain. He should have told her he'd been involved with Brielle. They both should have brought it up. That was the reason Constance had avoided speaking to Brielle all week.

What hurt the most was that she knew deep down that she would have to forgive Brielle. They were family. That fact alone would force her to accept that the past was the past.

With James it was different. She'd trusted him, and he hadn't proven himself worthy of that. When Constance opened her eyes, she shifted her focus around the room. Everyone seemed so happy together—so free to choose their path when it came to love.

A familiar head of dark hair caught her attention. The locks were wavy at the man's neck just like James. His skin was sun-kissed and bronzed like many of the men who worked long hours outside. Her heart leapt in her chest and her grasp on Dianna tightened. The man couldn't be James. He was dancing with a woman whose arms were wrapped securely around his neck.

James wouldn't move on that fast—not so soon after he'd confessed his feelings for her.

"You okay?"

Constance's gaze darted to Dianna. "What?"

"Your hands—they're a little tight on mine. You okay?"

She grimaced and released Dianna quickly. "Yeah. I'm fine. I just—" Her focus shifted toward the man and everything in her body went cold and stiff. He turned just enough for her to get a clear view of his profile.

It *was* James. And he was dancing with Chloe.

Constance's stomach knotted, crumbling and rolling together until she could barely breathe.

No.

She *couldn't* breathe. It was like her lungs had forgotten their only purpose in this life.

James's dark eyes lifted to meet hers briefly before she spun on her heel. Her eyes sought the exit. She needed to get out of there. It was too soon to talk to James about what had happened. He'd called, he'd left messages, and she still didn't know what to tell him about her refusal to call back. Even Monday seemed too soon to speak to him, but at least at the clinic she had Chloe as a buffer.

Only now, that concept somehow made things one hundred times worse.

By the time she made it out the front door, her breaths were coming out in sharp, short puffs. She could barely hear Dianna's frantic voice calling for her but refused to turn around until she heard her name from the one voice she'd been terrified to hear.

"Constance." The door to the club shut and James's soft voice somehow thundered through the evening air, wrapping around her and refusing to let her take another step.

25

James

James stood on the steps of the country club. His whole body felt weighed down and heavy. His heart thundered and he was lightheaded. This was the last place he had expected to see Constance. Even when they were together, she preferred to spend time with him in a quieter setting.

He took a step toward her, wishing she'd turn around and meet his gaze but also dreading that moment at the same time. There was so much he wanted to say to her and ask her. It felt like an eternity since their last dinner. And ever since Brielle had told him that Constance knew he'd been involved with her, he had this gut feeling that Constance wasn't going to be very open to discussing much of anything.

Clearing his throat, he said, "Can we talk?"

She hugged herself, her shoulders tight, but she still didn't face him. "Unless this is about work, I don't have anything I need to speak to you about."

Her words hurt more than he'd anticipated. A sharp pain sliced through his insides, and he winced. "Brielle came to see me."

She stiffened, then whirled around. Her accusatory eyes flashed with pain. "Do you want her back? Are you two finally rekindling whatever love affair you once had?"

His head reared back and irritation flickered to life deep down in his stomach. "Of course not. We dated in *high school*. I haven't been interested in her for a long time."

Constance snorted. "Really? Because it sure looked like you were still interested a few months ago when you started seeing Clio."

"What are you talking about?"

"I'm not blind. I could see it so clearly."

"Then why did we even start dating?" he shot back at her. Her words had managed to make him far more uncomfortable than he'd been prepared for. This mess could have been avoided if he'd only told her about Brielle in the beginning, but he'd listened to her sister rather than really considering what the consequences could be.

"Maybe I was just in deep denial." She folded her arms and looked away, her voice softening. "I had this crush on you since we were younger. I never even looked at anyone else. I knew in my heart that you were the kind of guy I wanted to be with."

James took another step toward her. "Then what are we doing this for? Why break it off with me?"

The anger returned to her gaze as she lifted her face, and the light from the building reflected off her pale skin. She glowered at him. "You lied to me."

"I didn't *lie*. I did tell you I had a small crush on Brielle. I just never told you we dated." Even as the words left his lips, he knew that was the wrong thing to say. He grimaced, bracing himself for her reaction.

"Omission is a kind of lying, James," she spat. "I can't ask about something I don't know about."

"She was an ex. Since when do couples discuss exes?"

"She is my *sister*. Don't you think that would bother me? I know Brielle. I know how often she used to sneak out just to be with the newest flavor of the month. For all I know, you two were far more intimate than you should have ever been." Her face flushed and she shook her head. "Why *wouldn't* that bother me? Every time I close my eyes, I see you kissing *her*. I don't know if I can get over that."

He clenched his jaw; the irritation inside him had mutated into something ugly—something desperate. The fact that she was insinuating he'd been inappropriate with Brielle had wounded his pride. "If you think that my character is so tarnished, then why bother dating me? Oh, that's right. Because I was so good at lying to you and keeping secrets. Maybe I'm just damaged goods."

She pressed her lips into a thin line, her eyes never leaving his face.

"But you know what? If I'm damaged, then you have a lot of growing up to do. Not only that, but if you cared about me as much as you said you do, you'd be willing to risk making your father angry."

Her eyes widened and she dropped her arms to her sides.

James continued even though there was a small part of his brain that told him he needed to cool it. He could fix this if he'd just take a deep breath and appeal to her softer side. But he didn't. He opened his big mouth and just kept talking. "You insist on staying under your father's thumb because he needs to feel secure, and you don't want to hurt him. But you want to know what I think? You're just terrified that if you step across that line he's drawn in the sand, you'll actually find happiness."

"Why would that scare me? Everyone wants to be happy," she shot back.

He closed the distance between them, his voice lowering to a sharp, husky whisper. "Because if you find happiness—true happiness—then you have to actually work to keep it. You have to dig your nails into it and clutch it so it doesn't slip through your fingers. Once you have found that happiness, you know deep down that losing it might be the end of you. You know that your heart won't be able to take returning to what used to be normal." His voice broke and he hooked his finger under her chin to lift her face toward him. "That kind of love, that kind of happiness is rare. Once you've tasted it, there's no going back."

She didn't pull away from him. They stood like that, staring into each other's eyes as if the world had stopped spinning. It was almost like his words had made a difference. Was it possible? Was he going to win her back? His heart pounded a little harder and he leaned closer, dipping his head toward her.

Ever since their dinner, he'd suffered withdrawal simply because he hadn't been able to drink in her beauty or caress her skin with his touch. He'd experienced the kind of happiness he'd spoken to her about. He knew right to his core that if the roles were reversed, he would have defied the rules her father had made right from the beginning.

Especially after he'd experienced the love he had for Constance.

She blinked and in a heart-wrenching second, Constance stepped back, shaking her head. "It's not just the lies, James," she murmured.

"Then what is it?"

Constance brushed at her face and turned to walk away, but he reached out and grasped her wrist, forcing her to turn and face him.

"What's holding you back?" he pleaded.

She wouldn't meet his gaze. "It's just not going to work out. We went about this wrong from the very start. I should have never—" Her eyes darted up to meet his. "Maybe if things were different, we could fix this. But there's just too many moving parts. Just trust me when I say that breaking it off now is for the best."

"I can't," he muttered. "I can't just let you walk away without knowing why.

Her voice rose and she yanked her hand from his grasp. "You *know* why. My dad. Brielle. All of the secrets. This relationship was doomed from the beginning."

"But we can start over. I'll come talk to your father—"

"No!"

He stiffened.

"No," she said more softly. "I've already talked to him. I'm not going to break my father's heart for the sake of my own. You might think that I should because it's my life. But it's his too. I can't be the daughter that does that to him." She spun around and charged for the truck in the parking lot. Dianna ran after her.

James stood there listlessly. His arms dangled at his sides as he watched them drive away. The only thing that conversation had helped him figure out was that Constance wasn't willing to fight for his love.

Either he cared for her more than she did for him, or she was holding back because of her father.

He scowled at the fading taillights.

Her father. That was the person he should have confronted this whole time. He had her so brainwashed she wasn't willing to do anything for her own happiness. Zeke was the villain in their love story, and he deserved a good talking to.

As soon as he took Chloe home, he was making one important stop.

∼

JAMES SAT IN HIS CAR, the darkness of the night swallowing him up like he was nothing. At least that's how he felt at the moment. He was doing this out of love. Or maybe he was just crazy. But Zeke needed to be told he was making a big mistake in the way he was handling his daughters. James was the one stupid enough to be the messenger.

He placed his hand on the car door handle and hesitated. Zeke was a big guy. He'd spent his whole life running this ranch and building it from the ground up. He had a reputation, too. One that had men shying away from his younger daughters from the very beginning.

James had been too scared to do much about it when he was a teenager. Then again, perhaps he hadn't been as invested in his relationship with Brielle as he was with Constance.

The explanation for that was easy. He'd cared for Brielle. He'd thought he might even love her. But he wasn't willing to risk his life to change the situation they were in.

Constance was different. If he went up to that door and Zeke answered, he could very well be thrown out on his behind. But it would be worth it. Someone had to tell him.

James squeezed his eyes shut tight and pushed the door open. The crisp fall air hit him in the face, cooling the heat that hadn't left since he'd confronted Constance at the club. James shut the door with a resounding thud, focusing on the smell of dirt and fresh-cut straw that wafted around him. He'd confronted Zeke on other things before, but never about this. There was no telling what might happen.

He trudged toward the door, his feet dragging, having not gotten the message that this was happening whether they liked it or not. James lifted his fist and pounded on the door, then stepped back a few paces to make room between himself and whoever was going to answer.

Footsteps sounded inside and he fidgeted with the hem of his shirt for a moment before shoving his hands deep into his pockets. The door opened a crack at first, then widened, revealing Brielle's face. "James? What are you doing here?"

He cleared his throat and lifted his chin. "I'm here to speak to your father. Is he home?"

She glanced over her shoulder, then slipped out onto the porch and closed the door just enough to leave it a crack open. "Whatever you want to speak to him about, you should probably reconsider."

James shook his head resolutely. "I'm not going anywhere until I give him a piece of my mind."

Her eyes narrowed. "He'll probably take a lot more than that if you're going to do what I think you're going to."

"He needs to know that I love Constance and I'm not giving up on her. I fully intend on fixing things with her whether or not you're married. This stupid rule of his has got to end."

The door lurched open and both of them sent startled looks at the intruder. Zeke held a Remington hunting rifle out the door, pointed directly at James. His eyes were dark and hooded, his jaw tight. "Brielle, get back inside."

She shot James a concerned look as if she didn't know whether she should leave him alone with her father.

James didn't have an answer. His eyes were glued to the business end of that rifle. His heart was pounding hard enough that he was certain both of the Callahans present could hear it. He nodded, not shifting his focus to Brielle. "You should listen to him, Bri."

She turned toward her father. "That's enough, Dad. You know you can't shoot him." When Zeke didn't respond, she sighed and slipped inside, then shut the door with a resounding thud.

"What do you want, Pratt?" Zeke muttered.

All the confidence and reasoning James had before this moment had disappeared completely. Everything people had said about Zeke was right. How on earth had Sean managed to win him over to marry Adeline?

James attempted to clear the lump in his throat but was unsuccessful and his words came out in a squeak. "I love—" he cleared his throat once more. "I love your daughter."

"You're going to have to be more specific. None of my daughters have breathed a word about you." Zeke gestured with his gun, forcing James to take a few steps back. He stumbled down the top step but managed to stay upright.

"Constance."

If there was any surprise on Zeke's face, he hid it well.

"I've fallen in love with her over the last few months, and I want to make it clear to you that I intend on marrying her."

His brows lifted. "Is that so?"

James nodded. "The rules you've set out for your daughters are outdated and ridiculous."

Zeke's features hardened, the surprise no longer present.

"They're adults who ought to be able to make that choice on their own."

"And you think they all feel the same way you do? Because if that were true, why wouldn't they tell me themselves?"

"Because they don't want to hurt you," James grit out. "You probably have the closest family I know of. Everyone works together on this ranch, and no one steps out of line." Well, besides Brielle, that he knew of. "But they're not happy."

Zeke's dark expression got darker. There was a storm brewing behind his eyes that made him even scarier. He didn't need the gun anymore to intimidate. "My daughters are as happy as they need to be."

"Really? Tell me something then. When you met your wife, would you say you could have been happy without her?"

Shock filtered through the anger emanating from the gruff man before him.

"When you find love, you know that you won't be able to

live without her. That's how I feel about Constance. And for reasons I can only assume are related to your ancient rules—"

Zeke charged forward and pressed the tip of the gun to James's chest. "You better leave my property before I have to call the coroner to remove you."

James stumbled back a few more paces until he landed on the ground. They glowered at one another, and James tightened his hands into fists. "I'm not going to give up on her. I know she wants to be with me. If you think she's happy with her life the way it is, you better take a good look at her—at all of them." He let out a mirthless laugh. "And maybe think a little bit harder about what your wife would think about all of this. Because I'd wager she wouldn't want her daughters locked up like some fairytale princesses waiting for their turn to find love that might have already found them."

He spun on his heel, adrenaline pulsing through his body and his nerves humming with energy. His hands shook and his legs felt numb. He'd never been so terrified in his entire life. And he prayed it was worth it.

26

Constance

*C*onstance fumed as she slumped down onto the chair in her room. Anger, depression, longing—her heart couldn't make up its mind. Seeing James at the club shouldn't have been a surprise, but seeing him with Chloe had been a total shock.

The pain that their conversation had elicited was almost more than she could bear. Deep down she knew that his relationship with Brielle wasn't as big of a deal. Yes, it had hurt her to hear about it. But the betrayal over not being told was short-lived.

While Copper Creek was growing, it was almost impossible to find someone that Brielle hadn't gone on at least one date with. That was just who she was. Constance had come to that realization rather easily.

At this point, the only thing that held her back was her father. The conversation she'd had with him and the one she'd had with Sarah, plus everything Dianna had mentioned—all of that had helped her settle on her decision.

She wasn't going to push her father into anything he didn't think was a good idea.

Her thoughts drifted to the Keagan household and how she'd been so quick to judge their living situation. James had put her in her place so fast it had nearly made her head spin. Her life was far from perfect. Yes, she wished there were other options when it came to dating, but it was all she knew.

Someone knocked loudly on the front door.

Whoever it was, they were probably here for Brielle. Dianna wasn't home yet. Adeline had moved into a small cottage on the property. And the rest of her sisters were around here somewhere.

She sighed and reached for a veterinary book nearby. Her life had already changed so much that she should just be grateful she had something she loved. James had helped her get it.

Her heart twisted. James had been the common denominator when it came to everything that made her happy. She tossed the book aside and stood up to stare out the window, surprised when she noticed a familiar car out in the driveway.

Constance's pulse roared and chills raced through her body. Why was James here and who was he speaking to? No one had come to get her. She turned to head for the door, then froze and strode back to the window. If he wasn't here to see her, then he was here to speak to someone else.

She twisted her hands together. Curiosity burning within her. Hadn't she ended their relationship? James knew exactly where she stood. So if he was here and he wasn't here to see her...

Constance's blood ran cold.

He wouldn't.

She stormed toward her door and yanked it open, then froze. Her sister Grace blocked her path. Her green eyes were wide and a small smile touched her lips. Her hand was poised ready to knock. "You won't believe what's going on right now," she whispered.

Constance's brows furrowed. "Well, are you going to tell me? Because if you aren't, then you need to move so I can go check it out for myself."

Grace shook her head, her blonde curls swaying with the movement. "You don't want to do that. If you do, you'll probably be interrupting a pretty intense conversation."

That didn't sound good. Constance sighed and gave her sister a pointed look. "Then *tell* me."

"James came to talk to Dad."

Oh no. He knew better than that.

"And when Dad went outside, he took his hunting rifle with him."

Constance's mouth fell open as she let the words sink in. Then she attempted to lunge past her sister but didn't quite make it.

"I told you that you'd go intervene. You can't go down there."

"Why not?" Constance had her hands on her hips and she scowled at Grace. "He's my boy—" She cut herself off. Grace hadn't known about that tidbit of information. But based on the way she didn't seem surprised by the statement, James must have said something. Constance attempted to push past Grace once more. "I can't let Dad do that."

"I don't think you have a choice. It sounded like he was just about to leave when I came up here." As if to confirm her statement, the front door slammed shut.

Constance let out a sigh. "Great. Do you think he scared him off?"

"From the sounds of it, you did a decent job of that all on

your own." Grace probably hadn't meant for her words to hurt, but they did all the same.

Shoulder's slumped and heart lagging, Constance leaned against the door jamb. "What else did you hear?"

Before Grace could get anything out, angry voices exploded downstairs. Both Grace and Constance jumped, exchanging looks of confusion but also concern. Grace spun around and hurried toward the stairway with Constance right behind her. They headed down the stairs, careful not to move with heavy steps.

Once at the bottom, they slowed and came to a stop just out of sight from the living room. Brielle and their father were the ones arguing.

"You think he's right?" Zeke growled.

"I *know* he's right. I dated him once."

There was silence for a full minute as if their father needed additional time to come to terms with what she'd just said. "You *what*? I'm going to kill him."

Brielle let out a sigh. "It was in high school."

"*In high school?*"

"What did you expect, Dad? I wanted to date, and Adeline wasn't ready to get married. So I kept it from you."

His voice hardened. "How many of you have been doing this behind my back?"

"That's not the point."

"Then what is?"

"It's—we're adults, like James said. We should be able to make our own choices."

"You mean your own mistakes," he muttered.

"Exactly."

More silence that seemed to stretch longer than before.

Brielle's voice softened. "How else are we going to find the men that we want to marry? How are we going to find someone who means as much to us as Mom meant to you?" Emotion caught in her throat. "Constance loves James. I've seen it first-hand. And he loves her. They're good for each other."

"How can you know that?" Her father's voice was softer now, too. And their frantic steps had stopped. It almost felt like the house was so quiet it would cave in on all of them.

"I just—know." Brielle let out another sigh. "All I'm trying to say is that we're different. You might not realize this, but Adeline and Sean got married because she wanted to give the rest of us a chance to find love sooner rather than later." Her voice shook a little. "As much as I wish I could do the same for Constance, I... can't. I haven't found love yet. And I'm not sure I'm ready for a relationship. But Constance shouldn't suffer because I'm not willing to make a sacrifice like Adeline."

Zeke didn't speak right away. Grace glanced in Constance's direction but didn't breathe a word. This fight was about Constance, but it was about so much more than that. The decision their father made would affect Grace and all the others.

Constance held her breath, waiting for her father to make any indication that he understood what Brielle was saying.

"Is this why Constance has seemed so distant all week?" The sound of someone settling into a chair came next. "I don't know if I feel comfortable with making that kind of change."

Constance's heart faltered, but she regained control. Even if he did change the rule, what would that mean for her failed relationship with James? It wasn't like she could just walk up to him and tell him that she'd broken up with him because she wasn't brave enough to be in Brielle's current situation. Constance had either been terrified or too set in her own ways to stand up for her own relationship. Maybe a little bit of both.

And now she had Brielle fighting her battle for her.

Brielle's soft voice broke through the silence. "It's not really up to you. We all live here, helping out at the ranch because we love you. We're all really close. None of us want to break the family up. But there will ultimately come a day when one of us breaks free from your rules and you're going to have to decide how you will handle it." Footsteps shuffled across the wood floor and Brielle arrived in the doorway. Her eyes landed on Constance and she gave her a wry smile before moving toward the stairs.

Constance's gaze followed her sister until she was no longer visible, then she glanced toward Grace.

"What do you think he's going to do?" she whispered.

Constance shrugged. "Doesn't really matter, does it? None of us have someone to fight for right now." She headed toward the stairs, her heart heavier than before. That should have been the conversation she had with her father. She should have been brave enough to stick up for what she wanted. She'd been a doormat from the beginning.

Grace hurried to walk beside her. "Yes, you do. You have James."

"I don't think I do anymore."

"Why not?" Grace touched Constance's arm, forcing her to stop and face her at the top of the stairs. "He's obviously crazy about you. He came here to fight for your hand."

Constance snorted. "This isn't some fairytale. Princes who come to save the damsel don't exist."

"James is as close to a *prince* as you're going to get, and you should probably do something before you lose him altogether." Brielle stood in the doorway of her room, her voice causing both Grace and Constance to jump. "If *I* were you, I'd go after him and tell him you made a mistake."

The hurt feelings from Brielle's deception hovered just below the surface. Constance wanted so much to give her older sister the cold shoulder. It would be easier to avoid a conversation about wounds that were still healing.

At the same time, she almost wanted to throw her arms around Brielle for doing the one thing she hadn't been capable of doing.

Grace nudged her. "Aren't you going to do something?"

Constance glanced from one sister to the other, then nodded. "Yes. But it's not what you think." She turned and headed down the stairs and straight for the living room. Her father was seated by the fireplace, staring at the empty contents. He didn't stir when she arrived and didn't show her that he'd noticed her appearance whatsoever.

She moved closer and plopped down on the couch that sat across from him, making as much noise as possible when sitting on the overstuffed furniture.

Zeke lifted his head and turned toward her. For the most part, his expression was unreadable—all except his eyes. Behind his grey eyes was worry. She hadn't expected to find that emotion from her father. He was the head of the family—always ready for anything and prepared to take on a stampeding bull if need be.

He groaned as he shifted in his seat and leaned over, resting his elbows on his knees. "I suppose you're here to give your two cents, too."

She opened her mouth, shut it, then opened it again. All she could muster was a nod.

"Well, get to it. I'm sure I've heard it all between your boyfriend and your sister. But I'll listen."

Her face flushed and she scooted to the edge of the cushion. "He's not my boyfriend—not anymore."

Zeke arched one brow.

Constance swallowed hard and glanced away, hating the discerning look her father was capable of throwing in her direction. "I heard the argument you had with Brielle."

"I figured you would."

She brought her gaze back to meet his. "She's right, you know."

"About what part?" He let out a strangled chuckle. "The part where I'm too controlling. Or how about the part where one day my family will fall apart because I was too scared to give you the freedom you all deserved?"

"You're not too controlling." The comment escaped her lips before she knew what had happened.

He gave her a pointed look. "The fact that you're here right now having this discussion with me makes me think otherwise."

She squirmed in her seat. "Okay, maybe you're controlling, but I get it. You had to raise all seven of us by yourself. It's easier to put us all in a pen than to let us roam free."

"Like cattle," he muttered.

Constance bit back a smile. "It's what you know best." He shot her a sharp look and she snickered, then after a little while she sobered as she continued. "Brielle was right that we need to find our own way. You've raised us right. We're hard workers and we have a strong family bond. But now we need to grow and stretch our wings." She bit down on her lower lip to prevent herself from saying she was ready for that stage of her life. It was hard to tell if Zeke had finally accepted everything he'd been told today.

"Do you love him?"

Her voice caught in her throat and she nodded.

He took in a deep breath, then let it out as he got to his feet. "If you're really in love with that boy, then I'm not going to stop you."

She gasped and jumped up from her seat. "Really?"

Zeke reached out and cupped her cheek with his palm. His hand dropped and he nodded. "If that's what will make you happy. Who am I to stand in the way? Pratt is a decent man— not good enough for you—but he's alright."

Constance threw her arms around her father's neck and gave him a hug. "Thank you, Daddy."

"I suppose we're overdue for a family meeting."

She pulled back and her brows creased.

"Your sisters are going to want to know they're free to fall in love whenever they please." He gave her a stern look. "But I'm not putting away my hunting rifle. Those men have to prove themselves like Pratt did tonight."

Constance let out a laugh.

27

James

The following morning, James sat in a booth at Sal's Diner with a coffee in his hands. He hadn't slept at all after his interaction with Constance's father. Zeke knew how to really scare a man.

What man needed to make a rule that his daughters couldn't date when he had a hunting rifle at the ready?

James raked a hand through his hair and let out a groan. His head pounded and his eyesight was blurry. He'd told Zeke the truth last night and now he needed to make good on his promises. He had to come up with something to get Constance to give him a chance. There was only one problematic thing he could foresee.

If he'd really riled up Zeke, he wouldn't put it past the guy to double down on his rules. The way James saw it, he could try the usual route of flowers and gifts. He'd be seeing Constance on Monday for work. She wasn't going to be able to avoid him forever.

He lifted the mug to his lips as the bell over the diner door rang and more customers entered. The man's sandy-colored hair was familiar. Wade. Wade Keagan. The woman who entered with him had to be his sister, the resemblance uncanny. They took a seat at the bar and the waitress wasted no time in serving them.

Constance probably wouldn't want flowers. She was a romantic, but she'd want something more meaningful. The problem with that was coming up with something that was as priceless as she was.

James stiffened as the door opened and the one person he hadn't wanted to see strode in. Zeke stood in the doorway and glanced around the room until his focus landed on James. His features were tight and he looked about as exhausted as James felt.

Don't come over here. Please don't come over here.

Zeke headed over in James's direction.

Shoot.

James straightened, his back stiff against the booth as Zeke took a seat across from him. James didn't take his wary eyes off the man. Rifle or no rifle, this man wasn't to be trusted.

Zeke's focus bounced up to James and he tapped his finger on the menu that had been left behind by the waitress. "I've had some time to think about what you said last night."

Eyes widening, James couldn't drag his attention away from Zeke if he wanted to. The man was going to string him up by his toes. He'd take him out into the woods and let the animals get to him.

"And I admire your courage."

Wait, what?

"It took a lot of guts to come tell me I'm raising my seven children wrong." He raised one bushy brow.

"I never said—"

Zeke held up a hand. "It takes even more guts to stay in town after being poked by my rifle."

James blinked. Was the man making a joke? None of that was funny.

Zeke's steady gaze locked onto James and he went quiet. Time slowed down and James's breathing all but stopped. "I've been convinced to change a few things about the rules of my house."

It was at that very moment that everything started back in motion. James glanced around the room, his gaze seeking out anything that would make it clear this was a dream or some kind of practical joke. People didn't just change their ways that fast. Something else had to have happened. Did Constance finally speak to him?

James focused on Zeke once more. "What exactly are you saying?"

Zeke got to his feet and set his steely eyes on James. "I'm saying that if you break her heart, I'm more than happy to get some hunting practice in. Have a good day, Dr. Pratt." He gave James a short nod and headed for the counter.

This had to be a dream. He hadn't slept well last night. Now he'd managed to fall asleep in his booth. Someone was bound to come poke him to wake him up. James set his head in his hands.

But if this was real, it meant there was nothing standing in his way of being with Constance. Nothing but the woman herself.

He shot out of his seat only to come face to face with the woman he couldn't get out of his mind.

"Hi, James." Constance gestured toward the booth. "Chloe said you might be here. Mind if I sit?"

His hand reached for the table and he lowered himself slowly into the booth. His gaze shot toward Zeke who he found giving him a warning look. James dragged his attention to Constance once more. "After last night—"

Constance reached for his hand across the table. "Can I go first this time?"

He clamped his mouth shut. If she was willing to talk now, he wasn't going to fight her on it. She was here, sitting in front of him. What more could he ask for in this exact moment?

She worried her lower lip and traced her finger on the back of his hand, causing fresh chills to overwhelm him. When she looked up, her eyes shined with emotion. "I wanted to say I was sorry."

James stiffened. "But you didn't—"

"I didn't stand up for what I wanted, and it wasn't fair to either of us. I should have known better from the start that if I planned on dating someone, I'd have to figure out how to make it okay with my dad." She glanced over her shoulder to where her dad sat, but he wasn't looking their way anymore. "I tried once, but I gave up too easily."

Constance brought her focus back to James and offered him a sad smile. "There are still a lot of things that I have to work through, but there's one thing I know I wanted to tell you."

The way she was speaking, he could tell she wanted to put their relationship on hold. Maybe it wasn't a complete breakup. But it still wasn't a rekindling. "Constance, before you say anything—"

"I know you visited my dad last night."

Once again, he was rendered speechless.

"I know that you told him you didn't like his rules and he needed to change them. Or something like that." She let out a soft laugh. "But after you left, your words spurred Brielle to say more."

James lifted his brows. "Brielle?"

She nodded. "I guess she was feeling the same as you. The pressure she was under to find someone to marry so that I could have my happiness had finally gotten to her." Her eyes dipped to their hands and her voice softened. "I only wish I would have been brave enough to do it first."

He leaned forward and touched her chin, lifting her face so he could see her eyes. "It's not a race. People have to figure things out when they're good and ready."

There was no one more perfect for him than Constance. He firmly believed that fate or God played a part in the path his life had taken. He tilted his head and smiled at her. He didn't dare hope that this conversation was headed where he wanted it to go. She hadn't exactly asked him to take her back, though she would never need to.

"My father called a family meeting late last night. I guess the thought of ending this rule had crossed his mind a few times since Adeline got married. He just needed the right push."

James probably should have shown more surprise, but Zeke had already cleared this part for him. What was more important was that he needed to hear Constance say she wanted to return to the relationship they had—only more out in the open.

The diner was getting more crowded and once again another patron entered. Shane strode inside and waved to Wade and his sister. His gaze swept through the diner, landing briefly on Constance and James before he took a seat beside the two he'd come to meet. James shifted his attention to Constance and leaned forward as she continued.

"I guess I came here because I wanted to—"

Movement out of the corner of his eye drew his attention as Wade pushed away from the counter and strode toward them at a speed that was more than a little concerning.

James jumped up with the intention of shielding Constance from whatever was about to happen.

Wade reached out and grasped James's hand and pulled him in for a hug, then clapped his hand on James's back. When

Wade pulled back, his expression wasn't a smile. It was just as flat and unreadable as ever.

James glanced from him to where Shane still sat at the counter with who James assumed was Wade's sister. He brought his focus back to Wade when the man shook James's hand. "I want to thank you, Dr. Pratt."

Confusion flooded every part of James's mind. What would Wade have to thank him for?

"Mr. Owens just informed me of a giveaway he organized for a whole-home remodel."

James shot one more look toward Shane. It would have been nice if his friend could have warned him this was about to happen.

Wade continued, his voice still gruff. "Apparently, you had the forms at the clinic. My brother didn't remember applying for it, but he said you had him sign a lot of paperwork when he started working for you."

James could sense more than see Constance stiffen behind him. She would have known about any giveaway that had been organized in Copper Creek. Well, the cat was out of the bag. He flashed Wade a smile and nodded. "I thought your family the most deserving of the prize."

Wade shifted his weight from one foot to the other and leaned forward, his voice lowering. "For the record, I don't appreciate you manipulating my brother into applying for this, but my family needs it. I won't turn away from something we won fair and square." He pulled back and gave Constance a short nod. "Ma'am."

Both Constance and James watched Wade retreat, and when he'd arrived back at his seat, she leaned over the table, wearing a wide smile to match the emotion in her eyes. "You actually did it! I can't believe it! You have such a good heart."

He reached for her hand and held it tightly within his own. "It was your idea. I just figured out a way to put it in motion.

Besides, Shane's the one who is footing the bill. I can't really take any credit for it."

She squeezed his hand. "Don't sell yourself short. I don't know anyone who would have been willing to help a family they didn't know."

"You would have."

Constance smiled and broke eye contact with him. "I guess we're a good match then."

"I guess so."

28

One Year Later

Constance

*I*t didn't matter how much time had passed, Constance still felt like she was living in an alternate universe. It was strange to invite James to family dinner and even weirder when she would catch her father having a normal conversation with him like the events of last year had never occurred.

A lot had happened since this time last year. She had been accepted into a veterinary school after getting certified as a vet tech. Her sisters had started venturing out and going on dates. Adeline had a baby girl, and Sarah would be getting married within the next week.

At first it was nice to take things slow with James. They were able to ease back into a relationship that was still so new. But now it felt like her relationship had come to a standstill while the world moved on without her.

Constance wandered through the trails around her house, soaking in the fall colors. She pulled her sweater tighter around her as a biting chill whipped through the air. She should be happy. She had everything she wanted, right?

It would be selfish to demand more right now, especially if James wasn't ready. Yes, they were close. They knew they loved each other, and James had even mentioned that he planned on being with her forever.

And yet...

There was no proposal, no ring, no promise of how that was going to happen.

She was being ridiculous. After what she'd put him through, she knew he might need to become more secure in their relationship.

But how long was that going to take?

She heaved a sigh as she came up to a towering maple tree with scarlet-colored leaves. When the breeze picked up, a few fluttered to the ground, dancing and swaying without a care in the world. That was how she should be feeling. She needed to figure out a way to push through this feeling before it became a bigger problem.

That meant having a good sit-down talk with James about where they were headed. If they were as in love as she thought they were, then there shouldn't be any question. They both wanted a family.

Constance leaned back against the tree and let out a sigh as she dropped to the ground. Her head rested on the bark, and she closed her eyes.

Footsteps crunched against dry leaves and twigs a moment later. Constance opened her eyes to find Dianna wandering toward her. Dianna smiled but didn't speak as she approached and took a seat beside Constance.

They sat in silence for a few minutes until Dianna nudged Constance with her shoulder. "I haven't found you out here in a long time."

Constance peeked at her sister with one open eye. "I haven't really had much time to come out here."

Dianna nodded and stared out at the clearing where they sat. Trees, overgrown wildflowers, and the sound of a stream running over smooth stones made up their little escape.

"Do you remember the first time we found this place?" Constance opened her eyes and glanced at Dianna.

Her sister smiled. "We were trying to avoid our chores and you insisted this was the only way Dad and Adeline wouldn't find us."

Nodding, Constance settled deeper against the tree and let out a sigh. "I still don't think that anyone else comes out this far. I'm sure they're aware of it, but you're the only one I've ever bumped into."

"You're probably right." Dianna rested her head on Constance's shoulder. "I feel like we don't talk much anymore. You're always so busy."

Constance leaned her cheek against Dianna's head. Her heart tightened. Dianna was right. There was so much going on that her relationship with Dianna had suffered. She'd been so caught up with her own problems that she'd failed to see if Dianna needed anything. "I'm going to do better with that."

Minutes stretched on as neither one of them spoke. That was how it went when they came out here. Their thoughts kept them company, but it was nice to be with each other.

"Do you think you're going to marry James?" Dianna's soft voice broke the stillness.

Constance stiffened. "I don't know."

"If he doesn't ask you, would you ask him?"

A smile stole across her face. "I hadn't really thought about it. But I suppose that's where I'm headed."

Dianna sat up and faced Constance, her eyes wide. "Really?"

Constance laughed. "Well, I probably won't get on one knee and ask him officially. But I do think I need to say something. Otherwise, I feel like I'm doomed to continue living in this weird limbo."

Her sister's face scrunched up and she frowned. "If you get married, we'll spend even less time together."

"That's not true. I—"

"Yes, it is. You're working more hours at the clinic, and you'd be moving into his place. I doubt we'd get any more moments like this." Her voice sounded so heartbroken.

Constance cupped Dianna's face between her hands. "I'll always have time for you." She let that sink in. "But maybe you need to find something you love to do, too."

"But Dad needs me here to help at the ranch."

"Dad has the ability to hire as many men as he could possibly need. If you find something you love to do, he's going to support you just like he supported me." Constance's eyes widened. "I know Shane is looking for some help with his equine therapy program. He needs people who can help with the children. You'd be great with that." Constance could see it in her sister's eyes. There was the same kind of longing that Constance had experienced when she wanted to learn more about becoming a veterinarian.

"I don't know..."

"You don't have to commit to anything, but go visit with Shane. You never know. This could be the one thing that has been missing from your life that you never realized you wanted. James and I could go with you if you need us to."

Dianna's gaze bounced between Constance's eyes until finally, she nodded and smiled. "Maybe you're right. I do like working with children. If nothing else, it will get me off the ranch for a few hours every day."

"Exactly."

They spent the rest of the afternoon under the tree, just enjoying one another's company, until Constance got a text message from James.

JAMES: Come to the barn. I need your help with Clio.

CONSTANCE STARED AT THE MESSAGE, hating the way her pulse accelerated. Something must be wrong with her horse if James was asking her to help.

Dianna peered over Constance's shoulder at the message and immediately got to her feet. "Let's go."

Neither one of them had brought an ATV or ridden a horse to their little getaway. They ran for short spurts and speed walked the rest of the way until they made it to the barn.

By the time Constance arrived, her lungs burned and her throat was too dry to say anything. She hurried down the aisle toward Clio's stall with Dianna at her heels. Her shaking hand yanked open the door and she froze as she sucked in a gasp.

James knelt beside the horse they'd both brought into the world, holding a small white box in his hand. He offered her a crooked smile, then shifted his focus to Dianna who was behind her right shoulder. "Thanks for making sure she got here okay."

Constance whirled around and whacked Dianna on the shoulder. "You *knew*?"

Dianna pressed her lips together and shrugged.

Dragging her attention back to James, Constance willed her heart to return to a normal pace, but it refused. She probably looked a complete mess. The back of her neck was damp and her hair was probably sticking out at odd angles. She still breathed heavily, but the moment James grasped her left hand, all of that disappeared. It was just the two of them.

"Constance, I've known since—"

She shook her head and pulled him to stand in front of her. "I've *always* loved you. And there is no one I want to spend the rest of my life with other than you." She placed her hand against his cheek. "I want you to know that I'm just as invested in this relationship. We're a partnership."

His eyes bounced toward Dianna, then back to Constance. "But you don't want to marry me?"

Constance laughed. "Of course, I want to marry you. I just didn't want you to ask me."

His brows furrowed and he scratched his head. "I'm confused."

Dianna cleared her throat. "I think she's trying to say that you're both coming to this proposal willing to offer yourself rather than having to ask the big question."

Constance's face flushed red. Her sister had hit the nail on the head. "I want to marry you more than anything. There's not a doubt in my mind. You make me want to be more, do more, and follow my dreams. I want someone who will help me realize those goals without a second thought... and that's you. I just wasn't sure if you were ready for it—ready for me?"

James pulled her into a firm hug, crushing her against his chest. "I've been ready for this from the moment your father aimed his rifle at me. There's nothing like looking down the business end of a weapon to make you put your priorities in order." He pulled back and tilted her chin up so their eyes met. "You're my everything."

His lips came down, claiming hers with a force she hadn't experienced since the beginning of their relationship. Her heart soared as she wrapped her arms around his neck and held him like her life depended on it. James had given her more than she could have ever dreamed possible. He'd helped her find herself and grow into someone she was proud of.

The way he held her made her legs feel like jelly. A spark of electricity burst to life inside her and flickered into an erratic flame. James deepened their kiss, stealing her breath. She dug her fingers into his hair, allowing these sensations to sweep over her and consume her.

Dianna cleared her throat, and Constance pulled back sharply. She shot James an embarrassed smile as he chuckled and grabbed her left hand once again. "Okay, so to make it clear, I'm not asking you to marry me. We're agreeing to tie the knot together."

Her already flushed face warmed even more, and she nodded.

"It's a good thing I'm head over heels in love with you," he murmured as his arms slipped around her waist and he pressed his forehead to hers.

"I couldn't have said it better myself."

Dianna let out an exaggerated groan and headed toward the exit. "You too are so mushy."

EPILOGUE

James

J ames stood on his toes and his heart nearly leapt out of his chest as the ladder beneath his feet tipped slightly. His hands gripped the edge of the barn roof while he waited for his heart to find its rightful place.

"Be careful," Constance demanded from her safe place on firm earth.

He shot her a dark look. "Maybe you should be the one to come up here and put up the Christmas lights."

"Shane didn't ask me. He asked you." She smirked.

He didn't even know why he'd agreed to help out. It wasn't like anyone was going to come out to get therapeutic services this coming month. People spent time with their families during the month of December. Shane was putting on a show for nothing.

James attached the strand of lights where it needed to be and then carefully climbed down. They'd decorated every structure on the premises when Shane had more than enough money to hire a crew.

Constance stepped aside as he finally made it safely to the snow-covered ground.

"What plans did Shane say he had for next month?"

Constance held out a new strand of lights and motioned toward the nearest corral. "What do you mean?"

"He said he wanted to turn this place into some kind of Christmas getaway. I just don't see why anyone in their right minds would want to come out here in the cold and—"

"Shane has a lot of things planned. Besides the regular therapeutic services, he's going to have sleigh rides, ice-skating at the pond, Christmas Cookie stations at the club—"

"Okay, I get it. He wants to turn this place into a glorified North Pole."

Constance's eyes brightened. "That's an awesome idea. You should tell him that's what he should call it."

He shook his head. "I was kidding. I told you, I don't think anyone is going to come here—"

Snow flung everywhere as Dianna came running toward them. "James! Shane wants your help putting up the big sleigh and reindeer set on the roof at the club."

James fought back the urge to groan as Constance giggled. He spun around, crouching like a predator. "Oh, you think this is funny, do you?"

Her eyes widened and she laughed again. "He's *your* friend. It's not my fault that you are so willing to volunteer when he asks you to."

He stalked toward her, and she squealed as she dropped another coiled string of lights and darted toward the club. James easily closed the distance, quickly grabbing her and tumbling to the snow together. His face hovered over hers, snow in her hair and eyes bright. This was his future wife, the future mother of his children, his whole reason for living.

James dipped and kissed the tip of her nose, only to be interrupted by Dianna clearing her throat once more.

She had her arms folded and she was tapping her toe. "I think I told you that Shane needs your help."

He rolled off Constance and got to his feet, dusting the powdery snow from his clothes with a chuckle. "I'm coming, I'm coming."

Constance lifted herself up on her elbows, a wide smile stretching from one side of her face to the other. "Speaking of Shane, you two seem to be getting along really well."

Dianna wrinkled her nose. "Don't even think about it. Shane is definitely not my type."

James chuckled. "You never know. Sometimes you bump into a person you've never met and bam, it hits you—you know you're going to marry them from that very second. Other times," he said as he reached down to help Constance to her feet, "you look into the eyes of someone you feel you've known your whole life and little by little, you realize you could never live without them."

Dianna rolled her eyes and stomped toward the club, muttering under her breath. "When is this lovey-dovey stuff going to end?"

James laughed as he grasped Constance's hand and they followed after Dianna. "Do you think we should tone it down?"

Constance shook her head. "Nah. It's good for her. Besides, when she ends up falling in love, we'll be able to rub it in her face."

They made it to the front entrance of the club and Shane waved James over to the ladder. "I'm going to need your help getting this stuff up there."

A car pulled into the parking lot, wheels crunching against the salt that had just been distributed to melt the ice. James glanced over his shoulder just as it came to a stop and a tall man wearing jeans and a fur-lined red jacket emerged. He waved toward Shane, then moved to the back of the car.

"I didn't think you had much family—none that you were close to."

Shane glanced once more toward the newcomer. "I don't. That's a friend from college."

"You have a friend coming to visit you at Christmas time?"

His friend smiled. "Is it so surprising that I might have more friends than you? Perhaps I was only being nice to the lowly, local veterinarian."

James slugged Shane in the arm.

"Hey!" Shane laughed. "But to answer your question, no. He wasn't really coming to visit for Christmas. He wanted to bring his son out here."

"Okay..."

"They've had it rough. His wife left him and now he has to raise his son alone." Shane's gaze bounced to the newcomers. "His son has autism. He's quiet, and he struggles with his social skills, but he's really smart. I told Tristan that his son might benefit from visiting. They're going to stay for the next month in one of the new cabins I built."

James dragged his attention back to where Tristan had pulled a boy who couldn't be more than seven out of the car. He was bundled up in a coat and boots, but from this distance he couldn't see much.

Dianna headed toward them and James turned to Shane. "Is that why you've requested to have Dianna working full-time this month?"

Shane glanced at him as he put his first foot on the ladder. "Of course. What other reason is there?"

James bit back a smile. "Constance is going to be sorely disappointed. She thought the two of you were hitting it off."

Shane shook his head. "You can tell her I make it a point

not to date my employees. If she wants to match her sister up with someone, she's going to have to look elsewhere."

James gave him a pointed look. "You know as well as I do that there is no telling Constance what to do. If I were you, I'd just try to steer clear of her."

His friend laughed. "Okay, point taken. Now, are you going to help me get Santa's sleigh on the roof? Or am I going to have to find a new best friend?"

"Who's finding a new best friend?" Constance said as she walked towards the ladder.

James was looking over her shoulder toward Tristan when he answered her. "I'm not, but looks like Dianna might be."

Constance turned around to see Dianna and Tristan shaking hands and looking at each other a *little* longer than one might expect from total strangers.

He didn't look like Dianna's type. But she'd be lying if she said she wasn't hoping Dianna was the next sister up for love. Because Constance was bursting at the seams with happiness with James and the thought of forming a family with him. And she couldn't help but envision a dreamy future of her and her sister's kids running around playing with each other on Slate Rock Ranch.

～

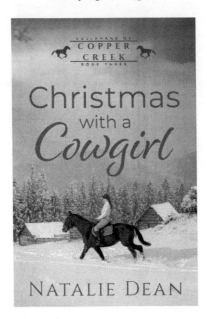

HELLO READERS! I sure hope you enjoyed reading Constance and Dr. Pratt's love story. Up next is Dianna and Tristan... Here it is! Waiting for you to read it...

EXCLUSIVE BOOKS BY NATALIE DEAN

GET THREE FREE BOOKS when you join my Sweet Romance Newsletter :)

Get One Free Contemporary Western Romance:
The New Cowboy at Miller Ranch, Miller Brothers of Texas Prologue - He's a rich Texas rancher. She's just a tomboy ranch employee. Can she make him see life can still be happy without all that money?

AND Two Free Historical Western Romances:
Spring Rose - A feel good historical western mail-order groom novelette about a broken widow finding love and faith.

Fools Rush In- A historical western mail-order bride novelette based off a true story!

Go to nataliedeanauthor.com to find out how to join!

ABOUT AUTHOR - NATALIE DEAN

Born and raised in a small coastal town in the south I realized at a young age that I was more adventurous than my conservative friends and family. I loved to travel. My passion for travel opened up a whole new world and new cultures to me that I will always be grateful for.

I was raised to treasure family. I always knew that at some point in my life I would leave my storybook life behind and become someone's mother, someone's aunt and hopefully someone's grandmother. Little did I know that the birth of my son later in life would make me the happiest I've ever been. He will always be my biggest achievement. The strong desire to be a work-from-home mom is what lead me down this path of publishing books.

While I have always loved reading I never realized how much I would love writing until I started. I feel like each one of my books have been influenced by someone or something I've experienced in my life. To be able to share this gift has become a dream come true.

I hope you enjoy reading them as much as I have enjoyed creating them. I truly hope to develop an ongoing relationship with all of my readers that lasts into my last days :)

www.nataliedeanauthor.com

 facebook.com/nataliedeanromance

Made in the USA
Middletown, DE
02 November 2022

13991396R00161